DAVID WIND

GODDESS

DAVID WIND

GODDESS

by: David Wind

A Forerunner Story

GODDESS

This is a work of science fiction. The names, places, and events are fictitious. Any similarity to persons living or dead is coincidental: and, unless you are a time traveler, impossible.

ISBN: 979-8-9871841-6-5
Copyright: 2023 by David Wind
A ColSaw Publication
Cover by: Steven Novak
Editing by: Lacie Redding

DAVID WIND

What the early reviews are saying about GODDESS.

BOOKBUB REVIEW:

"*I just finished reading the above book and WOW! I received my copy yesterday and I couldn't put it down. I really enjoyed it and felt a if I was actually part of what was happening. This book pulls you in right from the beginning and keeps you on the edge of your seat. I really liked the inclusion of the Navaho Nation. I can't wait to start reading the Tales of the Nevaeh. I am hooked! If you are looking for a new author, this one is golden!*" M.P.

"*Another epic read from Wind. It packs so much: Space-exploration.; set in the future, humans have colonized various planets & galaxies; Military vibes; Fresh start / adventure / discovery; Epic world-building; (Evil) fun with genetics, psi abilities and Aliens; Strong, brilliant, relatable male lead / Hero; Snarky AI; Completely twisted villain; Laugh-out-loud banter. Written in multiple POVs ... mostly we get the POV of the hero, Roke, but at times the reader is provided with others as well, and it's fun to have the insight. Before long, I found myself submerged in this world and I feel like I could never get enough. The book wrapped up nicely, but had a sort-of cliffie, if that makes sense. Wind brilliantly ties up the most immediate issues, but makes it clear there's more to come. I don't want to spoil anything, so you'll have to either take my word for it, or read it & see for yourself. Beautifully done—as someone with a very visual mind, I was treated to stunning landscapes and basically traveled in time and space. I could read this book over and over again.*" L.R.

GOODREADS REVIEW:

...[GODDESS] is very easy to read and it is entertaining. I had a hard time putting it down last night to go to sleep. It is full of twists and turns that I didn't imagine until I read it. It is kind of scary in a way. It is a page turner for sure. Some might think it is romantic, but I didn't think so. It could trigger some people, but the power play is

GODDESS

from the female instead of the male. There are a few adult scenes in it, but they are essential to the story and not just to fill in pages to make the story longer or titillate you.

What I like most about this book is that it is a complete story and there is no cliffhanger like books from years ago. It does leave open the possibility for more stories to come in the future and I hope to read more in this universe. If I could give this story 10 stars, I would, but since I can't, I will tell you I loved it and would highly recommend this book..." W.J

DAVID WIND

DEDICATION

This one's for Colby Levi
Who will have to wait until he's at least eighteen to read this.

GODDESS

GODDESS

A FORERUNNER STORY

By: David Wind

ONE

Swooping down from the sky like oversized bats out of hell, they dove straight at the running figures, firing weapons, and blistering whatever moved below them. Roke dove behind a thick tree, pressing his back to it. Several voices went off in his ears from those lucky enough to survive the initial attack.

One in particular was the panicked voice of the youngest of the apprentices, Jami, on his first exploration mission. The Guild always put a new apprentice with the more seasoned veterans and apprentices. The kid was at best twenty-two and scared shitless. One of the other scouts, Garon Prince, was talking him down.

Roke Stenner, the most senior of the scout apprentices, and on his last mission as an apprentice, swiped across a button on his EXO suit. A map hologram projected above his forearm displayed the area and each scout's position. Red showed the injured, black the dead, and the blue were those still alive and unhurt.

There were seven black, three red, and six blue, including himself and Caruso, the master scout to whom he was apprenticed.

"There were no signs of Scav here. Where the hell did these Scav come from?" shouted Sarina Gomez, a senior scout. She and her apprentice, Albin Walker, were off to Roke's left. Jami was alone, his scout dead at his feet. Prince was ten feet from Caruso.

"Up there," Caruso said sarcastically. "Who has a looksee?"

Roke glanced quickly to where Caruso hid in the thick grass before turning to look from behind the tree. The three Scav he spotted were hovering about a hundred feet up, their wings buzzing as they maintained their altitude, an altitude Roke knew they could not hold much longer.

"Three above me, hundred feet high, and ah …" He paused for another quick peek. "Seventy yards south. There have to be more. They don't come in with only three."

"I've got them now," Gomez called. "They're just north of me."

"Anyone volunteering to be bait?" called Caruso.

Roke looked across to where Caruso hid. He didn't see his mentor, but knew he was there. Before offering up bait, they had to locate the other Scav. "Jami, focus! Take a breath, a deep one." He waited a few seconds before saying, "Look at your screen. Tell me what you see. Anyone else as well."

The green apprentice was silent for several seconds. "I've got five dots on my screen. West. Three hundred yards. On the ground, moving at us." His words clipped and precise, the panic gone.

Roke looked around. A Scav ship held a crew of between three and eight. There were eight surrounding them. They were all there and no one was manning the ship's weapons. It was time to put some of his Diné ancestry to work. "Caruso, I'm bait. Keep me alive."

"Gomez," Caruso called, "You're with me. Prince, you take the apprentices and get ready for the Scavs on the west flank. Take as many down as possible." He paused to look in Roke's direction. "Anytime—hero." He drew out the word 'hero' until it sounded like wind blowing through a hollow tree.

Caruso was riding him as he always did; and he was the only member of the landing team who could. He was the strongest runner of any of them, having been trained from birth to run as part of the tribal heritage his planet, Kryon-Three, was bound by. Kryon's surface—the whole surface—was a mirror image of Old Earth's section of the Western United States, Rocky Mountains, and all.

Bending his head, Roke drew in a deep, preparatory breath, closed his eyes, and pictured the three alien Scav flying above. Their bodies were long, seven feet at average, fully humanoid with scale-like skin, two legs and two arms and hands with opposing thumbs. That's where the similarity between human and Scav ended. Scavs had claws for nails, and the bald circle on their heads, ringed by short, feather-like hair, looked exactly like the Old Earth pictures of birds—more specifically the scavengers of Old Earth—vultures.

It was a uniquely unappealing look at another supposedly intelligent creature—one that sent shivers down almost any human being's spine. They should be the stars of a Tri-D horror projection, but sadly, Scavs were far from fiction, and they were most definitely set upon ending the ever-spreading human race in favor of their own expansion.

Their bones were like earth birds: hollow; but, unlike earthly creatures, titanium-like fiber ran through their bones, giving them far more strength than human bones. Although it wasn't exactly titanium, it was close enough on the spectrum to be labelled as such.

Human scientists had discovered that the Scav, as babies, matured within a sealed egg, which contained an ammonia-based atmospheric supply until they were mature enough to be weaned from the gas, which was then slowly converted into an oxygen-rich atmosphere. The ammonia compound gas is what produced the metal fibers in their bones.

Once the surviving offspring in the egg were ready to be released, the shell opened. How they were able to move the infant from ammonia to oxygen was still beyond the scientists' understanding; yet, it was because of the oxygen they became our competitors for those planets capable of sustaining human or Scav life. There were plenty of planets out there, but only one in two or three hundred would support human life.

The most frightening aspect of the Scav, was their intelligence. Their DNA was as close to human as any scientist had ever seen in an alien, and they'd already conquered one galaxy, our neighboring galaxy, Canis Major. Some scientists believe they originated in Andromeda. Now the Scav were making inroads into the Milky Way. The Scav, unlike most humans, left no survivors to threaten their own race.

"Not today," Roke whispered. He stood, keeping his back to the tree. "On my count." Pausing, he took another breath. "Three, two, one … now!" The instant the word passed his lips, he spun to his left and ran straight at the three.

He went fifteen feet, waiting for their knee-jerk response. The instant they reacted, he zagged left, ran another ten, and zigged right. When his left foot came down for his spinning turn, the first whispers of their sub-sonics spattered the ground bare inches from his feet, the dirt spraying him from the waist-down. A microsecond later, the louder hard-shell firing of Caruso's large-caliber antique repro of a twentieth century S & W fifty-millimeter hunting pistol boomed.

Behind him, a body fell. He zigged right as more shots peppered the ground where he'd just been. Another shot rang out, this one from Gomez's burst gun. The stream of laser fire hit the second Scav, tearing through a wing, and sending it plummeting to the ground three feet in front of Roke, who had his eleven-inch battle knife out. Before the Scav could get to its feet, Roke was on it, the blade's razor-edge slicing across its most vulnerable acreage, the neck, cutting easily through muscle, veins, and arteries until its titanium spine stopped the blade. The Scav was dead before its partially severed head touched the ground.

Roke kept running. The nape of his neck was suddenly pricked by a thousand needles, as his inner warning went ballistic. Then from behind and above, the wings of the third Scav beat heavily, as it raced toward the ship. Roke took another three steps before Caruso's big boom went off for the second time. Two strides later, a heavy thud signaled the third Scav's body striking the ground.

Behind him, the battle raged on. A hundred yards in front sat the Scav ship with no one guarding it. Because their ships could only hold a max crew of eight, he was confident there were no Scav onboard.

He didn't slow as the battle raged on; rather, he ran even faster, until he reached the ship. There, he spun toward the sounds of fighting, and saw flashes of laser rifles flashing through the trees.. "Take them out. Do not let any get away. I'm at the Scav ship." The urgency in his voice was not lost through the helmet's mic.

With that, he slid the knife into its sheath, hit a button on the hip of his EXO suit, and drew his stunner from its extended holster. He flipped the switch from stun to lethal and waited in case one of the Scav escaped the other scouts.

"Four down," Prince called. "Fifth wounded but flying at you."

Roke watched the sky. He spotted the Scav cutting through the thinner high branches of two tall trees and heading directly toward its ship. He waited, kneeling in a firing position while the wounded Scav flew erratically toward him.

The instant the Scav spied him, it raised its weapon. Roke didn't hesitate. He pulled the trigger and released a lethal pulse. The shot hit the Scav's bird face point-blank. The flying alien tumbled downward through the air, and crashed into the ground, its headless, metal, heavy body rolling for ten feet before it stopped a foot from Roke.

Not taking any chances, Roke fired once more to be sure. He stood and released his held breath. It was over.

Turning to the hatch, he pressed a button. As he expected, nothing happened. "I can't open the hatch. Unless someone has a better idea, we'll have to blow it."

"No," Caruso responded. "The Scav fingers may work. Do it before the body cools."

Roke turned to look at the dead Scav. Shaking his head, he went to it, lifted its arm, and dragged it to the ship, not an easy task given the alien's body was three hundred pounds of dead weight. It was slow work, and just as he got the body to the ship, Caruso reached him to help him lift the Scav. With Caruso holding the Scav, Roke pressed its hand to the switch plate's surface.

The plate flashed a series of colors; the hatch opened. "Go," Caruso told him. "First in honors, Stenner. Go!"

Unable to hide his grin, Roke climbed into the ship. He went to the bridge, squeezed into the narrow and deep pilot's seat, and stared at the instrument panel. Having been fully trained in Scav tech, he hit two switches.

A screen rose from the center console with a star map centered on it. He stared at the map, and at the three highlighted planets, all seemingly in a row The first was the planet they were on, the second was in a system eighty light years distant from here, and the other planet was close to a 150 lightyears from this planet.

Even as he shook his head, Caruso's low voice echoed behind him. "This is not good."

GODDESS

TWO:

The exit from hyperspace kicked them about until Caruso steadied his scout ship, maneuvering out of the path of the moons, while gentling the ship into a smooth orbit two thousand miles above the planet.

The first sight of the planet hit Roke like a punch to the solar plexus, making his heart twitch. "Damn," he whispered, calming himself as the blue, white and green planet came into full view.

"You found a beauty." Caruso reached across the distance to grasp Roke's shoulder and squeeze. "A beauty."

Glancing at Caruso's face, he studied the master scout, whose pale, blue eyes were framed by deep grooves radiating from their corners to spread down along his cheeks. His thick, blond hair was cropped short, which accented a strong face and jawline. "Only if it's habitable," he finally replied.

"If the Scav marked it for exploration, it will be. And it should have a good climate, at eighty million miles from the sun."

"And we'd better hope they haven't gotten here yet."

Apprentice Scout Roke Stenner looked at the instruments, then, without a word, hit three switches on a panel of twelve. He pushed the red button beneath it. There was a light, triple thump as three bots shot into the atmosphere, each going its own preprogrammed way. "There's no Scav ship in orbit, but we'll know soon enough if any landed."

Caruso set the ship into high orbit. Then they went about their normal duties and two hours later, the ship's computer had synched the three bots' reports into one and projected on the center of the cabin.

When the report closed, Caruso turned to Roke. "Think hard about what to name it, because this is your find."

Roke stared at the planet, his mind almost but not quite rejecting the thought that this was his first planet.

"When do we go down?"

Caruso laughed. "You know when."

The apprentice shook his head. "I don't want to wait … but I will."

The Guild's third-highest ranking master scout surveyed him with an intense gaze. "This is only the first of many, Roke. Enjoy the feel, and the flavor of naming it, because it will never be the same, not in this way."

Yet, Roke sensed it would be repeated in the future, but like old lovers reacquainting themselves. He looked at his mentor for several seconds. "I hear you, boss."

<<>>

The next day, they sent the bots out again, and had them crisscross the planet in a different pattern than the first flyover. One bot traced each line of the north-south longitude, while a second bot flew the east-west lines of latitude. Both bots flew at an altitude of 200 miles, their instruments plunging deeper into the surface with each revolution of their routes.

GODDESS

When the bots returned, and the sun had set on the landmasses below, the ship's computer integrated the combined reports and opened a Tri-D projection. The two Exploration Guild scouts sat glued to their seats watching the large projection in the center of the cockpit give a three-dimensional view of the planet, while Adrianne, the computer's female voice, analyzed the report.

The computer spat out facts and figures, as the two scouts scanned the single ocean covering thirty- percent of the planet. They saw fish and larger water creatures swimming fearlessly before the camera's scene shifted to the land masses of the northern hemisphere. Amazing amounts of animal life wandered the planet, but they found nothing to indicate any life forms of sentient, intelligent beings.

"It's an old planet," Caruso half-whispered, concentrating on the instrumentation beneath the images.

The planet's two circular mountain ranges formed unusually perfect lines of demarcation dividing the east from the west,, which followed the equator, while the north-south mountain range bisected the east-west mountain range at zero degrees longitude and zero degrees latitude began and ended at zero degrees longitude, marked it as the prime meridian..

There were no cities, no construction of any kind, and no ruins. Only animals, reptiles, and birds populated the planet. "Adrianne, confirm no sentient life forms."

```
"The instruments detect no evolved life, no
sentient beings."
```

Caruso shut the report down and stared at Roke for a few seconds before saying, "It's strange, and surprising that there's been no intelligent evolution, not with the amount of animal life here." He paused, stared at the screen, and then looked at Roke. "It's unusual, but there's only one way to verify. Tomorrow, we take the sled."

Roke stood, and stretched. He'd been up for almost thirty hours. "Watches?"

"The ship will warn us if there's anything. I'll send out more bots to run nighttime sweeps as a safeguard."

Roke headed to his bunk. No matter his level of excitement at the planet below, it took him less than five minutes to fall sleep.

He slept for six hours, and fifteen minutes after he woke, he was in his chair on the bridge, drinking caf, and looking at the planet.

"Morning." Caruso came up behind him, his own cup of caf steaming in his right hand. "Anything show up during the night?"

"Nothing. I woke up an hour ago. It seems like there's nothing indigenous down there we need to worry about as far as security goes. But we'll still have look for Scav signs; we can't take chances."

<<>>

It's beautiful, Roke thought, his sled skimming a hundred miles above the ground of the Galactic Union designated planet ET-87310.2.

The planet spread dramatically below him. There was a lushness to the planet, which was almost foreign to him, but was closely reminiscent of the the documentaries he'd watched of Old Earth. Yet, there was one place in total opposition to any other on the planet. At the juncture of the equator and prime meridian was a valley five klicks long separating the two mountain ranges.

In the center of the valley a river flowed from one end to the other. The land and the water were rock-strewn, and devoid of vegetation for several hundred feet in every direction. But even in this place of desolation, it projected a strange beauty, one which called to him.

Included in the last week of scanning the planet, were intense security searches to make certain there were no traces of anything Scav or other alien species. At the same time, they ran a full internal scan of the planet. The ship's computer worked twenty-four hours a day for three days using a form of deep sonar and laser-band imaging. The final readings showed no underground structures or remnants, no machinery, nor were there any traces of a prior civilization. However, there were three blank spots—unreadable blips on the report—which Caruso said, "I've come across this before. See these half-visible wavy lines?" He pointed to the edge of the screen. "They're mineral formations outside of the computer's knowledge base—new minerals, which will be mined after colonization."

On the eighth day, with no reading other than non-sentient animals, and backed up by the solid evidence of the computer's scanning, the two scouts touched down on the planet.

Caruso, unable to control the smile breaking across his face, waved his hand in a sweeping motion for his apprentice to take the honor of being first to plant a foot on the planet; an award well deserved, for it was also the moment of Roke's graduation from apprentice to full scout.

On the first night after making landfall, Roke was restless. They were a 100 klicks from the rocky valley marking the intersection of the planet's prime meridian and the equator, and he was plagued by strange dreams about the valley, which he did not discuss with Caruso.

These dreams were of people and creatures he'd never before seen. He knew they were not simply dream images—they were more. Yet, he could not share them with Caruso. His grandfather had warned him throughout his childhood and had continued to do so until the day he left for Guild Academy; no one was to know he had any special senses—senses warning him of dangers to come.

The old man had told him about the men in his family—, his ancestors who for generations were so attuned to the ground, the air, and the universe they could not help but sense things others did not. And the last thing he should do was let the guild know he had psi abilities. It would doom him to becoming a lab rat. So he'd spent years hiding his ability from others.

On the day following the strange dreams, everything was fine. The second night was dreamless, and by the end of the first week, he'd almost forgotten about the dreams … almost, except for the magnificent woman who had turned into a mythical creature.

They spent the next few months travelling the planet, mapping out the livable regions, spending nights in different areas, analyzing the vegetation, and the nutritional value of any grains, vegetables, and fruits. Almost all were fit for human consumption; and the nutrients in the soil would support the seeds the colonists would bring with them. They killed three types of animals and analyzed them. Each contained human-digestible proteins and fats.

While humanity had adapted to the diaspora of space, it forced most to adapt to a vegetarian diet, supplemented with manufactured proteins. The truth being plants and grains proved to survive better than Old Earth animals on most of the earth-type planets. However, when animals were found to be fit for consumption, most people had no issues with eating them.

One night they ate a small animal. Roke thought of it as rabbit-type because it propelled itself by not quite hopping but popping into the air. Both scouts found it delicious.

When they finished eating, Caruso held up one of the animal's clean-picked bones and laughed. "How about we call them poppers?"

<<>>

Seventy-six days after arriving, they lifted off-planet and hyper-jumped to the nearest Explorer Guild oversight planet, Norton's Landing, which was one of the three Galactic Union's level- two Guild outposts, the second highest Guild outpost designation in the GU. The only higher designation was Guild Prime.

Guild Prime was the only level-one planet in the galaxy, and the capital of the Galactic Union. Guild Prime was home to the galactic government, the GU military and defense headquarters, and five Guild headquarters. Each GU level two planets were smaller duplicates of Prime.

During the twenty-six hours of hyperspace flight, Caruso filled out the reports and prepared them for filing. During the flight, he gave a lot of thought to the five years he and Roke had spent together, and the potential his apprentice had not only shown, but was reaching. Caruso admitted he had trained nine apprentice scouts over the last twenty-four years, and Roke Stenner was among the very best. An unusual wash of emotions rolled through him when he acknowledged how this had been their last trip as scout and apprentice.

The moment they set down, Caruso ordered Adrianne to file the reports and the final scout release naming Roke Stenner a full Guild first-in scout and requisition a new single pilot scout ship for the new scout.

Roke left for his new planet two days later, to complete the official first-in preparation for the engineers, construction crews, and first wave of colonists. Roke's job was to secure the best possible location for the first colony, survey, and prepare.

When the two stood at the hatch of his scout ship, framed from behind by the thirty-foot statue of the grandmotherly woman holding a cat in one hand, and a book in another, Caruso placed both meaty hands-on Roke's shoulders. He stared keenly at him; the master scout's ice-blue eyes intense. Then a twinkle replaced the intensity in the twin pools when Caruso's mouth twisted into as much of a smile as Roke had ever seen on his face. "Don't fuck it up before the rest of us get there, injun boy."

GODDESS

THREE

Roke Stenner's approach to ET-87310.2 was perfect. Skirting the twin moons to slide into orbit halfway between the moons and planet they circled, he gazed at the blue and green globe, and smiled. The planet was eighty-six percent the size of Old Earth and spent its solar year revolving around the G-2 sun for 337 Old Earth days.

"I discovered you; I name you *ni-hooká-á' á-nii-díi.*" He smiled, carefully enunciating the words *nihookáá' ániidíi*. The meaning was simple, New Earth. Of course, the Guild would never allow that name to stick, but he knew how to work around their naming formulas. When he and Caruso had returned to Guild Prime, and he'd formally requested to name the planet, he'd said, "Anadi," aloud and in English, not in the language of his ancestors, the Diné— the Navajo people of the long-dead planet once called home to the human species—Old Earth.

Settling the ship into orbit for the second time, he breathed a little easier. He and Caruso had spent enough time and done enough exploration to know no sentient life existed on Anadi. When they'd returned to Norton's Landing, Caruso had begun to coordinate the preparations for colonization he would lead.

The Guild council believed the planet to be one of the great finds of the last quarter-century, for it would support human life without any type of terra forming, or atmospheric scrubbing and tampering. It meant a savings of years, if not decades, and of credits as well, so they set preparations to run at the fastest possible speed—they wanted Anadi settled immediately.

And while Roke would spend the next two months alone, preparing for the colonization, Leon Caruso would receive every bit of information Roke sent to make certain of the coming colony's survival. It was also up to Roke to select which of the four areas would host the initial colony. It was a job he'd spent the last eight years of his life preparing for.

The three years at the Guild academy taught him both theory and actuality of everything from basic survival to planetary engineering concepts for first-in scouts. Apprenticing for Caruso had done the rest. Once their job was done, it would be the colonists, engineers, and builders who took it from there. First-in scouts were done and off to hunt for more planets, seek dead and lost civilizations, and those that might yet be present and living. Scouts always chased possibilities for the survival of the ever-expanding human species.

Standing, he went to the galley and pulled out a bottle of protein. He would be out there for six hours; he needed to maintain his body. He took his time, drinking the protein while containing his building excitement the way his mentor had taught him. He needed to conserve his energy until he was ready to land.

"The more internal energy you have," Leon Caruso had explained, "The safer you'll be. A new planet needs you cautious, smart, and scared as shit!"

His problem was in being too excited to sense his fear, but he knew scared would slip in when it was least expected it. A drop of fear

GODDESS

would also bring out his smart part; this part was what would keep him alive if the planet was displeased to be trespassed upon.

Following Guild protocol, he would continue to survey the planet until he was satisfied all was in order. Guild guidelines called for first-in scouts to monitor the planet for a minimum of six months, except the Guild was in a hurry this time because they'd gotten the map from the Scav ship. So Roke was lucky to have gotten two months. Two months would give Caruso barely enough time to assemble the colonization team and bring them to Anadi after Roke's all-clear signal. The colonization team consisted of Construction Guild engineers and builders, a complete medical staff, an administration staff, a detachment of Marines for security, and the first 100 colonist families.

Before Roke left for Anadi, he learned Gomez had chosen the second of the three earth-type planets on the Scav star map. The third was 200 lightyears distant and would be the last of the three if they decided to venture that far at this time.

The Scav's ship, one of the newest of the Scav fleet, had been taken back to Guild Prime, for the Galactic Union Engineering and Manufacturing Guild to take apart, piece by piece and reverse engineer any advanced tech.

Roke had checked on the Scav transmissions, and after backtracking to the point of their discovery, he was certain the map he'd found had not yet been transmitted to the Scav's home base.

When he took off from Norton's Landing, he peered at his console screen, and watched the large statue of the legendary woman for whom the planet was named, recede in his wake. It was an image he would never forget.

Suddenly, for the first time in five years, he had two months on his own—Old Earth months and not the shorter Anadi months—Roke planned on making his time worthwhile, and get everything done quickly. He was eager to get his first planet settled; but, not until he knew Anadi was absolutely livable for the colonists—no scout ever wanted to make a mistake of that magnitude.

Although he was certain he had selected the perfect area for the first colony, which was almost 800 klicks west on the northern continent, there was a lot he had to do before he went there. Only when he as certain all was right with the planet, would he signal the oncoming guild personnel; but if the planet was unsafe, if there was an issue, he would call in Caruso and the other scouts for assistance. Using hyperspace jump points—hops—they could be here in twenty-six to thirty hours.

Roke finished his protein and put on his EXO suit. He waited the twenty seconds it took the suit to adapt to his body, and for the sensors to send out their initial monitoring signals to the computer. He snapped on his helmet before going through the deck hatch, and stepping onto the small flyer sled for his final inspection of the planet: the sole purpose to determine if there had been any changes since his last time here.

Strapping himself in as the scrubbing filters in the helmet kicked on, he locked the belt into its catch, took a deep breath, and hit the release switch. The sled dropped through the hatch, and the

GODDESS

connection between himself and the ship opened, allowing the sensors monitoring his vitals and communicate with the ship's computer.

If three check-ins failed, or if an emergency signal was sent, the colonization would be halted, a Guild scout crew sent to find out what happened to their scout, and the colonization might or might not go ahead. Everything would depend on the circumstances.

Shaking off the what-ifs, he concentrated on the now of flying. At 10,000 feet, the air was cold, or so the monitor on the EXO suit told him. But he was comfortable. The off-ship monitoring was important for a first-in scout, and was broadcast on a special band to the waiting scout ship once every four hours.

The sled dropped to 2,500 feet. The temperature warmed at the new height. He was over the eastern ocean, a body of water that covered over one-third of the planet, and was neatly divided between the northern and the southern hemispheres. The colors of the water ran in shades from the turquoise jewels of his Navajo heritage to the center of the ocean, where the water color went from azure-blue to a sapphire-blue so deep it verged on black.

The depth of the ocean varied from twenty to 115 miles; its waters filled with wandering masses of life. The aquarian life, according to the ship's instruments, was all edible for humans. Although there was no western ocean, there were several smaller seas spreading out across western Anadi.

Despite the beauty of the ocean and seas of Anadi, it was the land which intrigued Roke the most. The mountains were blanketed with lush vegetation, The colors were almost but not quite the same as the pictures he'd seen of Old Earth in the twentieth century. The greens were so luminous they jumped out at you, the amazing shades of browns were unlike those of other worlds, and there was a species of trees with a sharper blue color than any tree color he had ever seen. The reds ... well, the shades of red vegetation glowed with spectacular power. The color spectrum of the planet was slightly different, not just from Old Earth, but from any oxygen-rich planet, and the colors themselves seemed more brilliant.

Roke's thoughts formed in direct opposition to the way a scientist would look at Anadi, and he took Anadi into himself, as does a person gazing upon the rarest and most beautiful of jewels. Finding an inhabitable planet with an earth-like atmosphere was among the rarest of finds.

He dropped low to fly over the valley he'd dubbed Point Zero because it was set in the center of the equatorial line and the prime meridian, and an area at odds with the rest of the planet. It consisted of a valley of large rocks and smaller stones instead of grass. He dropped to a few hundred feet above the tallest peak of the valley and gazed downward.

The mountains north of the Point Zero were part of a chain reminding him of a large animal's spine, where the mountains, like the bumpy lamina nodes of a spine, pressed against the skin of the planet's surface. The mountains began on the northern side of the valley, at the crossing point of the prime meridian and equator, followed the prime meridian to encircle the planet, and ended at the southern side of the valley, creating an almost closed but perfect circle.

The northern mountains, like rivers, also had branches jutting east and west, creating foothills encroaching the greener lush areas. These were smaller mountain chains, running only a few hundred miles, and creating several wide valleys. The east west mountains were different. Some were high, while at times the mountains disappeared into the ocean waters.

There was an unusual uniqueness to the planet Roke had never seen before, for it was the two mountain chains which divided the planet into four distinct hemispheres.

The ground at Point Zero valley was a gray sandy dirt, covered with neither grass nor vegetation, but by gray rocks and stones. The river flowing through the valley was filled with enough rocks to make the rushing water look like rolling river rapids. But although it gave the appearance of rapids, it wasn't.

It was here, where the equator and prime meridian crossed at the center of the valley, Roke intended to start his Anadian exploration. There was something about the valley that called to him in ways he didn't understand, but needed to, and it wasn't the first time this had happened on Anadi.

Six hours after he'd left, and right on schedule, Roke returned to his scout ship. He filed the verbal report of his last six hours, emphasizing he had discovered no life above those of the indigenous animals. Verbal reports were required to sync up with all data from the sensors in his suit and on the ship.

While the instruments had confirmed the animal life was, for the most part, safe for humans to eat, the colonists would bring food supplies, grain and vegetable seeds, and frozen embryos of cattle, chicken, and fish to add certainty to their food supply. Colonization had many risks, and contamination from indigenous animal species was only one.

Roke stood, stretched, and showered, before dropping into his bunk, exhausted from the last twenty-two hours. He needed a full shift of sleep to be fresh when he made landfall tomorrow.

Just as he slipped into sleep, there was a slight tug in his mind, a bare whisper, not unlike a soft breeze flowing through the leaves. He remembered a similar touch the last time he was here, after visiting the river valley. He tried to follow the whispering touch, but fell asleep before he could.

<<>>

Roke woke with the nape of his neck tingling. He stayed in the bunk, remembering the unusual dream. It had been so intense it had burned into his mind, and he needed to work through all of it, as his *acheii*—his grandfather—had taught him.

His grandfather words, when he'd instructed Roke in the intricacies of being a Navajo, hung in a corner of his mind. His grandfather's face had never changed in the years Roke lived with him after his parents' deaths.

His lined face looked like the skin of dried fruit, his grandfather's eyes, one deep brown, the other a pale hazel, would watch him carefully as he taught him the history and the language of

GODDESS

his people. He would sit with Roke for hours, explaining how powerful and how important it was, his having the blood of his people flowing through him. No matter if his mother was not of the Diné, his grandfather explained, his father's blood was of the people.

"The most potent dreams, those you remember vividly, are but spirit visions of what might come to be, or a powerful warning gifted to you for your protection," the old Navajo told him. If his acheii had been born 800 years earlier, he would have either been a tribal chief, or a medicine man. In the twenty-fifth century, he was among the last of his people, and one of the last Diné Guardians, the historians who devoted their lives to keeping the heritage and long history of the Diné — 'The People'—alive through the centuries.

His grandfather had done his job well, passing on the knowledge to Roke, and to Roke's brother, Jacob. At the same time he taught his grandsons their lessons, each was recorded, and filed with the libraries at the various universities on Guild Prime.

Thinking of his grandfather, he closed his eyes and replayed the dream, but its symbolism was lost on him. It showed him this world, this planet he'd named Anadi, filled with life—human, but slightly different. Then it showed him a vision of a woman whose face was of breathtaking beauty, with large, aquamarine eyes, and long, silver hair. Her body matched the beauty of her face.

He'd seen himself walking with her in the forest, lying down next to her on the soft grass, and learning about each other's bodies, as they touched, caressed, until they could take no more and joined together with a thundering passion.

Afterward, she'd risen and walked a few feet away from him, her eyes sweeping over him as her body shimmered and morphed into an iridescent creature resembling the drawing of dragons he'd seen in children's books. In the next moment, she'd spread her wings and lifted into the air, the sun's rays turning her wings into a colorful shower of shimmering light.

He had no idea what it meant, nor could he dig beneath the surface of what he'd seen, and especially what he'd felt. Then he remembered the fragmented earlier dreams, when he and Caruso had come to Anadi the first time.

Sitting up on the bunk, he stared blankly, his body physically remembering the feel of her, even though it had been a dream. The tingling in the nape of his neck was still there. His eyes focused. He stared at the wall in front of him, wondering if it was a vision of the future, or a warning of danger he was about to face. The one thing he didn't doubt was the tingling in his neck reflecting his strange ability to sense danger. His grandfather called it a gift; Roke wasn't so sure. A warning, perhaps.

Was it a warning about the dragon-like creature in the dream? A *tl'iishtsoh*, his grandfather would have called her; a mythical creature, a winged reptile with magical abilities, or spiritual qualities—in other words, a dragon. And the woman? Was she some kind of alien witch?

Standing, he shook his head to rid himself of the dream, and the nonsense of his thoughts. "Move," he ordered himself, knowing

GODDESS

today would be the best day of his life. He was going to stand on 'his' planet.

FOUR

He circled the planet one last time, following the north-south spine of mountains across the two poles, back to the equator, and into the valley. He hovered over the rock-strewn anomaly for several minutes before sending out his communication to inform the Guild he was landing.

The instant the transmission left the ship, he dropped to the planet's surface, settling the scout vessel on a level grassy area several hundred yards from the river, and a quarter-mile from the foothills.

Wearing his EXO suit, he held his helmet in one hand and disembarked. Once on the ground, he took in several deep breaths of air, returned to the ship, and put his helmet on a shelf near the hatch. When he stepped back out, he drew on his gloves. Each glove contained dozens of embedded digital sensors, which would analyze and record everything he touched, from the temperature of grass to an animal's tissues.

The EXO suit, his Exploration Outer suit, was a scout's lifeline. The skin of the body-hugging suit would resist everything except a direct explosive charge or weapon beam, and was aided by internal nanites used to fortify the suit's skin. There were hundreds of sensors built into the suit, some for him, the rest for everything around him. The suit contained earbud communications electrodes, similar to the helmet's speakers.

The gloves were fitted with sensors and ten curved, razor-sharp, metal, retractable claw-style talons, for protection, exploration,

GODDESS

and climbing. He had two knives, his eleven-inch Guild blade, and the six-inch antique buffalo bone-handle hunting knife his grandfather had gifted him when he'd been accepted into the Exploration Guild—the knife had been handed down for centuries.

He completed his weaponry with a stunner and a projectile weapon. The two pistol-shaped weapons were in the suit's built-in holsters. All he need do was touch the release plate on either side and the weapons would be extended. The EXO suit's four-inch-thick backpack was connected by the nanobots and balanced so perfectly it was close to weightless.

The pack contained enough rations to last a week should he need to be gone that long, a full medical kit, extra ammunition, rope, and antibacterial tablets for any microbial life in still-water ponds, and a shelter. They'd already tested the fresh water and found it safe for human consumption.

Ready to move, he took another deep breath of sweet, oxygen-rich Anadian air, which was purer than any other planet he'd stepped foot upon. Anadi's gravity was nine-tenths earth-standard, and seven-tenths of Kryon-Three's heavier gravity. The temperature was twenty-seven degrees Celsius. The smile stayed glued to his face during his walk to the river bank. There, he followed it north, stopping just before the grass ended and the gray stones began.

Standing still for just a moment, he looked to his left and then panned slowly to the right. The valley's length was fourteen klicks—eight miles—and its width was a quarter-mile. The river joined the north and south mountains together. The east-west mountains rose high on each side as well; the foothills were more gentle mountainside slopes than bumps rising toward the peaks. It was a fascinating place begging for answers as to why it was the way it was; it was his job to find out.

He bent his head, closed his eyes, and said, "*Ahéhe,*" 'thank you' in the ancient Diné tongue.

After uttering the single word, he entered into the valley. The moment his feet left the grass and stepped onto the rocky, grayish ground there was another whip-like touch in his mind. It was gone before he could even think about it. He stayed still, waiting to see if it would happen again. It did not. Imagination?

It took him an hour to maneuver through the rocks to the center of the valley, where the river was the widest. All the while the rushing waters struck the rocks in the river, at times so powerfully the wet spray reached him from where he walked, 100 feet to the side. Each time the droplets of water touched him, an urge to go to the river's edge pushed at him, but he kept on with the task he'd assigned himself.

Roke stopped at the center of the valley. The river had doubled in width, leaving a bare few feet between himself and the slope of the mountainside. He climbed onto a long egg-shaped rock to get a closer look at the river. When he did, another strange touch flicked through him. It was different this time, like a tickle in his mind. He frowned, remembering the touch on the shipboard just before he'd fallen asleep was similar.

Climbing over two large stones, he made his way to the river's edge, where he sat on a flat rock wedged into the river bank. He wiped sweat from his forehead as he looked at the river. The water cast off reflections of blue sky, yellow sun, and gray rocks; the rushing waters shifting from yellow to blue to gray, and at times swirling all three into the currents pushing the water against the rocks.

He was fascinated by the rainbow spectrum bouncing along the water's surface. Then he blinked to ward off the glare, looked at the chrono in the arm of the EXO suit, and saw he'd been staring at the water and rocks for almost a half-hour.

Knowing how dangerous this kind of hypnotic effect was, he stood and moved, needing movement to get back to himself. Strange … very strange.

He went a few hundred feet further, then veered to the water's edge. When he did, a six-inch-long fish swam by, not caught within the powerful current but navigating easily between the rocks.

Puzzled, for this size fish should be carried by the ferocious current, he lay flat on the wet ground at the edge of the river, ignored the water splashing over him, and plunged his arm into the water. The moment his arm entered the water, he had his answer. The surface rushed madly against his upper arm, making it difficult to hold it still; but his hand and wrist, which were over a foot and a half deep, sensed the current ending just above his wrist. It was as if there were two layers of water, one rushing powerfully upstream, the other calm, still, and gentle without any discernable movement. Interestingly, the deeper water was warmer than it should be.

When he took his arm out to check the instrument panel image on the inside of his arm, it showed exactly what he'd felt. The current stopped an inch above his wrist, which meant the current went about a foot deep and stopped. He frowned, puzzled as to how it was even remotely possible, but continued to stare into the multi-hued water. It took a moment to realize the colors he'd seen were not reflections of sun on water; rather the reflections cast off by the stones below.

The stones and rocks filling the river's bottom were iridescent. He reached down to where a fist-sized sparkling stone lay and lifted it from the water. The moment it touched the air, it turned gray. He frowned. It was lighter than he expected. Hollow? Or were the stones alive? Were the stones some sort of lifeform living beneath the surface?

Although unlikely, he still looked at his arm panel again. All he saw was the temperature and the mineral makeup of the rock—no biological info. He tossed the stone back into the water. By the time it settled on the bottom, its iridescence had returned.

He glanced at the other rocks in the water, ignoring the low tingle in his neck. They ranged from small stones to larger rocks: most but not all were iridescent. He would investigate this later; there was a lot to accomplish over the next four weeks, and he had to move on.

Looking across the river at the mountain's slope, he spotted an animal watching him. Deerlike in appearance, it stood about three feet at the shoulders, its brown coat making it nearly invisible against the brownish gray slope of the mountainside. The animal showed no fear at his presence. This one was new to him; he had not seen its type before.

GODDESS

Roke stood and jumping from stone to stone, he crossed the river. The animal didn't run. When he stepped onto the other side, and walked up the foothill's gentle slope, the animal still remained motionless.

Ten feet short of it, he stopped. Four legged and tailless, the animal's fur was a combination of browns running from nose to rear. Its ears were positioned forward, as were its strangely colored pink eyes, which had no white surrounding them. Its pupils were a deep blue and slightly oval rather than round.

When Roke took another step forward, the animal stiffened. He held his palms outward, showing an empty hand. After taking another step, he held for a moment. He took two more steps but stopped when the animal bared its teeth at him.

Its canines were three inches long, and slightly curved. No, not canines, he corrected himself, fangs. Roke spoke in a low and soothing voice. "I will not harm you." He took another step forward. When he did, his left hand unintentionally brushed his side, and the stunner popped out. The animal's ears flicked forward at the low click from the EXO suit.

Freezing when his foot touched the ground, Roke held still for a three-count, before moving forward again. On his second stride, he stepped on something slick, and his foot went out from under him. He fought to keep his footing but failed and he fell backwards toward the river. The animal backed up fast.

Roke hit the sloping ground hard. A loud grunt torn from between his lips when he luckily struck dirt, narrowly missing one of the outcropping rocks as he slid downward. The animal spun and ran while Roke rolled down to the river's bank and into the water. His body stopped when his head struck a large rock.

Stunned and barely conscious, he sank into the river, one arm clinging desperately to the rock. The surface current jerked him around, working hard to dislodge his hold on the rock. The metal blades had extended from his gloved fingertips the moment he'd fallen, and as his awareness came back, he turned his hand into a claw and dug the curved metal talons into the rock to stop him from getting pushed further into the water.

Battered and twisted by the rushing current, his head spinning from the blow to the rock, he struggled to hold on. He pressed his clawed hand to the rock, digging the talons against its hard surface. The talons screeched as he fought for purchase. Then one taloned finger hit a small crevice, which it clicked into and held.

Ignoring the fire streaking through the straining muscles of his shoulder, he drew on his willpower, and on his physical strength to hold his fingers into the rock. His shoulder screamed, sending lances of pain through this twisting muscles. Yet, he fought to get his other hand onto the rock.

At the very moment he swung his right arm up, the current surged, and the hard, rushing water slammed across his chest and face. He choked as another swell of the pounding water cascaded over him, ripping his hand viciously out of the taloned EXO glove, and shoving him into the river's raging surface current.

GODDESS

He sucked in a quick breath before the current carried him, tossing, and twisting to a point in the pounding waters where the river bottom dropped steeply, and the surface current deepened. The increased current pushed him down, spinning him head-over-heels toward the river's sloping bottom. He struck another iridescent rock just before the river dropped another twenty feet.

Grabbing wildly at the rock's slick surface with his bare hand, and disoriented by the spinning water, he held on while he worked out which way was up.

When he dragged his hand across the stone's face, his fingers and palm tingled. Ignoring the sensation, he drew his legs beneath him, planted his booted feet on the stone, and looked for the surface. He found it as his lungs screamed for air.

Concentrating on the water-distorted globe of the sun, he thrust, using his powerful thigh muscles to push off the bottom, and shoot upward, cutting knife-like through the current to catch the edge of a huge rock sticking half out of the river.

He pulled himself onto the rock, sat on its slippery, smooth face, bent his legs, and pressed his forehead to his knees. He coughed out water while he gasped for air. When his breathing settled, and he lifted his head, he told himself it could have been worse, he could have drowned.

"I was lucky," he said aloud, looking down into the clear water, and at the rectangular iridescent stone laying on the river bottom. He stared at the streaks of his hand and fingers across the iridescent coating. Then he remembered the tingling in his hand and turned his palm up. There were several lines of sparkling gray dust embedded in his skin. But as he stared at it, and the water evaporated, the sparkling dust faded and disappeared, leaving him with only a few speckles of gray on his palm.

Dipping his hand into the water to wash it off, he laughed, thinking of one of Caruso's theories about scouts. Caruso had voiced his belief for someone to be a good scout, a scout who lasted a lifetime, you had to be lucky.

Roke had laughed at his mentor, and Caruso shook his head, his face as serious as Roke had ever seen it, his eyes fiercer than he thought possible. "Go to the Scout Memorial when we get back to Guild Prime. Look at their plaques, and at their length of service. Any scout who is not lucky is there, and by the end of their first solo year. The others commemorated there had careers spanning decades."

Caruso had shaken his head. "No, if you aren't lucky, you don't survive. You'll understand when you go solo."

Today, and on his first solo day on the planet, he'd been lucky.

GODDESS

FIVE

Before he did anything else, he climbed back up the slope, searched the ground for the lost stunner, and looked for the animal as he did. He found the weapon lodged in a pile of small stones. There was no sign of the animal.

Retrieving the weapon, he sat on a clear patch of ground, took a food packet from his backpack, and ripped off its plascover. The packet warmed in his hand, and a half-minute later, he ate. When he finished, he took a drink from his canteen, and pulled the tab of the meal packet and dropped it. The empty packet disappeared in a flash, leaving a single ash to reach the ground. Re-energized, Roke left the slope, and when he was on level ground, walked north toward the far end of the valley.

He spent the next two hours walking slowly along the side of the river. He'd made it two-thirds of the way through the valley before the leading edge of the sun began its descent behind the western mountains. He had an hour of daylight left before the blanket of dusk would cover the valley.

He tapped a few keys on his sleeve. An oval four-inch-long mini drone dropped from one of the three bottom pouches on his backpack, while the screen hologram rose from the sleeve of his left arm. He sent the drone into the air and watched the screen show everything within camera range. When it became darker, the drone's night vision would activate.

The mini drone leveled off 100 feet above the river, its three lenses giving Roke a perfect view. Within minutes, he found a flat area for a camp between where he was now, and the end of the valley. The drone hovered on the river's northern mountainside, over the small area on the northern foothills, which was the mountain's line of demarcation between the rock-scattered ground and the beginning of grass and trees. Shelf-like, the area was a miniature plateau, its only vegetation being stiff and prickly grass.

An hour later, in the darkening night, he reached the small plateau. Without further thought, he stepped onto the grass and went to the center of the area.

Releasing his backpack from the suit, Roke withdrew a ten-inch rolled piece of material from a side pocket. He untied it, pushed a corner of it, and dropped it to the ground. It landed with a loud hissing. The material expanded and rose upward. Twelve seconds later, a full-sized scout shelter, ten feet by eight feet, stood on the plateau, and was anchored solidly into the ground. A moment later, two antennas rose above the tent.

The fabric of the tent was similar to his EXO suit, and filled with sensors to alert him of any dangers while he was inside. Sensors controlled heating and cooling and would adjust the internal temperature to keep it stable. The twin antennas were sending and receiving units.

Although the tent appeared flimsy to the casual eye, if any danger was perceived, and the shelter needed extra protection, its internal sensors would release nanites to bolster the metallic fabric.

GODDESS

Once set up, and his gear stowed, he stepped outside, sealed the tent, and went down to the riverside. Tomorrow, he would finish his exploration of the valley and return to the ship for a new glove. In the meantime, he sat near the water, which was now a deep blue-black, and according to his instruments reached a depth of 100 feet. In this section of the river there was no shimmering of color, not because it was night, but the water was deeper here, and there were no rocks close to the surface.

While he stared at the river, a school of multi-colored fish swam upstream, perhaps three feet below the surface. His stomach growled. He stood and went back to the camp.

<<>>

Caruso waited in the temporary office he'd been assigned in Guild Headquarters on Norton Landing. He hated being planet-bound, but in this there was no choice. A low chime sounded. He glanced at his screen readout, announcing his new apprentice waited outside.

Ignoring it, he punched in a high-priority code, and a moment later, Roke's daily report filled the screen. *Good*, he said to himself, seeing everything going exactly as they'd discussed. His own job was coming along smoothy as well.

He had all the guilds working together: Exploration, Construction, and the two sub-guilds, science and medical, which had branches in each guild. Even the colonists had been pulled into the guild preparations. All he had to do now, beside ride them to completion, was wait for Roke's final colonization approval signal so he could get the hell off the planet.

He flicked on the com. "Come in."

The door slid into the wall, exposing his six-foot, short-haired, and brown-eyed new apprentice. The woman walked in and up to his desk. She stopped, her body ramrod straight, and saluted.

"Thea Laanestret, scout apprentice reporting in."

"Apprentice Laanestret, this is the explorer Guild not the military, and not the Guild Academy. We do not salute here, and I do not stand on formality. You need to relax; former marine, yes?"

"Yes, sir."

He stared at her, his eyebrows raised, waiting.

"Yes," she said, dropping the 'sir.'

"Good. Apprentice, you, and I will be together for the next five years. Let's get one thing straight between us. You will never do anything on your own unless I say so. Is this understood?"

"Yes, s—" She caught herself quickly. Caruso liked that.

"Pull up a chair, Thea. Let's go over the ground rules."

<<>>

He was outside the shelter, his attention fixed on the twin moons of Anadi locked in their dual orbits, each close to the other. The moons' reflections glowed pale blue due to the gaseous atmosphere enshrouding both satellites—an atmosphere unbreathable to humans, and which also distorted light within the range of human vision.

Disregarding the scientific principles, Roke smiled, naming the moons 'Blue Eyes', for they resembled two eyes staring down at him—pretty blue eyes to be exact.

GODDESS

He yawned, acknowledged his growing tiredness, and entered the shelter. After undressing, he lay on the soft, air-cushioned floor, and the area he stretched out on lifted six inches as the shelter created a sleep pallet. He couldn't stop his laugh when he thought of how his grandfather would have shaken his head at seeing him in the shelter.

"We are Diné," he would have said. "We seek not to separate ourselves from the kiss and touch of the ground; rather, do we seek its comfort, and beneath the sky as we were meant to do."

"Yes, Acheii," he would have replied, his face serious while he smiled inside. And perhaps soon he would lie on the ground without the shelter's protection, but not yet. Not until he knew Anadi better, and what might lie beneath its surface.

He fell asleep slowly as his thoughts wandered over the day.

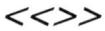

<<>>

At first he thought it was a large bird, its skin reflecting the sunlight of Anadi's yellow dwarf. But when it came closer, he realized it was anything but a bird. It landed amidst a surge of light, its wings shimmering beneath shafts of sunlight. Half blinded by the burst of light, he blinked.

When his eyes readjusted, the bird was gone, replaced by a tall woman striding toward him. She was magnificent, with silvery-blonde hair, which was more silver than blonde, and so long it covered the upper part of her naked body. When she came closer, he saw her face was oval with high cheekbones, a small Romanesque nose, and a wide mouth with full lips. Her eyes, when they locked on his, were a startling blue mixed with luminous shades of pale green—a color like the most perfect aquamarine gem from any part of the galaxy.

Although she was completely naked, he could not take his eyes from the beauty of her face. Something about it drew him to her. Suddenly, they were face-to-face on the small plateau.

Curiously, he was as naked as she and when she reached him, her arms went around him and pulled him to her. Her breasts flattened against his chest; her arms held him so tight she almost crushed the breath from him. Then her lips covered his, her tongue breaking through his closed mouth, forcing his tongue to dance with hers. He tried to pull away, but could not.

An instant later, he gave in, and returned her kiss. His passion took charge. He hardened against her. Moments later, they were on the grass, their bodies entwined. He entered her slowly, accepting the warmth around him and he pushed deep inside her. Her fingers pressed deep into the muscles on his back, crushing him against her breasts so powerfully her stiffened nipples poked the muscles of his chest.

Her legs locked around him. She held him still, her nails digging across his skin as she shuddered against him, and then shuddered again. When the pressure from her fingers eased, he moved slowly within her. When he moved, she responded. He shifted carefully, following the gentle swivel of her hips, and the welcoming upward push of her pelvis. Her inner muscles tightened around him. He held still, drew his lips from hers, and looked into her eyes.

GODDESS

For a millisecond, her eyes changed, her pupils going from round, to oval, and then back again. *A trick of light*, he thought. Lowering his lips to hers, he tasted their sweetness, while the incredible warmth of her body beneath his, and the searing heat surrounding him within her, increased his passion even more. Their lovemaking turned more and more physical, each giving, and each taking, until her body suddenly stiffened and arched against him.

She pushed hard, her pubis crushing against his as she drew him further in, her legs tightening again, and the heels of her feet digging into his buttocks. A moment later, she cried out in release. In that instant, something slipped around him, squeezing him tighter to her, deeper into her until she again spasmed around him, and he came within her. He lifted his head and pulled his lips from hers to look over his shoulder at the scaled tail securing him to her. He blinked and it was gone. When he turned back, her face had transformed into some sort of animal. He jerked himself free, sat up, and pushed away as fast as he could.

Drawing in breath after breath, his body drenched in sweat, he looked around the empty shelter only to realize he'd been dreaming.

He sat in disbelief. He had never experienced a dream this intense, nor one so completely sexual. Still, it was a dream. It had to be a dream, but was unlike anything he had ever experienced before. He could still feel her skin against his, feel the heat from inside her lingering on him.

The dream concerned him. Part of the process in selecting first-in scouts was their ability to put sex on the back burner for long periods of time. Not because having sex wasn't enjoyable, for he was as virile as any man. It simply wasn't the driving force in his, or any scout's makeup, as it was in other men and women.

While his thoughts continued to puzzle him, he stretched out the tight muscles of his shoulder, and a stab of pain sliced across his back. He reached over his shoulder, his hand and fingers going down his back as far as they could, until he touched what seemed like cuts on his back.

"What the hell?" Then he sat on the floor, closed his eyes, and did his best to do what his grandfather had always told him when he'd had a powerful dream. Recreate it and look for its meaning.

Closing his eyes, he brought back the dream, watching the woman walk toward him, her beautiful face alight by the sun. Her body was the most feminine he'd ever seen, and athletically muscled, her breasts rode large and proud upon her chest, their brown circular tips aglow in the sun. Her waist was narrow. Her hips flared outward until they blended smoothly into the lean, muscled thighs of a long-distance runner. Her legs were long, and her calves perfectly muscled.

When she was close enough to touch, he looked into the aquamarine of her eyes, and even though he was visualizing his recall of the dream, he sensed himself being drawn into their blue-green depths. He shook the memory away, belatedly realizing she was the same woman as the dream he'd had on his scout ship when he'd been orbiting above Anadi before landing yesterday.

He was intrigued by the strange sexuality of the dream, and the weirdness as well. He thought back to the last time he'd had a

GODDESS

sexually driven dream—He'd been fourteen. He was certain this dream was connected to the others he'd been having since his arrival here, but none compared to this one.

He thought about the moment she'd reached the height of her passion, and the sensation of something going around him, even as her nails dug into the thick muscles of his back. He stood, went to his EXO suit, and activated the small drone he'd used to find this grassy ledge.

Seconds later, he was looking at his back, and was stunned to find long, red lines crisscrossing his skin. Then, unbelievably, as he studied the red lines, the scratches faded, and his skin was once again unmarked, except for the three scars that had already been there, a souvenir of an animal on Laius Twelve.

What the fuck? Frowning, he shut down the drone. He knew he'd seen the scratches, but had he? Was it his subconscious confirming his thinking about the dream? What else could it be? He knew the impossibility of anything entering the shelter last night without the sensors waking and warning him. A cold chill raced along his spine. Was something on the planet affecting his mind?

"What in the seven hells of Pronos just happened?"

DAVID WIND

SIX

Unable to sleep after the dream, Roke was packed and off the mini plateau with the dawn. He decided to hold off on the second part of the valley exploration, and was back on his ship by noon. His first stop was the medical monitor to check on his head to make sure he wasn't suffering some sort of injury causing him to hallucinate during the night. The medical response was negative. He grunted at the results: his head was as good as it would ever be.

His grandfather would say, "Your head is as thick as a rock." While that might be true, his mind wasn't. He was disturbed in a way he'd never experienced. How could a dream have done this, and why couldn't he cast off the haunting visions of the woman ... if that's what she was? How was it possible? He'd heard stories—everyone had, of ghost-like aliens who could come and go as they pleased, but no one had ever confirmed the stories used to scare children.

The sensors had shown he was alone all night. There were no violations to the enclosure, no alarms had woken him. He'd also heard the even older stories, the ones about the forerunners, of how they had populated almost all the earth-type planets of the galaxy, millions of years before. But according to the Guild archeologists, they mysteriously disappeared 100,000 years ago; and close to the same time scientists believed the evolution of sentient human life began on Earth.

Symbols and a strange language were discovered on sixteen earth-type worlds, all of them filled with unusual ruins and the mysterious glyph style writings. Some scouts had reported strange occurrences at forerunner sites, but none were verified. Still, that didn't explain his dream, or the lingering sensation of the scratches on his back. The scientists, alien archeologists, and linguists had all come to the same conclusion about the forerunners. The writings were warnings, but of what, they had no idea.

No matter, he needed to make certain it wasn't something alien—something he and Caruso had missed. If there was alien inhabitation the planet, he'd have to warn off the Guild before sending the builders and colonists. He tossed off the dream fragments and went to work.

Deciding to stay shipboard for what was left of the day, he set about planning his next moves. Tomorrow, he would fly the ship to the western end of the valley and explore the section he'd not reached yesterday.

Roke glanced around the ship's command console, then placed a neuro-electrode pad on each temple, which connected directly to the ship's main computer. For the most part, he used verbal commands and requests, but the pads gave him the ability to combine visualizations while speaking to better communicate with the computer. At the Guild Academy there was a standing joke about mind-reading computers.

"Place three stationary survey bots above the valley. 1 on each end, one over the spot where I went in," he ordered the computer. These larger drone-type bots cruised at altitudes between five and ten thousand feet, or could hovered over an area for up to three days without moving from their position. He was extremely uneasy about the whole episode, and had to make certain there was nothing there. His 'senses' were on high alert.

When the drones settled into place, he said. "Talk to me, Daho." Daho was the name he'd given to the ship, and the ship's single most important component, the ship's computer—the ship's heart—and by a logical extension the name of the ship. It was the abbreviation of the Navajo word for 'wise one', *dahóyánigíí*.

"What would you like me to talk about, Roke?"

"Tell me what your files have on the race we call Forerunners."

"There is much in my banks. What do you seek in particular?"

"Last discovery of artifacts."

"System Delta-3-1, outer galactic rim. Astro-survey ship Outreach Seventeen sent back the following report …" The date under the vid file was fifty-seven years earlier, thirty-two years before he was born. Roke watched the screen as the ruins came up. They appeared the same as all the surface forerunner ruins: so old the remnants were piles of crumbled rocks.

The structures found underground on three of the planets had remained standing; however, the moment anyone touched them, pieces would fall and turn to powder. There were machines too, but by assumption only, because the remnants lay in corroded piles of an

GODDESS

unknown type of metallic rust. Still, writings were found, but to this day, they remained undecipherable.

In one underground find, the ruins were built around a lake filled with large rocks. He stared at them. Their shapes were similar to the ones in the valley. But then, even on Anadi, rocks were rocks.

"Show me the writings salvaged from the other worlds."

It took less than a quarter-minute to fill the screen with the strange symbols.

"Has anyone found a key to this?"

`"Negative."`

<<>>

Roke was outside, staring up at the sky and glad to be in the night air. He'd spent the last half-hour running a wide circle around the ship, loosening the stiffness of his muscles from sitting all afternoon. Being cooped up had never been easy for him, and he didn't want to use the exercise equipment on the ship, as he did when spacing.

He'd spent his time watching the stationary drones' relayed images from over the valley. He had seen nothing concrete, yet twice something blurry passed across on the screen, as though there was a shifting movement beneath the water where he'd gone under.

When he'd gone to the close-up, the large underwater rock he'd grabbed onto with his bare hand seemed more iridescent. He was certain it was a trick of light from the sun and the fish. The streaks from his hand and fingers, which had disturbed the iridescence, were gone as well. Nothing moving except the fish.

Shrugging away his thoughts as his breathing eased from the run, he looked up at the twin moons, which were directly overhead. They had the exact same orbital route as the sun, but at 180-degrees opposition. The scientists had yet to explain this in terms he could understand, or even care about, but he'd never seen a planet's suns and moons at exact opposition and following identically similar orbits throughout an entire solar year.

Midnight. Time for sleep, yet he wasn't sure he wanted to, not after last night's dream, but at the same time, he was intrigued by its unusual eroticism. He wished he had someone to talk with who might understand the implications of his dreams; not one of the Guild's psych docs, but someone like his grandfather.

However, the most senior Navajo Elder on the Diné Council, and the Planetary Council, had died three years ago. Roke had been lucky enough to have been back at Guild Prime when he was notified of his grandfather's condition. He'd taken emergency leave and made it home before his acheii moved on.

His grandfather had wakened when Roke came in; it was as if he'd been waiting for him. The moment Roke entered, his acheii's weathered eyes locked on Roke's face. "Tsé nitsaa," he said, Big Rock, his usual name for Roke—that or Stubborn Rock, *Tsé nil-ta*, depending on what Roke had done.

"I'm here, Acheii."

His grandfather nodded, then gave him a half-smile. "Live long, my blood, do so with honor. Forget not from where you come, and bring from where you come with you, always." His eyes went

GODDESS

opaque. He grabbed Roke's hand, his grip so tight it cut off circulation. "You have made me proud, bitsóóké. You have made my life one of great honor for having been able to raise you."

He didn't speak, he simply grasped his grandfather's hand and held it. His grandfather died minutes later.

Roke, along with the remaining Diné and planetary tribal council elders, three blended Apache, and four Cherokee elders gave him a traditional Navajo funeral. Roke bathed and dressed his grandfather, following the millennia-old traditions of the Diné. After which, he sat through the night, watching over him as ritual dictated. And unlike most other cultures, on most planets, Roke buried him in the land he loved rather than cremated him.

When Roke returned to Guild Prime, he doubted he would ever go back to the planet of his birth.

Exhaling away the memory, he returned to the ship, knowing full well he needed to sleep in order to do his job. Inside, he instructed Daho to go to sleep lighting, undressed, and climbed into his bunk.

As soon as he lay back, the computer turned down the lighting even further, and his bunk darkened enough for sleep. Once he was fully settled on the bunk, the computer opened the sleep program. Roke closed his eyes, listened to the soft sounds flowing from the speakers, and drifted along with them. He was asleep sixty seconds later.

<<>>

Waking from his dreamless sleep refreshed, and after having a cup of caffeinated protein, he went to the console to check the images from the stationary bots. The ones above the entrance and exits to the valley showed nothing had happened during the night. The one over the spot he'd gone under showed the same.

"Daho, did anything happen during the night?"

`"Nothing occurred; animals drank from the river. One rose to the surface and walked away."`

Pinpricks played a tattoo on the nape of his neck. He stared at the middle bot's screen, not paying attention to Daho's words. Something wasn't right. "Close-up on number two bot."

The camera lenses widened, and the water's surface came close, fast. He stared at the image on the screen, and at the bottom of the river, at where the stone he'd touched should have been. It wasn't there. There were several smaller stones, each perhaps ten inches long. "What the hell?"

`"Is there a problem?"`

"Negative. Send the bot to the river bottom."

The bot dropped stonelike into the water, stopping ten inches from the bottom. "Scan 360 degrees."

The bot scanned in two directions, first horizontally, and then vertically. When it showed the river bottom, he saw the large rock was gone, and there were only those few small grey stones nearby. "Daho, replay from midnight to dawn, stop when the large rock disappears."

The computer began its replay, and everything on the screen blurred, except for the time designation in the bottom corner. At four, the screen froze on the small stones. "Back, slow motion."

GODDESS

When the small stones disappeared, the large rock reappeared. "Stop. Forward. Slow." The computer went into slow mode. He watched the large rock begin to blur. The rock's iridescent surface somehow grew brighter under the light of the two moons. The picture moved forward, the rock's shimmering grew more intense until, a few minutes later, there was a flash of light momentarily blacking out the camera with its luminescence.

When the lens cleared, the scene had changed. Off to one side, a strange-looking animal swam toward the surface, but Roke's eyes were locked on the stone as the larger stone disappeared and a small stone lay in its place. "Daho, what happened to the large stone?"

The screen shifted, blurring as the computer reran the scene 100 times per minute. Three minutes later, the picture settled onto the small stone.

"It is uncertain what happened to the large rock. I have analyzed everything. The large rock vanishing is a fact. The small stones appearing is a fact."

"In other words, you don't know how or why this happened."

"Affirmative."

He shook his head. He translated Daho's words into what his acheii would have said, 'What happened, happened. Accept it as such.' Translation: *it is what it is.*

"Prepare to raise the ship." He hit a sequence of four switches. The ship came alive, and he did his best to settle his thoughts. How could the stone he'd struck on the bottom disappear? It made no sense, and he couldn't leave it at it is what it is.

"Daho, are there any unusual readings on the rocks in the river?"

It took the computer a half-minute to respond. `"Affirmative, Roke. Every rock, even the smallest, appears to be the same shape with the same relational dimensions. Their width is thirty percent of their length with a thickness of five percent of the length."`

"Every rock?"

`"Yes."`

How was that possible?

Seven minutes later, he landed on the western side of the valley, at the point where the northern mountains began. This morning, he would check this area, then he would move northwest, over the landmasses.

The planet was unusual and differed greatly from most earth-type planets, for a full two-thirds of the eastern continent was ocean, an earth-like saline-based ocean. The ocean fed all the lakes, rivers, and small seas throughout the planet, except, of course, for the massive deserts in the southern hemisphere. Fresh water had a saline base of zero-point-four percent: drinkable.

Between the ocean and the deserts, the habitable regions were in the western hemisphere, north of the equator and included parts of the eastern hemisphere, north of the equator.

GODDESS

Putting on his EXO suit, he attached his backpack, stepped onto the surface, and gazed thoughtfully around. The only sound was rushing water. He itched to move on but had to make sure there were no issues here, before heading northeast to the location he and Caruso had determined to be the best initial location for the colonists.

Roke walked to the edge of the river bank, looked at river's entrance into the mountain, raised his left arm, and pressed two buttons. The view screen projection rose, and a mini drone dropped from his pack. "Daho, have the drone follow the river underground."

When the drone dove onto the river and disappeared from view, Roke watched the screen. The river flowed into the mountain, then descending on a thirty-degree angle. Within ninety seconds the drone was 1,000 feet beneath ground. It stopped and forked in the underground river, where three quarters of the flowing water went north, and the smaller fork went east.

Something about the fork was off; he sent the drone into it. The fork continued east for another for another two klicks then took a sudden ninety-degree angle south. Seven klicks later, the drone hit a wave of strong current and was tossed around.

Daho automatically took control of the drone, leveling it and holding it steady within the new current. "Scan the area." The drone did two three-sixties: vertically and then one horizontally. The bottom was now covered with enough small stones it could only be seen in patches.

The lights of the drone, streaking a few inches above the riverbed, sent out the iridescent reflections of the rocks in all directions. He sent the drone forward. Six klicks later, the water made another left and slowly ascended. As it went higher, small rocks began rising from the riverbed, its current now strong enough to carry the stones with it.

Roke again turned control of the drone to Daho as it zigzagged between the rocks to avoid being hit. He tore his eyes from the images to check the readouts below the screen. The fork of the river rose quickly toward the southeast end of the river. At the same time, the current increased,

"Show me where it reaches the surface." The screen flicked and Roke found himself starting at the entrance to the valley.

"It does not reach the surface. It empties into the river," Daho reported.

The screened flicked and he watched the riverbed rise until it fed into the valley's river, the current moving even faster as the water propelled the the stones upward toward the junction with the river.

Stunned, he watched the stones spit into the river until the drone reappeared at the entrance to the valley. He had never seen a river that fed itself. He wondered if anyone had. Creeping through his mind came the certainty there was something very strange about this phenomena.

"Retrace course. Show the sides and top of the underground river." He squatted and stared at the images flowing across his screen. "Oh … shit!" Alarm bells rang in his head. "Return," he commanded the drone.

GODDESS

"How could we have missed this?" he hissed; his anger barely contained. The underground river's strange fork and double-back return wasn't a natural phenomenon, it was too perfectly engineered.

By whom ... or what?

SEVEN

The unexpected implications of his discovery rocked him. He had no option but to return to the ship. There were Guild protocols in place to determine what came next. The drone slipped into his backpack as he opened the hatch and stepped inside. He would have to report this, but not until he investigated further—a first-in scout had certain leeways when confirming alien presence.

While there had been more than a few incidents in Explorer Guild history of alien planets, only the Scav had proven to be a danger. The Guild had found the handful of other races peaceful for the most part. Almost all were humanoid to some degree, and many were not oxygen breathers. Those who inhabited earth-type planets, including the humans of the GU soon learned it was mutually beneficial to become allies rather than enemies.

Most of the alien species stayed within their own solar systems, content with their ways. The GU over two and a half centuries, had formed treaties with all but one alien race. It was the Scav who were aggressive, destructive, and combatant to all other oxygen-breathing races.

Dropping his pack, he went to the pilot's seat, hit a switch, and the engines came to life. He flipped two more switches. "Taking flight command."

When the computer switched control to him, he lifted off and retraced his flight back to the southern end of the valley to land in the same spot he had two days before. Once on the ground, he had Daho

GODDESS

replay the drone's recording. He watched, then replayed it again, slower this time. He bent closer to the screen. "Magnify by two."

The image expanded, showing the drone moving through the new fork until it reached the southern end of the valley. "Impossible!"

Standing, he started toward the hatch. `"Roke, your physical readings tell me sustenance is required."` He was about to argue but remembered he'd only had a cup of procaf. He was hungry. He went to the galley, pulled out a protein pack, and devoured it.

"Satisfied, oh wise-one?" Without expecting a reply, he went to the hatch, withdrew a rebreather, and attached it to the side of his helmet. Once in the water, the rebreather would seal the scrubber from any gas or liquid outside the helmet.

Debarking, he walked the hundred yards to the river edge, stopping near the point where the underground river-fork emptied into the valley. He snapped on his helmet, entered a double combination on his arm pad to increase his weight and counteract his buoyancy, and jumped into the water.

He floated until the weight of his suit increased enough for him to sink to the bottom. He dug his feet into the silty river bottom and looked around.

Not three feet before him, was the oval opening from the circling river fork, its rushing water forcefully entering the equatorial river. He'd missed seeing this because he'd walked into the valley 100 feet from the river.

Watching the intensity of the water entering the river, and the rocks tumbling within it, he wondered if the rocks were part of the process, whatever 'process' meant. This was what he had to discover before reporting to the Guild.

Roke glanced back. The river bottom was clear of any of the sparkling rectangular rocks or stones populating river through the valley. The water current, before reaching the spot where the fork joined it, flowed gently around him, and unlike the river within the valley, its current was normal, the water's pull gradually easing the lower he went rather than the current reaching to only a foot or so in depth and ending.

Turning back, he bottom-walked to the edge of the fork's opening, watched stones emerge, and pushed further into the main part of the river. Some of the rocks sank quickly with enough force to roll along the bottom a few feet before stopping in the bottom's still water. The ones caught within the higher current were carried downstream, falling randomly.

He leaned over the opening and watched batches of small stones spin by. When only a few flew out, he still waited, all the time judging the patterns of speed and amount of stones. Being cautious was the only way to make it safely into the fork and see what was happening. He had to have a firsthand look—not one through a camera lens.

In the space of a minute, two small bunches of stones went by, followed by a group of larger rocks, perhaps two feet in length … Just as he was about to go into the fork, he held back, a question floated in

GODDESS

his mind. How could the water move rocks as big as the ones that just passed? It made no sense for something as heavy as a rock to be pushed this way.

With the pattern and timing of the stones set in his mind, he gripped the edge of the opening and flipped himself inside. The weight of his suit dragged him down into the path of the oncoming rocks. He managed to hold onto the opening's lip, but couldn't reach his arm pad. "Daho," he called instead. "Reduce my suit weight by half."

"Dangerous."

"Do it!"

A heartbeat later, the suit's weight dropped, and he was no longer being dragged by the current. He let go of the lip, and pushed into the tunnel, for that was what he now believe it to be. It wasn't flat-bottomed, but the rocks and stones made it appear so.

Spinning in the water, and looking at the walls, confirmed that this was not a natural underground river trunk, it was too perfect. He reached out and grabbed a small stone. He could barely feel the weight, which was even stranger. Yesterday, when he'd picked up the rock, its weight was right for its size. This wasn't.

Across from him, he watched a medium-sized rock, caught in the current, spin into the side of the tunnel. When it ricocheted off the wall it left a shiny mark in its wake.

Puzzled, Roke reached up above him and rubbed across the dirt and algae coating the surface, revealing the sheen of polished metal which reflected the lights of his helmet.

Roke had no doubts the river fork was not natural; it was manufactured. But more significantly, the area he'd wiped his hand across had no corrosion on its surface, nor scratches from rock strikes.

Every shipboard instrument they'd used had confirmed this planet had no intelligent life. No remains of a previous civilizations had registered on sonar, radar, or any of the twenty-seven other planetary exploration instruments, biological sensors, nor was anything seen by camera. There were no readings from beneath the surface, yet this was here—it wasn't possible.

He took in a deep breath and, disappointed by his discovery, yet excited at the same time, flipped himself over and headed back. At the point where the tunnel bent upward, a sudden surge of current driving a cluster of small stones shot past him an instant before the rushing water caught him and swept him upward.

Spinning out of control because of the lighter buoyancy, he couldn't stop himself from veering directly into the path of another batch of stones heading directly for him. Before he could raise his arms to protect himself, one of the stones smashed into his helmet, shattering the clear crystal into a thousand cracks.

He took a deep breath a half-second before the crystal fell apart and the water rushed in. Kicking his legs and using his arms, Roke pushed himself upward. He almost made it to the surface before a larger rock in the middle of a group of smaller ones rammed into the already-shattered side of his helmet.

<<>>

GODDESS

Above the river, sparkling lances of sunlight bounced from the scaled wings of the small iridescent dragon-like creature who flew above the river, watching the spinning stone strike Roke. It followed as his body was thrust into the river by the current. The small creature drew its wings to its sides, stretched out its front arms, and dove straight into the water.

It sliced through the water, ignoring the small stones striking its scales to catch the unconscious form in its arms. Although the creature was a third the size of Roke, its taloned fingers held him tightly while it rose to the surface.

Breaking into the air, its wings unfolded, and the creature carried the larger man over the water's surface, and over the river's edge to his ship. It landed on the ground before the hatch and set him carefully down.

Using talon-tipped fingered hands to detach the remnants of his helmet, it pressed the two buttons in the sequence to open his EXO suit. The moment the suit shrank into itself, Roke, still unconscious, began to shake.

The being lay next to him, wrapped its wings around him, and did its best to hold him while the tremors shook his body. While it held him, its shape transformed from the scaled dragon-like creature to a silvery blonde haired human girl of seven or eight.

Once Roke's body temperature was elevated, the girl rose, went to the ship, and pressed on the almost invisible panel next to the hatch. When it opened, she tapped a code with one finger.

"You are not authorized."

Ignoring the computer, the child reached to the emergency box on the other side of the hatch, pressed the single button, and said, "Íidoolííł."

The hatch slid into the hull wall. She returned to Roke, knelt, and doing what seemed impossible for so small a girl, lifted him and brought him into the ship. She went directly to his bunk, as if she'd been there before, and set him upon it.

Bending close to Roke's face, she examined the cut on his forehead. She wiped away the blood, after which she stared silently down at him, taking in the planes of his face. Then she knelt on the floor next to the bunk, traced his jawline with one finger, moving it from his jaw, upward along his cheek until it reached his ear.

The child took a moment to glance down the length of his well-muscled body. Her eyes, the depth of an aquamarine jewel, seemed to glow. She traced her fingers along the length of his side, then looked at the lens across from the bunk, turned back, and leaned over him. She reached out with both hands, and pressed them to each side of his head. She shifted slightly, turning her back to the lens to block her mouth, and Roke, from its view.

She pressed her forehead to his, and moved her mouth to a hairsbreadth from his ear. "Call to me when you are ready." This time she spoke English. With her last word, her body reformed into the iridescent creature.

Standing gracefully, the dragon-creature went to the hatch, left the ship, and ran across the grass, wings extended. Soon, the

GODDESS

shimmering wide-winged mini dragon was framed against a pale blue sky, a small shadow outlined by the sun.

DAVID WIND

EIGHT

Roke woke with a massive headache. Disoriented, he sat up, planted his feet on the ship's deck to ground himself, and looked around: he was on his ship. His last memory was of being underwater, getting swept into the current, and something smashing into his helmet. *How did I get here?*

He touched his forehead and explored the cut and the lump beneath his fingers. "Daho, what happened?"

"An alien saved you."

He shook his head and groaned at the stab of the pain from the movement. He pressed his fingers to his temple to ease the headache. "Daho, we are the aliens here." He went to the med cabinet, took out a hypo, and sprayed it into each nostril. Thirty long seconds later, the headache was gone. "Daho, vitals?"

"All is normal. An alien saved you. You went into shock. The alien kept you warm."

"Like hell. Was everything monitored?"

"Affirmative"

"Show me!"

"Commencing."

The playback ended twenty minutes later, leaving Roke to stare at the screen. *Na'ashǫ'iitsoh,* he heard his grandfather whisper from deep within his mind. *Mythical creature.*

"Mythical my ass. That's a dragon! A little dragon, and a ... a little girl," he whispered at the impossible scenes he'd witnessed. No

GODDESS

… not impossible, just … He was at a loss for words. How could it be a dragon and a child? "Replay security breech." He scrutinized every frame of the recording, from the very first frame, knowing everything he watched was as real as the ship he was in.

He observed the creature place him on the ground. She … it … was not large; barely a third of his own six-two, but incredibly strong, judging by the ease with which she'd carried him.

Unlike the mythical dragons in children's Tri-D shows, she didn't have four legs with clawed feet, she had two feet, and two arms as well. The dragon's tail was the length of her body, and the wings had a wide span. A mane of silver blonde hair flowed halfway down her back.

But when she'd folded him in her wings, and brought him against the scales covering her body, her body fluttered between the shape of the creature and that of a child. When she released herself from around him, her wings and tail disappeared, leaving a young child.

He watched her override the computer and manually open the hatch, the lens capturing every feature of her face. The color of her eyes haunted him for they were the same color as the woman in his dream—her hair too.

How could she know the codes, know what he called the computer, and how to open the hatch using a Diné word? Who in all the planetary hells was it—she—whatever?

He'd overcome his initial astonishment, while following every movement from entering the ship, to her placing him on the bunk. He did not miss the way she trailed her hand along the length of his body, and questioned what she did when she leaned over him and whispered into his ear.

But the words she'd whispered made him sit straight with the realization those words did not come from Daho's recording but from his own mind. *"Call to me when you are ready."*

Ready for what? And how could he know what she'd said, he'd been unconscious. How was it possible? And how could she speak Navajo and English? It made no sense.

Staring at her back, and the long, silvery hair, his problem turned palpable. He had come face-to-face with an unforeseen quandary, a predicament effecting the entire mission, and one he'd never considered as a remote possibility.

How did we miss something of his magnitude? He and Caruso had spent three months studying every square inch of the planet, both from above, within, and on the planet's surface. They'd swept the planet, entering everything into the data banks of Caruso's ship. Their findings were communicated to the main computer banks of Guild Prime, and verified one hundred percent. There was no sentient life on Anadi. None!

Did the valley have something to do with this? "Daho, replay first entry into the valley."

<<>>

He shifted the food aimlessly around his plate, too nauseated to eat. Everything about the planet changed when the little dragon made its presence known. He had no doubt it was intelligent, which

GODDESS

meant there was sentient life on the planet, alien, and not human … or was it another some other form of humanity?

"Roke. I have finished."

He put the fork down, the slice of protein untouched. An hour before, he'd asked the computer to see if it could analyze what the creature was, and if it was indigenous.

"There is insufficient data to confirm or deny. The image she presents is non-humanoid. In opposition, her internal organs are identical to a human, including reproductive organs. Proteins and hormones are identical; but a single gland next to the pituitary exits. This is not part of earth-normal humans. I cannot analyze this gland. In addition, I cannot confirm if the being is indigenous because we have no knowledge of what is and what is not indigenous on Anadi."

"Does it activate when she changes into the … creature?"

The computer was silent for a moment, the images on the screen flashed by so quickly they were blurred into one sparkling run of colors. A moment later the screen cleared, and a Tri-D projection of the girl as a dragon appeared.

"Confirmed. The gland produces the change, but it is more as well. She is human, but she is not human as we know it."

"You're not helping."

"Apologies. What can I do to help you better?"

"Tell me what to do."

"I am a computer I can only make suggestions. I am not permitted to tell you what to do."

"Then give me a few fucking suggestions." The computer went silent for almost three minutes.

"Roke, this is not about sex. But I have gone through all my programming. I have reached a conclusion: there is only one possible option."

Roke didn't say a word.

"Guild protocol requires immediate notification."

"Negative."

The computer went silent. "Daho?"

"The primary first-in scout protocol is to report a sentient presence, and or an alien presence, leave the planet, and call off colonization. The second protocol is, when possible, examine the alien to determine if the alien is a danger to human life. May I call in the notice of sentient or alien presence now?"

Roke closed his eyes. "Negative."

"It is required."

"Your prime directive is to listen and obey your scout. Correct?"

"Yes."

"No matter the circumstances as long as I am alive?"

"Yes."

GODDESS

"My instructions are as follows. We do not notify Guild Prime until we know what we are dealing with. Understood?"

`"I understand, Roke; I am recording this for later playback."`

"Of course you are." He shook his head. He had trained the computer to respond to him as if it were a person. He almost regretted it now. He shook his head. He'd been unconscious when she leaned over him, blocking the computer lens's view. But he knew she had whispered in his ear, "Call to me when you are ready." He didn't know how he'd known what she'd said, he just knew. And she did not say 'call me'; rather 'call to me'.

He sat; his eyes were unfocused `in thought. There were several possible choices, but he wasn't sure if any were right.

Roke would eventually call to … it … to her, if for no other reason than to learn who, or what she was. He took down a bottle of scotch, opened it, and took a long deep pull. He leaned back without putting the bottle down.

<<>>

He woke refreshed; the scotch had helped him sleep dreamlessly. After a cup of caf and a full protein bowl, he sat at the computer and brought up a map of the northern land masses. He and Caruso had gone over this dozens of times. There were four viable settlement options, and they'd both decided on where the first colony should settle. To make certain one last time, he had Daho bring up Tri-D image of the land and hills surrounding it. This area was his personal choice as well.

"Daho, prepare for takeoff to sector N-8721."

`"Yes, Roke. Fifteen minutes."`

"Show me the substructure of N-8721." The sector was 900,000 square miles running 900 miles north along the northern mountains its boundary, and 1,000 miles west, along the western side of the east-west mountain divide, and crossing two climate zones.

A Tri-D representation appeared in the center of the deck, a circular slice of the planet from the surface down 10,000 feet. The planet's substructure was perfect, with layers of various rock interspersed with layers of dirt. The area he and had Caruso selected for the first colony had a rocky substructure, strong enough to hold buildings. This was also one of the areas where parts of the substructure blocked the instruments. The computers of both ships confirmed the assessment: the blocked areas were deposits of an as-yet unknown minerals.

The surface was composed of a ten-foot-deep layer of high-nutrient topsoil, below which contained layers of nutrient saturated dirt, creating a strong base to support decades of farming. It was perfect, except for one issue. Defensibility.

`"Take off six minutes,"` Daho announced.

In exactly six minutes and eleven seconds, ship reached the altitude of 4,000 feet, flying northwest. It reached the location in twelve minutes and descended until Roke said. "Hold! Give me a circular view 200 klicks diameter."

Below him, grass and growths of small tree groves showed it to be a suitable area for the colony's first settlement. He looked from the open fields to the large broad forests of multi-hued trees filling the sector, and then to the rivers which fed abundant lakes.

It was the ideal area for a settlement, especially knowing the forest was within thirty klicks. Yet, somehow, it seemed too much … too perfect, which it was.

Again, the strange sense of something being off crept through his mind, infiltrating the nape of his neck with irritating, tingling knife points, and brought out his sense of something not quite right.

"Go northwest to the line of trees," he instructed Daho.

Without comment, Daho sent the ship skimming the 200 klicks to the edge of the forest. When they arrived, Roke checked his weapons and made sure each area of his EXO suit was set.

Then, with his ancestor's buffalo knife on one side, and his scout's longer blade on the other, he went opened the floor panel to the lower bay. "Maintain altitude. Activate all sensors. Hold a hundred-yard security border around me."

Dropping onto the belly hatch, he mounted the sled. "Open hatch." The split opened, the sled dropped, and Roke spun it away from the scout ship. He flew a slow route over the forests, spending a half-hour skimming the treetops and found nothing wrong.

The forest was hundreds of square miles of hills, trees, and small lakes framing the open grassy land. At one section of the northern mountains, he found two unusual lakes. One was set several hundred feet above the other, and fed into the lower with a magnificent wide waterfall.

After circling the forest twice, he landed on the shore of the waterfall-fed lake, secured, and left the sled, before walking straight into the woods. The moment he'd stepped onto the surface of Anadi, the strange sensation at the base of his neck grew.

He sensed eyes on him, watching him, waiting for him to do something ... but what?

"Daho, are there any signs of life near me?"

"Animals are present. Birds too. There are two species of birds, three of animals. Two small animals. One ten feet to your left."

"Carnivorous?"

"Uncertain. I cannot get a clean scan. I offer caution."

"Suggest, not offer," corrected Roke.

"Noted."

Moving slowly, he turned left, and walked quietly into the woods toward where Daho said the animal was. If it were like the one he'd seen the other day, it might not run. Seven steps later, he spotted it. Small, perhaps ten inches tall. It had a strange body, both elongated and broad, with colors of brown and white. Its legs were no longer than five inches. Its head was elongated as well, almost doglike, with a long snout. He could not tell what its teeth were like, yet.

Its eyes were on the sides of its head, just below forward-facing ears. But when there was a sound behind it, the ears rotated backward, the eyes extended on stalks to look in the same direction.

GODDESS

Fascinated, he knelt three feet from the animal and watched it. "Daho?"

"Definitely carnivorous, young too. It has three stomachs. My instruments show readings of sexual duality. The animal can be either male or female. It was catalogued."

"A hermaphrodite? It can reproduce itself?" He stared at the strange-looking animal.

"Without tests I cannot give an answer with absolute certainty."

"Give me your best guess."

"I—"

"Do it!" Roke snapped.

"Negative hermaphrodite. If it follows the patterns discovered on other planets, it will be determined by its first mating. If a male seeks to mate with it, it will be female. The propagation of the species makes most forms of life adapt to a method assuring its survival."

"Always?"

"I'm a computer, Roke; I cannot answer without more data."

He reached out carefully toward the animal. It backed up two steps, sat on its rear, and lifted its body. It opened its mouth and exposed three rows of razor-sharp teeth.

DAVID WIND

NINE

"You do not want your hand near its mouth."

Roke's arm froze in mid-air. He glanced at the small bot hovering nearby, its laser red and waiting. "Do you not think I know what I'm doing?"

"Not the point. It is dangerous."

"We don't know ... yet." Roke inched his hand closer to the animal's face. He'd always been good with animals, he had a 'sense' of predators as well as prey. This one was definitely a predator, and while it exuded a sense of danger, it was not directed at anything.

A moment later, the animal resettled on all fours, its mouth closing as its nose came closer to Roke's hand. It sniffed the scout's long fingers, then pushed its head against Roke's hand. It lay on the ground, its eyes locked on Roke.

He inched closer, and placed his hand on the animal's head. The furry creature rolled over, presenting its belly to Roke in the way animals, no matter what planet they are on, offer themselves to one who is stronger—to the alpha.

Roke stroked the animal's belly, then stepped back. Hearing movement behind him, he spun. The animal jumped to its feet, scrambled next to Roke, and growled. Roke started forward. The animal growled again.

Kneeling, Roke stared into the animal's yellow eyes. A sharp warning raced through his neck. He stared down at the animal, whose

GODDESS

eyes never left Roke's face, until Roke nodded and turned from the woods.

"Send the bot into the woods. There's something there."

Thirty seconds later, Daho said, `There is nothing.` Roke looked at the animal, who peered one more time into the woods, spun, and ran in the opposite direction.

What the hell was that about?

Roke went into the denser area of trees. He bent low to scan the ground for tracks of whatever might have been there. What he found were footprints. Human footprints, perhaps a child. "Analyze!"

A warning spike ran through him, vibrating within every fiber of his being. Yet another impossibility had happened. How could there be human footprints on a planet without signs of human life?

Things were out of whack! Every new turn of the day brought something unexpected, and he was caught within the harsh grip of danger. He needed to find out what was causing this, what was wrong with Anadi. He needed to fix it before it was too late. He followed the footprints, which led him a half-klick deeper into the woods where they made a wide curve, reversed direction, and returned to the grassy plateau fifty feet from where they'd entered.

He followed the steps until he neared the lake with the waterfall. He stopped, a chill racing down his spine when the footprints ended twenty feet from the water's edge.

Shaking his head at this newest mystery, he picked a nearby rock, sat on it, and stared at the water cascading into the lake from above. After a few moments of puzzled thoughts, he went to the sled, lifted off, and flew to the open area he'd marked for the first colony. "Daho, land at my position."

The scout ship set down in the exact center of the green meadow and Roke entered it. "Send bots to monitor the forest."

"The alien creature is not there. I could not follow it with my sensors or scans, I do not know why."

He wasn't surprised by the news, only that Daho believed it was the alien. What about the footprints?

"Bring up the geological reports for this area."

A series of maps and charts spread across its surface. As he studied them, he realized this was the perfect place for the first colony. He lost himself in the sheets of analysis and by the time he finished the charts, and made his notes as complete as possible, it was late.

After eating, Roke went outside. He took a pop-up chair, the bottle of Glencovian scotch, and sat as the sun gave up its tenuous hold on the horizon. He deliberated on a simple question, was it ego making him hold onto his need for this planet to be perfect for colonization? He took a pull of scotch and looked up at the stars.

"What is wrong with me?" he asked aloud.

"There is nothing physically wrong."

"Privacy, Daho. Do not monitor me. Monitor everywhere but a yard circle around me. I want privacy."

"As you ask, Roke."

He pictured the woman and called to her in his mind as she had asked him to do.

GODDESS

Nothing happened. He laughed aloud, knowing the only explanation for what he believed he experienced after injuring his head was a hallucination. His mind had made up whatever he thought the creature was; he took another pull at the bottle and shook his head because he knew better.

Exhaling, he stood just as the last edge of the sun disappeared behind the forest. Sadness pressed down on him, as the growing likelihood of his sending the hold signal to Guild Prime became apparent, but only when he was absolutely certain.

He gave himself five days to find out what was wrong with Anadi.

TEN

Standing near the woods once again, the twin moons rising overhead in a cloudless night sky, Roke closed his eyes, and called to her. Within seconds the skin at the back of his neck tingled. Before he could take a breath, a light thud sounded behind him.

He turned to find the silvery-haired child shifting into her human form, but she was no longer a child, she was a … a teenager was his best guess. And she was naked.

Her shinning twin jewels of her green-blue eyes locked onto him for several seconds before she said, "It is time to talk."

"Why now?" he asked, not questioning her ability to speak his language.

"I'm maturing. Let us go to the lake. The water feels beautiful."

He cocked his head to look at her. "Feels beautiful?"

"Is there no more to beauty than what is before your eyes?"

Having no basis to argue, he said nothing. At the lake, they sat caddy-corner from the waterfall, and she dangled her feet in the water.

Illuminated by the pale blue moonlight, the water was so clear that even at night the beige sand on the bottom was completely visible. Again, he realized the difference between earth-normal colors, and those on Anadi were just enough to shift the blue spectrum to a different hue—to one that was almost white.

He avoided looking at what was now the fullness of her adult breasts by maintaining eye contact. "Who are you? What are you?"

GODDESS

"It is not time for that, not yet."

"Not yet time for what?"

"To answer your questions. Your mission here is important. More important than you know."

He studied her face, the way her eyes held his, the way her mouth formed words. "Important how?"

"To help keep humanity alive."

"And you are human?"

"I am as human as you," she said, her hands shifting, her arms bending, allowing her to motion from her head downward, outlining her body. "Perhaps a little more so."

Her words threw him off. "You have the form of a human, but there is more to being human than just a body."

"You speak of my mind. Of my intellect, yes?"

"How do you know English?"

"I learned it from you."

"And the language of the Diné?"

"From you."

He cocked his head slightly left and studied her. "From me or from my mind?"

"Is there a difference?"

"Yes. I didn't offer anything, you took it. What is your name?"

She stared at him, and then reached slowly across the space between, her fingertips danced lightly across his lips before drawing her hand back. "Yes, I took what I needed to help you. Give me one … a name, please. This is the purpose for our sharing this moment."

He stared at her, a sudden need to do this growing within him. He wanted to find not just a name, but the right name. Every female name he knew danced though his mind, He rejected them all. Then, a whisp of thought feathered through his mind and he remembered what his grandfather had once called a newly born baby as it was drawn from its mother's womb. *Haseya.* The word was more description than name, but was good enough until her father held the baby to the sky, and formally named it.

In the Diné tongue, Haseya means *she rises*. Although the word has several meanings in the language of the Navajo, his grandfather's use was more a reference to birth and growth. "Haseya," he said aloud.

A smile stretched across her lips forcing twin dimples to break into creases along her cheeks. "Yes, she rises … I rose. An appropriate name, Roke. Thank you." She reached out and took his hand.

"Now that you have a name, I have questions."

She smiled, her aquamarine eyes aglow in the blue light of the twin moons. "Not yet. I cannot answer you yet. What you need to ask, must be asked when you are awake. Know this, Roke, you called to me; I came. The next time you see me, I will be ready to answer. By then you will have formed the right ones and learned more about Anadi."

Leaning forward, she kissed him hard, her tongue spearing into his mouth to tangle with his. She grasped his shoulders, pressing him to her breasts.

GODDESS

She pulled away, tilted her head back, and smiled. "It is time for you to return to sleep."

<<>>

He woke suddenly, yanked out from sleep by a sense of urgency—the alarm ringing in his ears confirmed the urgency. "Daho?"

"The ship is surrounded by those creatures."

"What creatures, the dragons?"

"Negative, they are like the animal you played with."

"The dog?" he asked, not realizing he'd put a subconscious name to an unknown species of animal. But it had been very dog-like in its actions and reactions.

"It is not a dog. Yes, it is the same type."

He exhaled slowly. It had been four days since he'd come to this sector in his effort to make certain this was the best section for the colony. Four nights since he'd dreamed of Haseya. Was the dream a segment of reality? Had he really named her? He shrugged.

Today, he had to disprove or prove there was alien or intelligent life here. He'd explored as much as he could on foot, and done the rest on the ship's sled.

The lakes were still the most impressive sight in the sector. And beside his exploring them physically, he'd had dreams every night; but, for some reason he could not remember them, only that they were about Anadi. This too was something new—he always remembered his dreams., He used to ask his grandfather if there was a way to stop them.

Still, it appeared to be a confirmation of something wrong on Anadi. "What are the animals doing?"

"Nothing. They sit and stare at the ship."

GODDESS

ELEVEN

"Show me!"

The Tri-D projection appeared in the middle of the deck and showed the ship was surrounded by the small dog-like creatures. They were sitting patiently, waiting for something.

"How many?"

`"Thirty-two."`

Rubbing the remnants of sleep from his eyes, he glanced at the chrono readout. It was a little after sunrise. Then he remembered the dream, and the girl.

He stared at the circle of animals ... of 'dogs' and wondered if it was connected to his dreams—If they were dreams. The discordant note of his thoughts threw him off. He frowned at the image as he studied the dogs.

The first time he and Caruso had landed, they'd cataloged all types of animal, including these, and although they'd interacted with a few, none behaved the way these 'dogs' did. Then he thought about the silver-haired woman, Haseya. And knew, deep within his mind, he had not been dreaming; rather, he was certain what he considered a dream was a deep psi connection.

Turning from the Tri-D projection, he glanced at the instrument panel. "Are there any more anywhere close?"

`"Negative."`

"Okay." There was no rush, these 'dogs' were not threatening, just waiting, and there were none lurking anywhere else. Roke went about his normal waking routine, and when he finished and dressed, he had his first cup of procaf.

Still, the animals had not moved. "Daho, do they present a danger?"

"Unknown."

"You are monitoring them?"

"Yes. Since they surrounded us."

"And the readings?"

"Everything appears as normal as far as I can tell. Their heartrates are steady, and their brain activity is high."

"Intelligence?"

"Animal-level."

He looked at the image. "Are the lasers ready?"

"Yes."

"Set to stun only."

"As you wish."

"Monitor the animals' responses to me."

Roke went to the hatch, grabbing his EXO suit on the way. Once the suit was on and adjusted, his weapons set, and his helmet on, he hit the hatch's switch. The door whooshed into the hull, and the ramp slid toward the ground.

He stood in the opening and watched the animals during the time it took for the ramp to reach the surface. Not a single dog reacted to the oncoming metal, not one. Was it because they had no means of judging if this was a threat, or had they seen this before?

GODDESS

Deciding it made no difference, yet, he walked down the ramp, and stopped when he planted his feet on the ground. The heads of every animal turned to look at him.

"`The readings have not changed.`"

"Nothing? Brain activity?"

"`Brain activity steady without change. Their only response is to look at you. There are no altered bio readings.`"

What were they doing? Better yet, *why* were they doing whatever it was they were doing?

Knowing the ship—Daho—would be at the ready, Roke looked to see if he could find the animal he'd seen yesterday, the one with the small diamond mark on its head. Not a millisecond later, one of the dogs across from him took a step forward and sat. He could not miss the diamond mark on its head.

Roke exhaled sharply. *Really?*

He walked between himself and the dog and knelt on one knee.

"`You are making yourself vulnerable.`"

"Do nothing."

The instant his knee touched the ground, the dog came toward him. It stopped a foot away, and stared up at him, its brown eyes locked on his. He carefully reached out and slowly moved his hand toward the dog.

"`Its heartrate increased ten percent. No other reaction. Brain activity is high, but stable.`"

A good sign, he noted without slowing the movement of his arm. When his arm was outstretched, the animal leaned forward to sniff Roke's fingers. Then the dog-like animal stared into Roke's eyes, a picture of the upper lake, and an opening into the mountain appeared in his mind as if he were looking directly into a cave. No sense of danger emanated from the spot on his neck, but knew intuitively the connection was not the dog's but Haseya.

The animal leaned forward unexpectedly, caught Roke's hand in its mouth, and tugged gently. An image of himself entering the cave filled his mind before fading as the animal released Roke's hand.

"Did it break your skin?"

"It was gentle, not an attack."

"Just before it took your hand, its brain activity doubled."

"It was communicating with me."

How?"

Roke shook his head. "I'm not sure. It wants me to go with it."

"You cannot go."

"Of course I can."

"Guild Protocol requires two scouts in this situation."

"We are not doing this again, Daho. I am the only scout on Anadi. My decisions are final."

"I am only reminding you of the protocols."

"Enough!" Looking at the dog, he tried to figure out if he was doing what was needed to communicate with the animal. He pictured

GODDESS

the dog within his mind, and then pictured himself returning to the ship, and coming back out again.

Standing, he returned to the ship, set up his pack, and told Daho to have a drone follow him at a hundred-foot altitude.

`"Why do you do this?"`

He stared into the nearest lens, knowing the computer had not misspoken when it asked, 'Why do you do this?' instead of asking, 'What are you going to do?' The difference was subtle, but it was right. "Daho, you cannot see inside my head. You do not know the actuality of what is happening. Be silent unless I speak directly to you! Observation routines only. Secure the ship."

With his orders given, and three days of supplies in his backpack, he left the ship, and went to the dog with the mark on its head. "Let's go," he said, building a mental picture of them walking to the lake.

Apparently whatever he did worked, and when the strange procession moved toward the lake, the ship's hatch closed. The diamond-marked dog led the way, the other thirty-one trailed behind. A single small drone flew 100 feet above his head.

The dog led him to the waterfall lakes, skirted the edge of the lower lake, and followed the mountain to a second small plateau, and the lake feeding the waterfall. The walk took twenty minutes. By the time they reached the lake, the day was warming.

The oval lake, with crystal clear water, was narrow, but stretched inland for a quarter-mile. The water feeding the lake below flowed over the edge, falling a hundred or so feet to fill the lower lake with crystal clear water. The water in the upper lake was fed by the mountain's icy heights and flowed down deeply grooved channels carved by the water's passage over the centuries.

The lead dog continued toward the far end of the plateau. The animal stopped when it reached the cascading water and turned to stare at Roke. A picture filled the scout's mind, a picture of an opening in the mountain behind the water.

Then the animal stepped up to the water. Its eyes rose on their stalks, turned backward to look at Roke, and waited for him follow. Roke took a step forward, and the dog stepped into the water, and disappeared from sight.

"Shit." Roke looked up at the drone for a second before following the dog, only to discover the downpouring water was a bare six inches thick.

GODDESS

TWELVE

Going to where the dog disappeared, he saw its dark outline behind the water and took a step with his right foot. The footing was solid and level. He brought his left foot forward with the same result.

Exhaling, he unclipped his helmet from the side of the backpack, locked it on, and walked through the water and into a high tunnel. The ceiling was hidden in darkness but there was enough light filtering through the waterfall for him to see ahead. Half a dozen steps later, he turned a bend, took a step forward, and froze. Shafts of light streamed into a huge circular cavern through holes in the mountainside.

Halfway up the walls were rows of evenly spaced holes of light filtering into the large cavern. He pressed a button on the side of EXO suit, and whispered, "Daho, are you seeing this?"

"Affirmative. The suit cameras are working properly."

"Analyze the holes. They seem too perfect."

He fell silent, his eyes now fully adjusted to the new light. He looked around and knew what the computer's response would be.

Ten seconds later, Daho reported back. "Each is a meter in diameter. There are 337 holes in a perfect circle around the mountain."

"Is this natural light?"

"I cannot tell. The light spectrum is identical to Anadi sunlight; there are no holes in the mountainside."

Light, not sunlight, meant intelligence. One hole for each day. A calendar or something else? Something else, he decided. A calendar like this would have a means of marking the days. He blew a stream of air from between his lips. His meandering thoughts were on a meaningless treadmill because he had no way of judging if he was on the right path, at least not yet. But the evenly spaced holes could not possibly be natural.

Something tugged at his ankle. He looked down to see the dog's mouth around his ankle. When he pulled his leg away, the animal looked up, but there was no mind-picture. He wondered why.

What changed? Was it the helmet? He pressed the two switches at the neckband of his suit. There was a hiss as the helmet disengaged. He took it off and there was a tug in his mind followed by a vision of the dog walking forward. Was he doing this, or was she?

Interesting, he thought. "Yeah, I see you," Roke told the dog, who was still looking over its shoulder at him. He started forward, his eyes scouring the walls of the cavern for anything not feeling right, which he decided was everything.

"Daho, any reading?" he asked five minutes after entering, and a few moments after his inner senses told him the floor was angling down, but only marginally.

`"Nothing has changed."`

"Can your instruments reach deeper into this cavern? The floor seems on a downward slope." He looked up. "The holes appear higher than when we entered."

GODDESS

```
"Negative, Roke."
```

"Are you being blocked?"

```
"It is unclear. My instruments show nothing
200 meters ahead of you. That is the start of one
of the blank areas from the planetary survey—high
probability of unknown mineral types."
```

Roke stared into the darkness ahead. Not even the light from the holes could not reach. More than his senses were telling him, they may have been wrong about the minerals.

The dog moved toward the center of the cavern and Roke followed. A few minutes later, the ground angled noticeably steeper, and the light was fading. But he was able to make out another opening ahead.

Roke touched the suit's light switch. Two lights, one on each shoulder went on to illuminate the twenty feet before him with brilliant white light. The lights would last a minimum of forty hours; he didn't plan on being in the mountain that long.

"Where are you taking me?" he asked the dog when they reach the next opening. As expected, he didn't get a reply.

When he stepped through the opening, a light turned on above him. He took another step, and another light went on. This continued for another half-dozen steps before he stopped and turned in a full circle.

"Daho, are you seeing this?"

```
"Affirmative, Roke, but communication is
weak."
```

"Am I on a ramp or something else?"

"It appears to be a spiral ramp. You are below sea-level. "

A spiral ramp … how was that possible? But his question was more about how he hadn't sensed the amount of descent, rather than the impossibility of it.

"The signal is fading, Roke," Daho reported, static making the words hard to decipher.

"Daho, if we lose contact, activate protocol two. If you cannot reach me at that point, follow the full communication protocols. Understood?"

"Af-i—mat-i-v—."

He hoped what he'd heard through the static chatter was Daho. He waited, but his speaker was dead. He took a moment to debate returning to the ship, but decided to keep on, knowing there was an automatic safeguard in Daho's programming.

Because scouts could be out of contact with their ships while on exploration, a seven-day non-contact period was set in the protocols; but, on the first second of the eighth day, an emergency signal would go to Guild Prime with a missing scout notification.

Knowing he had seven days, he looked down at the animal, and said, "Lead on, MacDog," misquoting the misquote.

<<>>

According to Roke's chrono, he'd been inside the mountain for almost half an hour, and they were still walking. He'd had no choice but to accept he'd lost contact with his ship. A few minutes earlier, he heard faint sounds in the distance, but could not make them

GODDESS

out. His first thought was water, possibly an underground river, but as he walked on, the sounds grew more distinctive, and more and more like machinery. How was it possible?

After another few hundred feet, he sensed the rock floor leveling off. The sound was still present, and as muffled as it had been since he'd first heard it. Looking around, he took a deep breath. The curving ramp had straightened into a hall-like passage.

The air tasted fresher. He froze, realizing he was deep in the bowels of a mountain. The air should be stale and moldy; it wasn't, the air was fresh and sweet. He raised his right arm, twisted his wrist sharply, and three dials flashed above his arm. Their readings confirmed the air was oxygen-rich, even richer than on the surface of Anadi.

With this knowledge, the sounds confirmed machinery was producing the richer air. He froze in place. He had learned all about terraforming, and this cavern now made sense. Yet, nothing ever showed on the ship's instrumentation. The waning tingle at the nape of his neck began to pulse. Now he knew why this area couldn't be seen with the ship's instruments. It wasn't because of an unknown mineral deposit; it was blocked.

By whom, or by what? Every nerve in his body vibrated with warning. Was it the Scav? Had they been here already? No, he would have known—this had nothing to do with them.

Reversing himself, Roke headed back to the surface. He had to get to the ship, and off-planet to send a warn-off. There was a lot wrong with Anadi he and Caruso had missed.

He froze on his second step. Every one of the thirty-two dog-like animals were lined up, three deep before him, forming a solid block, and stopping him in his tracks. "Move!" he shouted and took a step forward.

The animal with the marking on its head rose onto its back legs, its jowls drawing back, a deep, dangerous growl emerging from low in its throat. The sound was accompanied by the dog opening its mouth to expose its three rows of razor-sharp teeth set aglow by the light above.

As he stared at the dog, the other thirty-one followed their leader and sat upright, their mouths open, exposing their teeth. The sound in the cavern was not unlike a fleet of hoover craft.

"Shit," Roke whispered.

GODDESS

THIRTEEN

Turning his back on the animals, Roke continued walking toward the sounds of machinery. A dozen minutes later, he reached a doorway-like opening with a stairway leading down. He looked over his shoulder at the shadowy outline of the animals behind him.

He moved onto the stairway. When he did, more lights flicked on ahead of him. He went down eighteen steps. When he stepped off the last one, he found himself in a square room, perhaps fifteen by fifteen, with shiny gray metallic walls, and not the rock walls of the cavern. There was one door ahead of him, and one to the left.

He went straight, stopping a foot from the door, which unexpectedly opened by disappearing into the wall. He took two steps inside and stopped as row after row of bright lights sped their way across a high ceiling.

After his eyes adjusted to the bright illumination, he surveyed the space, which was a vast room with a high vaulted ceiling. The sound of machinery was loud here, and as his eyes traversed the room, he spotted the mass of machinery from where the sounds emanated.

He noted the lighting was uniform in color and illumination. And there was no one in the room.

Off to his right, and lining the wall of the room was a structure with medium high walls and several doors. To his left were huge metallic vats. He walked toward the vats. The closer he came to them, the sound of running water grew louder. When he approached the first vat, he estimated its height at thirty feet. There were ten vats set in a line, and stretching the length of the wall from where he stood, to the machinery.

Each vat was attached to the other by a metal tube approximately three feet in diameter. Placing a hand on one tube, he felt a coolness within the vibrations on the metal skin. The last vat had a tube as well, but this one bent ninety degrees, and disappeared into the floor of the cavern.

He looked around, then back to the doorway he'd just entered, searching for the animals that brought him here. They were gone.

He pressed the suit's com button. "Daho?"

There was no response. He looked up; the bot was gone as well.

He walked back to the center of the room and sat cross-legged on the floor. *Why am I here? Why did the dogs bring me here?* He had no answers, only more questions.

He considered returning to the surface, even if he had to fight through the pack of dogs, but discarded the idea. He was brought for a purpose. He needed to know what this place was before he reported its existence to the Guild. Somehow, he did not doubt the dogs were guarding the upper cavern.

Glancing up at a vat, Roke saw lettering on its side. But its words were too high to make out clearly. He pulled a bot from his backpack and sent it upward. The hologram screen rose above his arm a moment before the bot reached the lettering, and his breath caught in his throat.

GODDESS

He'd seen symbols and glyphs like this before. A shockwave blew through him, stunning him with a punch to his mind. Sucking in breath after breath, he tried to control himself. It took a minute, but finally forced a calm over himself. The lettering was the unreadable symbols they'd discovered in forerunner remains. The realization hit hard. This was a Forerunner planet.

Does the signal block do anything here? He pulled a second bot from the compartment in his pack and sent it upward. He keyed in the instructions to search the entire room and all its contents, and sat dead still on the floor watching his screen.

It worked. He was glued to the screen for the entire time it took the bots to survey the cavern. When they returned to him, he knew exactly what was there. The machinery was split down the middle. One section produced air; the second section produced whatever was flowing through the vats.

The bots had been unable to see into the vats, as they had solid metal covers, but the separated and constructed area on the right side of the room had walls that were only seven feet of the room's thirty-foot height. Except for one area, there was no ceiling, and this section was was constructed into separate internal sections, which allowed the bots to see what was there.

Everything appeared normal and very human in design. Two of the sections had the appearance of working areas, and the section on the left of the others looked like a communal area. He wondered what mystery lay behind the section with a full ceiling, the one furthest on the right.

He tried one more time to communicate with the ship, and failed. He considered sending the bot to the surface, but realized if the transmissions were being blocked, as soon as the bot reached the edge of the block, he would lose control.

Rising from the floor, he walked to the right side and went to the middle door. The door was metal, without handle or knob. Roke pressed his fingertips against the cool surface and pushed. The door gave off a whirring and slid into a pocket within the wall. Roke went to a narrow hallway leading into a larger area. To his right were several clear doors showing small empty rooms.

He went on until he reached a moderately large and open room, with metal columns equipment twenty feet into the air. At mid-height, small dots of blue and green lights pulsed in a steady rhythm. The columns were monolithic in appearance, and made of a dull gray metal.

He put both hands on one; low vibrations trembled against his palms. *What is this?*

Stepping back, he looked at the rows of thin, rectangular pillars, which reminded him of the miles of computers banks in the bowels of the Guild's main headquarters; computers which ran the Guild, controlled the planet's machinery, the power, and everything else needed to support those living and working on Guild Prime.

The thought cut through him like a knife slicing a piece of meat. This may be the discovery of the century if what he thought was correct. Anadi would be the first Forerunner planet found with operating technology.

GODDESS

The enormity of the prospect took his breath away. At the same time, Anadi was doomed to be overridden by Guild personnel, tearing it down to its last molecule, while seeking the answers they've always been denied.

Roke stopped himself from going further on this route. He needed proof, and without being able to contact the ship, he could not send messages or images. "Better to stay and explore," he told himself aloud.

He inspected the section once more, turned, and retraced his steps. He went to the far end of the the walled in hallway, and tried the door to the covered section. It would not open. A sleeping area? Barracks? The answer would have to wait.

Backtracking to the huge open cavern, and then out the initial doorway, he went into the square room. He pressed on the second door, which opened into a long hallway, the floors, walls, and ceiling of the same smooth metallic material. There were evenly spaced doorways on the right, and left, and more hallways leading deeper inward. Those were spaces between every fourth door.

He chose one doorway at random and entered. The lighting was softer, warmer in the way it illuminated everything perfectly. He glanced around the room which was furnished with a table, several chairs, and a low platform he took for a bed. There was another door on the left side of the room. When he opened it, the wall across from him transformed, and he didn't need to guess what the room was when a grey metal sink slid out from the wall, and further down, a curved and strange looking metal toilet rolled out.

Back in the larger room, he went to the table, and sat in a chair. The moment he did, the chair shifted and flowed to conform to his shape. At the same time, a screen opened in the center of the table with rows of unreadable glyphs marching across its face.

This was definitely a Forerunner facility, and a working one as well!

He stood. The chair reformed and the screen disappeared from the tabletop. He looked at the platform, wondering what would happen. He went to it and sat. The platform shifted. A soft material rose beneath him.

He stood. The material disappeared.

Leaving the room, he retraced his steps back to the large cavern, and then into the walled section. He went down the corridor, and into what he'd thought was the communal area. When he entered the first room, the walls were the same color as everything else.

Something was off about this section, he sensed it viscerally. Nothing about the room indicated a gathering place or an area for eating. No, what he saw were rows after rows of clear booths, the tops of which he'd seen from the drone bot's camera, and assumed were tables.

He went in the first one, pushed against the clear window, and the front opened. Rather than step inside, he simply stood and watched a seat extend from one side, and a small shelf-like table opposite it.

When he sat, three clear cables descended in front of him, the ends of each had opaque disks. Following Guild protocol, he touched nothing; rather, he left the cubicle, and headed out of the section.

GODDESS

When the door closed behind him, the grumble of machinery swelled in his ears, and he realized he had not heard it in the constructed section. How could that be with open ceilings?

Letting the question go, he went straight to the entrance of the cavern, and started up the steps. The sounds of growling erupted as the dog-like animals charged down, filling the entryway, and circling behind him, each snarling and baring razor-sharp teeth.

The one with the head-marking let out a loud howl and leapt directly at him. The dog struck Roke's chest, harder than he could have imagined for so small a dog, and sent him backwards. He stumbled, caught his balance, but with his next step, tripped over two of the animals behind him.

He fell sideways, slamming his shoulder against the wall, hit the floor, and rolled down the last step and back into the gentry room. Before he could recover and stand, the diamond-marked dog pressed its front legs to his chest. An instant later, there was a loud hissing.

Roke pushed against the animal, but a wave of dizziness swept through him. There was a strange smell in the air. His breathing grew labored, his vision blurred, and darkness took him away.

FOURTEEN

Floating on a soft cushion of air, Roke stared at a plain gray wall. He looked up. The ceiling was gray too. "Daho, where am I?"

There was no answer. It took a few milliseconds for his memory to kick in. He remembered it all: the dogs charging at him, the diamond-marked dog jumping on him; and he remembered rolling back into the entrance and hearing a loud hissing sound. Then there was nothing.

Sitting up, he twisted himself until his feet touched the floor. His head spun. He grabbed the material beneath him to steady himself. "Shit!" he said aloud, realizing he was on one of the sleep pallets in the Forerunner living quarters. The hissing ... he'd been gassed. By whom?

Holding his head in both hands, he took a slow deep breath as he reoriented himself. *How the hell did I get here?* Warning bells belatedly sounded in his head; the nape of his neck buzzed in agreement. He hadn't walked here himself, someone put him here.

The alarm in the nape of his neck went off, his headache worsened. He closed his eyes and began to breath in the cadence he'd learned to keep himself relaxed in tense times. Only when the pain in his head eased did he open his eyes. He searched the room for his EXO suit: it was nowhere to be seen. Then he realized he was naked.

"You're awake," came a soft female voice. He turned toward the now open doorway, stunned at the vision of the silvery-blonde haired woman entering the room. No longer a child, nor a teenager;

GODDESS

she was very definitely a woman, a beautiful aquamarine-eyed woman wearing a white garment without adornment. Light shone through the thin material, outlining her body. Was this another dream?

"Haseya," he whispered.

A radiant smile formed at the sound of her name. "Yes, Roke, it is I."

He blinked twice. "How long have I been out?"

"Three days."

"Shit!" He shook his head, which he immediately regretted. He took a breath..

"You triggered an automatic defense mechanism. The gas made you unconscious, but you had a negative reaction, and there was an injury. It has been repaired. I brought your clothing." She placed the folded material on the pallet next to him, looking at him as she did.

"You're older."

"I am. You need to eat."

"I need to piss."

She frowned, then smiled. "Oh, I understand ... Urinate. Come with me. Can you stand?"

He did. He felt no weakness, no further dizziness, and followed her into the larger room, and then to a door on the opposite side. Once again, he watched the plumbing come out of the walls.

After leaving the bathroom, he found Haseya waiting where he'd left her. "Is there a place to wash? To shower or bathe?"

"Of course." She pointed to the door next to the one he'd just used. He went in and looked around. A moment later, in the center of the room, a spray of water came from the ceiling. When he stepped into it, a metal shelf extended from the wall, a bottle of liquid on it.

Not bad, he thought, and poured some in his hand. The liquid not only foamed, but ran up his arm. He used more, rubbing into his hair. Within seconds the liquid spread over his entire body, foaming even as the water washed it away.

When the water shut off, warm air whirled around the room, and by the time he reached the door, he was dry. He paused at the door to look around. He smiled, perhaps for the first time since leaving the ship. *Not bad.*

When he stepped out of the bathing room, Haseya handed him his clothing. which was the underclothing for his EXO suit, lightweight against his skin. His shirt closed by itself, the nanobots automatically sealing the shirt. After he pulled his pants up, the nanos connected the waist to the shirt, effectively making it a one-piece jumpsuit undergarment.

"I'm not thirsty. Why?" he asked.

"I've been giving you water."

He stared at her, puzzled. "How? I was unconscious."

"Auto-reflex. I held you up, you drank."

He thought about what she'd said, and dismissed it. There was no auto-reflex, which was why intravenous was used. "That's not true."

Her brows drew together. Then she shook her head. "Why would you say that? I held you up, I held the water to your lips, and I told you to drink. You did."

GODDESS

He remembered when his younger brother had been sick with sandworm fever, and his grandfather held him in a sitting position, a glass to his mouth, and whispered 'drink' into the child's ear. His brother drank.

Roke looked into her eyes, held them for several stretched-out seconds, and nodded. "Apologies."

She smiled. "Accepted."

"I am hungry. My pack has food."

"As do we."

"We?"

Her smile did not fade. "A figure of speech."

"Are there more of your people?"

The smile faded. "No, I am the only one."

"But you have food I can eat?"

"The animals, the fruits, the grains on this world are all edible for humans."

Roke gazed at her for a moment before nodding. "Would you turn around … please?"

Her brows drew together again, her features shifted into a puzzled expression, but she said nothing. She turned.

Roke looked at her back, stepped closer, and lifted her hair with his right hand to look beneath it. Then, using his left hand, he pressed his palms to her back, looking for the wings he knew were there. But all he found was her smooth skin beneath the material.

"What?" she finally asked.

"Your wings …"

A light laugh filtered into the air. She turned back to him. "Let's us eat and talk. All right?'

When he nodded, she turned and, with a wave, motioned him to follow.

Trailing silently behind her, his mind worked at warp speed, trying to figure out why he was here. He'd followed the dogs only to be trapped and later attacked. And Haseya appeared fully knowledgeable, not only about his situation, but this Forerunner installation.

How is this possible? A dream? An illusion? And her wings ... What happened to them? All these thoughts and more raced through his mind, turning his brain into a huge miserable ache.

When they reached their destination, which was the middle section of the living quarters, she went in, turned to the right, and led him into a medium size room without a ceiling. She went to the wall, pushed against it, and a panel slid open. When it did, a table, and two chairs rose up from the floor.

She motioned him to her, and pointed to the other chair. As she sat, but he remained standing, she raised her eyebrows in question. He shrugged, unable to find one question to ask that didn't involve a hundred other questions, he shook his head and sat down. The chair shifted and conform to his lower body.

"This place is old, yet everything appears as if new. How?"

"This was built 111,000 years ago by my ancestors, and—"

"—Who are your ancestors," he asked, jumping in the instant the word left her mouth.

GODDESS

She reached across the table and covered his hand with hers. Her skin was warm, bordering on hot. "Give me time to tell you, *tsé nil-ta*."

"Stubborn I am, but a rock, no." He looked at the hand covering his, his eyes tracing faint blue veins woven beneath pale skin, and slowly nodded.

Haseya pressed something on the table. A panel beneath their hands opened. She drew her hand away and he did the same when a large cup of steaming liquid rose before each of them. "Soup. High in nutrients."

He slid his fingers into the handle and brought the cup to his mouth. He stopped the cup before it reached his mouth, the scout in him rising to warn him off. He was on a new world, talking to some sort of a being who might or might not be a Forerunner, might or might not be a human; and might or might not be a dragon, but definitely was one of the most beautiful women he'd ever seen.

Am I being stupid, doing whatever she wants? He paused, looked at the soup, and back at her. He tilted his head to the side and waited.

"What?" Her features were puzzled again.

"What's in it?"

She stared at him, her aquamarine eyes growing large as the understanding of what he'd asked. Disappointment flashed across her face, a second later, her features were unreadable. "Don't your senses tell you you can trust me?"

"My—" He stopped talking. He had to admit he'd not had a single tingle of warning since he'd seen her. She was right, but how could she know about that? Then he remembered what she'd told him about learning English and Navajo.

"I will never hurt you, Roke. I cannot hurt you."

He didn't know how to respond, so he finished the movement, and drank from the cup. His first sip was an explosion of taste. He took another, trying to identify the flavors but could not. "This is very good."

Haseya lifted her cup, and drank. They fell silent until the cups were empty. "You will feel your energy return now. Come." She started to rise.

"Wait. I thought we were going to talk."

She half-closed her eyes as a low sigh escaping as she sat back down. "If we must."

"We must. You told me I had to wait until I was awake. I am." Then he wondered if this was a dream too. He'd not been able to tell the difference before. *Am I? No, this is different.*

She searched his face with her eyes, tracking every part of it until she finally said, "All right, Roke. I would rather be in bed with you, making love as we should, but ask your questions."

GODDESS

FIFTEEN

Ignoring her last comment, which was far from easy, he said, "I have done as you asked. I have named you; and I have waited for you to explain who you are. It's time."

She momentarily looked away, before reaching across the table, and taking his hand. She drew him to his feet. "Look around. My … my people came here a … a quarter-million years ago, intent on creating a new world, populating it, and watching it grow into a meaningful and civilized world; however, human life did not evolve here, so our seedpods lay dormant until you found us."

Her eyes swept across his face. "But now, when the colonists come, and they waken us, this planet will be filled with life."

"Unless the Scav get here before the world can be populated."

Haseya's eyes widened at the mention of the Scav. "Yes, and all because we made a terrible mistake."

"Mistake?"

She blinked several times. "As eventually happens to all species of life, our race was dying, and we did not know if the humanity on the worlds we had seeded had reached the point of sentience and found our seedpods—you would call them our embryos. When we seed a planet, we do so with ourselves. Just before a woman gives birth to her second child, the embryo is removed and placed within a seedpod. This had been done for so long no one remembered its origin. But the duty my race held, as the precursors of humanity for the universe, put us on a path to our own destruction. We seeded so many planets, our entire race giving forth their embryos, without regard to our own growth and survival."

Roke took in what she was saying, analyzed it as best he could, and came up with her only possible meaning. "You bred yourselves out of existence."

She held his gaze without blinking. "Our scientists were so secure in their purpose, our health sciences so advanced, they did not factor in unknown diseases from other planets, or premature deaths. We lost track of our purpose. Our entire civilization, which for untold generations, was so singularly focused on human-kind's survival, we were no longer able to look to ourselves to build a future, but look only to the worlds where life was beginning to flourish."

"When we realized what we had done, we withdrew to our home planet, abandoning everything, but our population continued to decrease. Our leaders were determined to stop our decline, and the contributing of embryos was ended. But it was too late. It was then we discovered our biggest mistake."

"What mistake?" His eyes hardened.

"You call them Scav. They were our mistake. We had populated this galaxy, and another hundred or so galaxies containing planets to support human life. Then, at the farthest edge of the universe, in a galaxy so far distant from here it takes millions of lightyears to reach—a galaxy at the very edge of the universe, we found another earth-type planet with human life just evolving. We seeded it to ensure its survival."

"This was the Scav."

GODDESS

"Yes," she whispered. "We were careless. What we did not know then, was that they were not human, but they appeared to have to a humanoid body and intelligence on the human scale. Their DNA presented as human, which was how they were able to bond with the seedpods. When they awakened the seedpods, and the pods bonded with them, our people, our progeny, were changed by the alien blood. The ramification of the interbreeding created an entirely new race, one with too much of our knowledge."

Everything she said had the feel of reality. But was it, or was she manipulating him with her story? "How could you have travelled millions of lightyears, and returned in the time you describe?"

"Science. Our race is old, so old our roots have been lost. Those who have found the artifacts and technology of our creation, call us Forerunners, Precursors, Gods, or any number of names. But we remained faithful to our duty, which was to keep sentient races alive."

"Why have we never found any of your ships or anything that enabled you to travel as you did?"

"We had gone far beyond mechanical vessels, we used portals. We could travel anywhere for which we had coordinates, but when the … the Scav took to them, we destroyed as many as possible to prevent them from gaining footholds in other galaxies. As their technology grew, and our race began to die out, we seeded as many human-supporting planets as possible, disabling each portal along with any technical data to recreate them." She paused for a breath.

"But before we could reach all the seeded planets, the Scav found a portal on one. They sent four groups of their fighters through to our home planet. As soon as they arrived, the leaders knew they had only one choice. They reactivated the portals and sent out our scientists and technicians to as many seeded planets as they could. There, they reprogramed the seedpods with the knowledge of what had happened. When the last was done, every portal was destroyed including those on our home planet."

Haseya looked into his eyes. "I was created 100,000 years ago, while the last of my people died out. I was an embryo, placed within the seedpod, and held in stasis to await the touch of a human."

"But you … you are not just human, you're something else as well. What?"

She shook her head, her eyes darkening slightly turning more green than blue as she stared at him. "No, I am human, thoroughly. The seedpod programming changes parts of my DNA."

"How is that possible?"

"The method for creating the seedpods creates a gene in the DNA. It is a protective gene so the child can protect itself by flying to safety until it is mature enough to survive."

"Each time we met, dream or not, you had wings, you had a tail, and your face changed. You were a dragon."

"Not a … a dragon, but yes, I change as I mature, until I am at the true level of the current evolutionary period. And what you call a dream is not in truth exactly a dream. It was a conceptual manifestation of ourselves."

GODDESS

Somehow, Roke stopped his jaw from dropping. "Excuse me, but what the fuck does that mean?"

She drew back slightly at the intensity of his voice and words, but took his hand, and squeezed it gently. "Roke, you have been hurt, and were unconscious for three days. You still need to rest."

"No."

"Then at least let's go back to the room so we can be more comfortable."

He started to say no again, then shrugged. He didn't feel tired, but it didn't matter where they were to have this conversation. "First, what does conceptual manifestation mean?"

"It means I ... I was able to bring our minds together for a little while and show you what the future can be."

"You were in my head." He digested her words. "Okay, continue, please."

"Understand we, my ancestors, have authored a huge number of scientific breakthroughs, including a way to assure our children are born with the memory of what has happened in the past. You could call it active genetic memory implantation. Our genetic coding is ancient ... My ancestors were born ... created ... whatever word you want to use, over 200 million years ago."

She took a breath. "Roke, we, my people, survived for a long, long time—longer than any other race ... ever. In that time, our discoveries enriched the galaxy, and not just ourselves. Each one of us was created to further humanity's evolution. When our scientists learned how to read the full genetic code, we discovered at the moment of birth, we have four individual types of DNA."

"Four?" Roke challenged.

"We have animal male and female, and human male and female DNA."

Did she put a drug in his food? Was he imagining this conversation? "It's not possible."

"Not only is it, but your scientists will discover the truth of it when our first child is born."

He stared at her as if she were insane. He snorted, then he realized what she had actually said, 'Our child…'

"Think about your evolutionary past. Humans evolved over time, but very quickly in the context of evolution, from ape to Cro-Magnon, to what you are today."

"You forgot Neanderthal."

"No, while Cro-Magnon may be considered having evolved from Neanderthal, they did not. They were two separate branches; however, Cro-Magnon came into existence over 100,000 years ago, and I believe that by the time one found a seedpod, they were more human-evolved than Neanderthal, and while they contained some Neanderthal DNA, it was different. They, Cro-Magnon, were the main factor of the evolution of modern humankind on your planet."

Roke knew his evolutionary history; it was a more-than-obvious required course for scout exploration Guild students. The course ran through every year of the Exploration Guild academy. "You said your people stopped creating embryos before then. How

GODDESS

could you know this when all evidence points to Cro-Magnon reaching a more human status, at the earliest, 35,000 years ago?"

"Cro-Magnon, not Neanderthal, was the only species that could awaken a seedpod, and they did so. But because our records stop before then, I have no information on why their offspring did not gain our knowledge."

"As I just said, you were a stored embryo here 100,000 years ago, how can you possibly know what happened after that time?"

"Since you awakened my seedpod, I have been in here, refreshing myself on our memory banks—computers. Although my genetic memory is strong, the computers not only refresh what is in my memories, but show me what has happened since my embryo was placed in the pod. And Roke, the memory banks still monitor all the planets we seeded."

"It doesn't explain the four DNA types."

"No," she agreed. "It doesn't, but it is a long, technical explanation. Let's say we seed a planet where intelligent life is a humanoid-shaped but has animal or avian—"

"Human-like or bird-like?"

"Yes. If the life is more human, then our DNA allows us to procreate with the species to produce a more human version during its evolution."

"Like the Scav?"

"No, there must be more than intelligence. There must be the potential for what the Scav lack, an instinctive sense of morality: what you call a conscience; empathy, morality, integrity, like you, and not like them. The Scav have animal tendencies and only show decency toward their own kind. As I said, they were our greatest mistake, and have cost us so much."

"But—"

"I'm not finished. When skin touches the seedpod, and there is human DNA, or the potential for human DNA—no matter the evolutionary stage—we receive the DNA."

Roke held up his hand. "How?"

"The dust, what you call the iridescence, collects the DNA, and two of our strands attach itself to the single strand. If it is male, our DNA selects the female strand. If it is a female, then our bodies select the male strand. If it is the wrong branch of humanity, one which will never fully evolve to human, like the Neanderthal, its seed will use the animal DNA and not breed with the animal."

"But Neanderthal DNA is often found in humans."

"Because the Cro-Magnon bred with anything similar to themselves. They had a large appetite for procreation. The breeding changed the way the Neanderthal evolved when Cro-Magnon bred with the Neanderthal."

"They liked sex."

"Yes, which is a part of my makeup as well."

Roke stared at her. He shook her words off. "That still doesn't explain it all."

"No, there is more, but not now. You were hurt. You need rest."

"No."

GODDESS

"Can we at least go back to the room so you can sit?" She took his hand and led him along.

He wasn't finished, not yet. "The rows of metal in the large room. What are they?"

"Our computers."

"And the tanks?"

"Where our seedpods are created and then sent to the river. Roke, you have woken me. Accept the fact we are bonded in a way that can never be changed."

He heard her but did not react. His face was as unreadable as a statue. "What happens now?"

"We will have children, and our children will have children, and they will populate this world, and move on to the next."

"What if I had been a woman?" he asked suddenly.

Haseya smiled. "As I said a moment ago, I would have been a male."

"So no matter who I was, I would become the father or mother of our race?"

Her smile widened and her eyes glowed. "You are wise, my Roke."

His mind darkened; his instincts and his senses saw through her words. He stared at her, unable to see the beauty she projected, afraid of what had just happened, and of the knowledge he had gained. Of all the stories, of the folklore of his people, and of the scientific papers written about them, the Forerunners were those who not only seeded the universe, but did so for their own benefit. They seeded the galaxies, not to give humanity a better chance at life, but to keep their race alive, which was the reason the guilds had found storehouses of goods and weapons on so many planets—all ready to be used.

And it was for-shit-sure he wasn't on this planet to be someone's prize stud, or to create a new race. No! The dreams he'd had were, as his grandfather told him, warnings. She may appear to be human, somehow, she was not … She was something else.

GODDESS

SIXTEEN

"It is time, Roke, come with me." Still holding his hand, she pulled him along the corridor to the room where he'd awoken. She let go of his hand and pointed to a flat area where where the bed was. "Rest, please."

He started to say something when her eyes locked on his. They took on a glow for so short an instant he wasn't sure he'd seen it, and then strangely, whatever he was thinking disappeared. Her arms went around him; she leaned toward him, her mouth seeking his.

Trying to draw back, he couldn't understand why he met her lips instead. A line of fire exploded across his buttocks when her hands cupped each side and pulled him to her. Haseya's tongue darted into his mouth to play with his.

A heartbeat later, she slid her right hand along his hip, then moved it between them to to cup his growing erection. Before he could react to her hand, she drew both her hands away, stepped back, and retook his hand. She led him to the bed, which was rising from the floor.

Turning him to her, she pressed the spot near his collar, and his shirt opened. Without releasing his hand, she leaned forward and took one nipple into her mouth, her teeth teasing it while her free hand drew circles along his chest.

She stepped back, stared into his eyes, and released his hand. She moved quickly to brush his shirt from his shoulders, and as the material floated to the floor, she pressed the closure on his pants, and they too dropped to the floor.

She put both hands on his chest and pushed him backwards. He landed on the cushion of air to lie there staring up at her. As he watched, still somehow under her control, she pressed the silver button on her shoulder, and the material covering her body fell to her feet.

All he could do was stare. Her body was magnificent. She moved, kneeling on the bed, one leg on each side of him. She leaned forward, and kissed him, her tongue darting in and out of his mouth. She drew her lips from his, and lowered her mouth to his neck, kissing it as she trailed her lips downward. Her tongue flicked across one nipple before slowly travelling to the next. She teased him with her lips, her tongue, and even her teeth until he groaned.

Shifting and moving up along his body, she slipped her hand downward along his belly, until she grasped his erection. She shifted again, rising up and centering herself over him. With her green-blue eyes holding his in thrall, she lowered herself, and took him slowly inside.

A low, drawn-out moan escaped her lips, her eyes rolled upward, and hands dug into the muscles of his shoulders. She pressed down on him until she could go no further. Then she took his hands and pressed them to her breasts before swiveling her hips, pushing against him, her hips rotating as she moved up and down. The need within her grew out of control, her passion bloomed stronger, bringing forth long, guttural moans from deep in her throat.

GODDESS

Lowering her head, she kissed him hard, and as she climbed toward her orgasm, she brought him with her, moving faster and faster. The very instant her orgasm began to race through her, her wings rushed out from within her to slide beneath him; her tail extended and wrapped itself around both of them until she could pull him no closer, and no further within her. Then as they each reached their fullest climax, both cried out.

She fell across him, her wings and tail disappearing as her breathing eased. She lay there for a few moments, rising and falling with each movement of his chest. When she rolled off him, she resettled herself in the crook of his arm, her head on his shoulder, and her hand caressing his chest.

<<>>

From the moment her eyes flashed at him, Roke became distant, his mind somewhere else, and his body reacting without his own participation. He was an observer to what was happening, a distant speck on the horizon—a single audience to a Tri-D. He watched her, her features woven by pleasure and passion, her body moving in ways he'd never experienced, yet, there was no emotional connection. He felt nothing except the knowledge she was using him. He could see in her eyes, her need to copulate with him was overwhelming.

It was not only a new experience, but a frightening understanding of how she—no, it—was using him to create something against everything he believed in.

When she slid from him, then cuddled next to him, he breathed a sigh of relief. But a few minutes later, her hand began to trace along his chest before dropping to outline the muscles of his abdomen. Then her fingers dipped lower, her hand cupping his testicles for a moment before rising to stroke his penis.

She raised her head to look into his eyes, but he turned from her.

"What is wrong?" she asked, her hand not stopping its movement.

"I ... I need to rest."

Smiling, she grasped him tighter. "This does not feel like it needs to rest."

He twisted from her and shook his head. "I am not a machine."

"Of course you are not. Look at me, Roke."

Somehow, he had no choice. The instant his eyes met hers, the world changed, and he was lost to her. He could feel everything happening to him, the warmth, the heat, and the incredible pleasure in the way her body merged with his. And, once again, his body gave her everything she asked of it, even while his mind was somewhere else.

When it was over, and she lay once more in the crook of his arm, he began to feel like himself, yet his mind was foggy, almost as if he were recovering from a hangover. This was not a feeling he'd ever had after sex.

On top of everything else, he realized the fear that he had known would eventually show up, struck into him like a knife.

GODDESS

He looked at her face, at the soft and beautiful lines, and then down at the perfection of her body, her full breasts, the graceful dip of her waist just before her hips curved out and looked back at her face again … and saw, in her sleep, a smile had formed on her lips. Then he remembered the way her wings had enfolded them, and her tail secured him to her.

In that moment, something inside him died.

DAVID WIND

SEVENTEEN

He woke slowly, his upper arm weighted down by something warm. He ached hangover-style, and it took a moment before he remembered what happened between them, and the memory of what she was. He recalled barely seeing a flash in her eyes. He looked at Haseya, whose eyes were now open and staring at him.

He shifted to his side and met her gaze. She put her hand to his cheek and searched his face. Too late to stop himself, he stiffened slightly at her touch.

She sat up, but held his gaze. "We made love, why do I sense fear coming from you? You do not need to fear me, I am here because you brought me here."

"Fear can be healthy," he said, glibly.

"But unnecessary. Roke, you will never need to fear me. I have told you we bonded together the moment your fingers went across my seedpod. We are one in this world; when your people arrive, we will build a world filled with humanity."

He shook his head, his thoughts speeding along a careful path. "I am an explorer, a first-in scout. I have devoted my life to finding habitable planets for my people, for the Galactic Union, and the Exploration Guild. I am not someone who settles in one place."

She smiled, then, as if speaking to a child, she said, "I understand. But do you not see how everything has changed since you touched my seedpod? Seeking new planets is unnecessary; the

GODDESS

computer banks will give us the location of every system holding a planet to support human life."

"I cannot stay."

"You must." Her words were softly spoken, almost sad. "You will father our children. You and I will create a world where we not only survive, but grow to become so much more than who we two are."

Again, his mind went cold. He had to stop this; he just didn't know how. One thing held strong above all else, he would not let the colonists come. He would find a way to prevent it from happening.

"Roke," she whispered just before sliding her hand upward along his inner thigh, her nails tracing lightly over his skin.

<<>>

Roke was alone. He had no idea where Haseya was, but he would take whatever free time he had. He needed to think, and think without someone who was able to get into his head—literally.

Cursing himself for a fool, and chastising himself for allowing this female being to get into his mind in the first place, he set about figuring a way out. Earlier, after they'd had sex yet again, he'd asked her about going to his ship so he could report in. Her response had been a simple and seemingly innocent, "Not yet."

When he'd asked why, she'd said, "We need a few more days to get everything set. We need to prepare the computers for those who are to come."

"Why don't I go, and you do that? Once I've sent the signal to bring the waiting ships, they will get the operation underway. It will still take weeks for the colonists to arrive."

"No, Roke, it is important to do this my way."

He let it go on the surface, while at the same time doing his best to create a mental wall to protect himself and keep her from sensing his thoughts. *Hopefully*, he told himself silently.

He was convinced everything he'd done was wrong. He had accepted her because she had enticed him in an unfamiliar, even foreign way. He wasn't used to a woman's charms, not as a boy, not as a man. The women he had been with were nothing remotely similar to Haseya.

He looked around the room and then left, following the hallway to where he knew she would be, at the computers. With each footstep, his thoughts centered on how to salvage his situation.

His overconfidence had done this, his need to prove himself had created this situation. He reached the entry to the data area, and as his foot went down and his hand rose toward the door, he froze. *Idiot!*

Staring at his hand, hovering a bare inch from the door, he realized he didn't have to leave; all he needed to do was keep her occupied for a few more days. He'd given Daho the protocol instructions. If there was no contact for seven days following his departure, the computer would notify Caruso first and then the Guild.

The leading edge of relief rose, but he refused let it go further than simple hope. It was possible she'd already seen this in his head.

GODDESS

Whatever ability she used to look into his mind didn't matter, he just needed her to have not discovered his fail-safe.

Looking at his wrist, he discovered the chrono wasn't there. Since he'd been out for three days, he guessed it was nighttime on day four. If that were the case, he needed to wait only three more days.

Concentrating, he tried to do what his grandfather had taught him as a child: build his inner strength and prepare for the psi tests. Eyes closed, he focused on the darkness behind his lids, building a mind-picture of a wall circling his head. Once the wall was erected, he topped it with a solid dome. The visualization trick had worked during the Guild's psychic testing.

When he finished, and praying it would hold against Haseya, he pressed on the door. The door whizzed into the wall. Inside the huge rock-manufacturing cave, which was how he thought of this place, he spotted Haseya at one of the tall data banks, wearing what looked like a wrap, or a toga. He was halfway toward her when she turned to smile at him.

The noise of the machinery was louder than the first time he had entered here, the sound of rushing water through the connected vats had added to it. "What are you doing?" he asked, smiling at her.

Aquamarine eyes sparkling, she returned his smile with a radiant one of her own. "I'm restarting the rock process and embedding the updated information."

Puzzled, he looked from her to the vat-shaped tanks and back. "Aren't there enough rocks in the water?"

"Yes, but it is better to have a quantity of the rocks, which are stored in stasis, activated. There is no need to have the newborn update via the databanks when it can be done this way." She pressed three buttons on two different rows of the vid panel. A new sound emerged from the first tank.

"Embryos in stasis are moved into this tank, transferred into a different stasis configuration, which is then formed into a stone."

He stared at her; his suspicion confirmed that the seedpods were not actually stones. "How long does the process take?" he asked, pushing her to think more about what she was doing than why he was trying to keep her out of his head.

"To create a stone, not long. The new stasis field is released by being touched. Following that, it takes an Anadi day for the rock to enlarge and release the child. It takes another three to four days for the child to fully mature."

"How can you grow from an infant to an adult in four days?"

"Our scientists inject the embryos with a growth protein."

"I see. What about the time to create each rock, you said not long? How much time does it require?"

"A quarter-hour or so to create, maybe an hour more to go through to the final processes." She waved her hand down the line of vats. "I am creating one now, testing to verify the process."

He stared at her. She spoke more like a scientist than the woman he'd ... had sex with—a woman who had been born only days before. He wondered if this was nothing more than an elaborate dream, or the ravings of a psionic lunatic. "And then?" he asked, realizing it didn't matter because there was nothing he could do about it.

"You said there would be at least a few hundred people landing to build the first colony, this is correct, yes?"

When he nodded, she smiled again. "Good. The entire process will take three full days. Then another day for each stone to harden properly before its coating is applied and the rock released into the water. When the coating is touched, it will grow."

"Why water?"

"It must be in water, or the coating, what you call the iridescence, will go inactive."

"What about the colonists' families?"

"What difference does it make? Procreation can be done by anyone."

"But many believe pro—sex is immoral once a man and a woman have bound themselves in marriage."

"Why?"

"Because it is their belief. They believe God told them to do this."

"Whose God?"

"They believe there is only one."

She stared at him. "This is interesting. We need to speak more about this."

"I understand," he said. He made a show of glancing around before saying, "I think I'll get something to eat. What about you?"

She looked at the first vat. The sound was growing louder. "We have time. Yes, I'd like to do that with you."

<<>>

They ate in a comfortable silence. When they finished, Roke said, "When they arrive, how do I explain … you? How do we get them to touch the stones?"

She shook her head. "You do not need to explain, I will remain here when they arrive. You will have those who lead, touch the stones first. They will be in the two lakes above us."

"The waterfall lakes?"

"Yes."

"What if they don't?"

"They will. The dust induces a natural curiosity to sentient beings. The coating … the dust as you call it, will attract them as it did you. It was created to do so."

He thought of an old trope, *you can lead a horse to water, but you can't make it drink.* In this case, it was *you can lead people to water, and they will drink.* It was true; the dust had made him curious, even though touching the stone was accidental. *Or was it?*

"No. I slipped and fell from the hillside; I didn't go in the river out of curiosity."

"Are you sure you didn't feel the urge to touch a rock?"

He closed his eyes and thought about it. He remembered everything about that day, seeing the rocks, wondering about them and the current. His eyes snapped open. He'd touched one or two of the rocks with his gloves on. It was only after he'd fallen into the water and lost a glove trying to hang onto the rock that he'd touch the rock below barehanded.

"Yes!" Haseya said, eyes dancing. "As I said."

Roke slowly rebuilt the wall, having realized by drawing up the memory, he had allowed her into his thoughts. "Yes, I see it now."

When he started to stand, she leaned across the table, and grasped his arm. Her smile changed, her eyes turned a deeper shade, more emerald than sapphire, and she kissed him, her tongue slipping between his lips to press against his and begin its seductive dance.

He was trapped as she climbed onto and across the table without breaking the kiss, and he not only had to give in, but keep his mental block strong. A few seconds later, she broke the kiss, sat, and wrapped her long legs around him.

"Here?" He forced himself to feel desire should she try to sense his thoughts. But before he could, his body reacted to hers. For some reason, he found he had no choice.

"Yes. Here, now!" she whispered urgently. She pressed the catch on his pants, and slipped them down, loosening her legs just enough for the material to drop to the floor. She arched her back to pull up her garment an instant before she tightened her legs around him, pulling him closer.

Rather than climb onto the table, he held back, standing as her hand brought him inside of her. He let his body take over then, concentrating on the power of their joining, which he could not deny.

Somehow, being inside of her made him want to go on and on without stopping. But this time she was fierce, groaning and pushing against him, drawing him deeper into her as their pubic bones ground against each other. Her hands dug into the muscles of his sides and back.

Looking down at her, watching her features twist with passion, he knew the only thing she was conscious of was blind desire. In a rare moment of clarity amidst his own roaring physical desires, he intuitively understood she had no control over herself. Her own genes—her Forerunner genes — had been designed to create an overriding sexual desire above all else. It was this desire, no, he corrected himself, this deep and powerful need pushing her to propagate at every chance so her race could be reborn.

In that fragmented instant, he'd found her only weakness; the genetic programming her ancestors had manipulated, forcing reproduction to be the highest function of life for the new generation of forerunners. Her hips bucked harder, the heat within turned volcanic, and he reached his climax.

A breath later, Haseya released a rolling groan. When her body rocked with the orgasm, she pressed her head against his chest. He held her close, their breathing overpowering the constant hum of machinery. It was then he understood with a fatal certainty, she would not let him go until she was pregnant, if then.

GODDESS

EIGHTEEN

Pacing in circles, Roke worked on his escape plan. He'd left Haseya to the vats and computer banks and returned to 'their' room. His chance of escape depended on his EXO suit and helmet, but he didn't know where they were. He'd been wracking his brain on ways to hide his intentions and remembered when he entered the cavern with the helmet on and lost the connection with the 'dogs' thoughts, and how the diamond-marked dog waited for him to take off his helmet.

The memory gave him promise that the helmet might block her ability to sense his thoughts better than his own desperate mental wall. And then there was his inability to tell if Haseya was sensing him like an empath, or able to go into his mind, and see what he was thinking. With luck, the helmet would stop either.

Growing up, Roke had not known anyone born with psionic abilities. His own grandfather believed Roke had a form of psi ability and assured him psi abilities were no fairytales. Backing up his grandfather's words, the guilds were always on the alert for those with psionic abilities. Perhaps it was a part of human makeup, a long-atrophied area of the brain humans lost at some point during their evolution.

Whatever it was, he had only one mission, to get free before Daho, his ship's computer, sent the missing scout message. His original idea of waiting would not work. He had to get out and warn them before they landed, and before any scout touched the stones

Haseya was now filling the lakes with; and he wanted the weapons in his suit—if they were still there.

No matter, suit or no suit, weapons, or no weapons, getting free and staying free until Caruso and the other scouts made planetfall was his only option.

I will get out! he told himself even as the skeleton of a plan began to sketch itself in his mind.

<<>>

They sat at a table in the food area, finishing up a meal of some light-colored protein, with the texture of pudding and the flavor of meat. It was a strange combination, but it was tasty, he thought as he finished and looked at Haseya. Holding his mental barrier, the walls surrounding his mind as best he could, he wondered if they worked at all.

Not knowing if his block was working, he decided on busy thinking to keep his mind jumbled, but concentrated on one underlying thought: how closed in he was becoming, focusing not on the closed space around him, but of being underground. In a small ship, in space, he could always look outside. He could not do that deep inside of Anadi.

He'd spent most of the meal running these thoughts through his head, growing his skeletal plan with flesh and muscle. By the end of the meal, he decided to test it. "Can we go outside and get some real air? I need to be out there, to feel the ground under my feet, not be under it, and to see the sky."

GODDESS

She gazed at him for a moment, then smiled. "What is bothering you?"

He waved his hands around the room. "This place ... being below ground. I was raised outdoors. The soil, and the stars are a part of me. You know my ancestry. I come from a line of people who lived outdoors."

"I know your DNA makeup. It is the same as my human strand, which will soon be my only DNA. But I do not know why you feel this way."

"I have always hated being inside something and unable to see outside. Haseya, you didn't grow up the way I did. The influences on my life are different from yours. You went from child to adult in a week. Your influences came from genetic programming and computers, while it took me years to mature. I have experienced things, done things, and been places you have not. Each left its own particular mark upon me."

He paused, smiled at her, and said, "But you have not."

She smiled. "Nor do I need to. The databanks gave me the experiences."

"Really? The databanks touched you, kissed you, fed you as an infant, told you children's tales, and surrounded you with warmth and love?" His eyebrows rose while his mind rolled on, the thoughts in his head caroming off the edges of his mind, the sound in his ears, which only he could hear, was a locomotive's roar chugging through his brain in time with his mantra ... *I must get outside. I cannot stay closed in. I must see the sky. I have to go outside so I can breathe. Am I dying in here? I need to see the sky, the sun, the stars.*

Haseya raised her hand and reached toward him. She stopped suddenly. Her eyelids closed. Her brows creased in concentration.

He studied her while the tingling sensation at the back of his neck grew strong, and knew she was attempting to get into his mind. He refused to let up.

A few seconds later her eyes snapped open, wider than he'd ever seen them as her blue-green irises floated in a sea of white. After another ten seconds of silence, she blinked. "Yes, I understand."

He exhaled his relief. "I'd like to wear my suit."

She stared at him and the tingling in his neck became intense. "Did you hear me?"

Her exhalation was long and sibilant. "Yes. I understand. Come."

<<>>

Twenty minutes later, wearing his EXO suit, but not the helmet, he followed Haseya up the long, curved ramp toward the surface. If he'd have forced the issue, she would have grown more suspicious. After all, why would someone claiming claustrophobia want to put on an enclosing helmet? More important than the helmet were the stunner and projectile weapons. Either she hadn't found them, or she didn't know he had them. But he was surprised she'd not taken away the knives.

It took ten minutes to reach the surface, and when he stepped through the waterfall opening, he took in lungfuls of air. It was dusk, the sky was darkening. He looked west, the horizon was alive with fading bands of colors as the night smothered the day.

He turned to the eastern horizon, where the leading edges of the twin moons were rising from the edge of darkness into the star-strewn sky. The air washing across his face held a tinge of coolness, along with an explosion of scents and sounds, which was a far different feeling than the tasteless machine cooled air generated below the surface. He didn't have to feign their effects on his mind and body.

Twisting his wrist, he glanced at the chrono: the hologram didn't appear. He pressed another switch against his side. Nothing. Had she found a way to shut the equipment down? Or was something inhibiting the EXO's sensors?

They walked along the edge of the lake, his eyes searching everywhere in the low light, looking for the 'dogs', the animals that had trapped him below, but of them, there were no signs. He scanned the ground. Wherever he looked the blades of grass were undisturbed, which meant the animals had left at least a day ago, allowing the grass to rise from where it had been stepped on—if Anadi followed the normal path of nature on an earth-typical planet.

He knew exactly where he was, and where his ship was. He turned to Haseya, a smile curling the corners of his lips. "Thank you. Can we go to the lake below?"

"It's getting dark. Can you see?"

"I'm fine."

"Alright," Haseya agreed.

They went down the trail on the side of the low mountain, following the same path the animals had led him up. *Two days*, he thought, then wiped it from his mind.

At the lower lake, Roke studied the waterfall. "The rocks with the ... dust, how do they get to the river?"

She waved her hand at the lake. "An underground channel runs from this lake to the underground channel recycling the river water. When the stones are fed into that tube, the stones are carried into the the river."

"I saw the inside of the tube, but not any opening where the stones came in."

"Perhaps there were no stones entering at that moment. There is a ... mechanism allowing the stone to drop into the tube, and then seal itself."

He glanced toward the lake, then up at the second lake. "The channels, the ones above the falls feeding the upper lake, those aren't natural are they?"

"No, both lakes were built, the upper to feed this lake, and this lake to carry the stones to the river." She turned and went to the water's edge, where she released her garment and stood naked. "Come, swim with me."

She dove into the water, cutting through its surface with knife-like smoothness. He watched her disappear, and kept watching until a full minute later, she rose to the surface, her silvery hair sparkling in the pale blue light of the twin moons. She held a small stone in the palm of her hand. She tossed it to Roke.

GODDESS

Catching the stone, he asked, "Won't the dust affect me?"

"No, you are bonded to me, as I am to you. This is not a simple thing. When you first touch it, the dust reads your DNA, and sees mine as well, then it blends together to make the bond. This is why the dust will not bond with you and bind you to another. Even so, it cannot work in the air. The dust is inactive without being in water."

He looked at the stone, which was a solid gray just like the stone he'd held the first time he'd been at the river. "Why?"

"I do not know," she admitted. "It is not a question I have thought about. I'll research it in the databanks."

He flipped the stone back to her, and she held it underwater. It took only a few seconds for the dust to be reborn.

"Come, swim with me," she repeated. He had no choice; he needed to keep her off-guard and unsuspicious. He also knew what would happen if he was naked.

She stared at him, waiting.

He pressed the catch buttons on his suit. The metallic fabric opened and dropped to the ground. He was naked beneath the suit, and when he stepped forward, he saw the change hit her, beginning with her eyes. Taking a deep breath, he dove into the water.

DAVID WIND

NINETEEN

The water accepted him with a caress of coolness flowing into every pore of his body. It was the first time since he'd followed the dogs into the cavern he had a sense of freedom. But when he broke the surface, and saw Haseya waiting for him, the feeling fled.

Forcing a smile, he turned and swam from her. A moment later she was next to him, swimming with him. He pushed forward, enjoying the sensation of the give and take of his muscles after the imprisonment below.

He cut through the water, his arms pulling him, his feet pushing as he kicked the water. Haseya swam effortlessly at his side, matching him stroke-for-stroke. He turned in a wide arc, not slowing, nor going faster.

After ten minutes swimming, Roke returned to shore at the exact spot he'd gone into the lake. When he climbed onto the ground, and into the thick, short grass, he lay back to let the air dry him. It was a cool evening, and his skin reacted with goosebumps.

Haseya left the lake and knelt next to him. "You are cold."

"No, it feels good."

Ignoring his answer, she lay on her side next to him, and pulled herself close. "I will warm you," she whispered, ignoring his words. Her hand went to his chest, skimming over the surface, her fingers outlining the muscles of his abdomen before dipping lower.

In a flash, he realized he could no longer use the mind trick he had been employing, and filled his mind with thoughts of he and

GODDESS

Haseya making love. He had no other option, and he couldn't let her get the slightest hint of what he planned.

With luck, he would get away soon, and this nightmare would end. The barest tingle rose in his nape, a hint of alarm as her nails played a teasing tattoo along his chest. When her fingers moved downward, gliding across his abdomen before continuing on their sensual path, he let himself go instead of thinking—it was safer.

<<>>

An hour later, he followed her to the upper lake. The twin moons, halfway between the horizon and the apex of the sky, lit the way with shafts of pale blue breaking through the clouds to spotlight their way.

He searched everywhere when they approached and then went through the channeled water and into the large cavern. There were no signs of the dogs anywhere, which eased his mind, and allowed him to breathe a sigh of relief.

Fighting a pack of animals was not a means to escape. He stopped his train of thought, shored up his mind wall, and made it stronger. He pushed out thoughts of being fatigued, of needing to sleep, and repeated them over and over.

By the time they reached the room they'd been using, Haseya pointed to the bed. "Get some sleep, Roke."

"What about you?" With a smile, he reached out to stroke her cheek.

She covered his hand with hers. There was an immediate increase in the heat coming from her hand. She drew it quickly away.

"I must keep everything moving. There are only a few hours of work left, and then we can await the arrival of your people. I will be back soon."

She leaned toward him, swept a kiss across his lips, and stepped back.

"Wake me when you do," he told her, again repeating his tiredness over and over.

Nodding, and obviously reluctant to leave, she sighed and walked out. He sat on the edge of the bed. The sleeping surface rose instantly. He closed his eyes and probed his memory. He pictured the path to where his EXO suit had been, in need of the helmet, gloves, and his boots.

He waited an hour to make certain she was totally involved. Then, careful to stay low and beneath the eye of the various lenses he'd spotted in the hallways, he went to the small room where she'd stored his suit.

His helmet was still on the shelf. He grabbed it and put it on. When the oxygen intake valves and scrubbers opened, he breathed in the highly oxygenated air of the cavern, and stepped into his boots. He looked around for his gloves, but couldn't find them. "Why?" His backpack was on a shelf, looking deflated. He checked its contents. All that remained were his medical kit, bacterial tabs, and one flare tube. There was a single protein bar, the rest were gone.

"Damnit!" he muttered, connecting the backpack to his suit with a pressure button. Then he studied the room and the shelves filed with unusually shaped objects. He recognized one in particular from the museum at Guild Prime—a Forerunner weapon.

The Guild weapons experts had no clean answer for how it worked. There were no triggers, and nothing on the weapon had a moving part. They had been unable to find a way to load it, or fire it. The majority of experts believed the weapons were imprinted with, and controlled by the wielders' minds, so advanced did they believe the Forerunners were. He looked at it, started to reach for it, but stopped himself.

The GU scientists had no idea what the weapon could do. He knew the Guilds, all of them, had tried using the Explorer Guild's Special Division's psi scouts to work it. Only one had been able to. The weapon exploded and killed him.

The working theory evolving from the incident was that the weapon could only be used by the imprinted mind.

All Roke could do was hope Haseya would be occupied for longer than it took him to put distance between them … a lot of distance. He needed to stay free for two days, so his ship's computer could send the missing scout signal. Unless his suit link to the ship was working.

He wasn't certain the material of the cavern was blocking com signals, and believed she'd activated some sort of block possibly covering the planet, or a radius around the installation. Forerunner technology was so far advanced over theirs; anything he could think of the Forerunners had already built—there was too much evidence in the galaxy to let him think otherwise. But he wouldn't know until he was out of the cavern, and at his ship, which he'd have to avoid for two days.

"Move!" he ordered himself.

Leaving the room, his footfalls as quiet as possible, he followed the exact same path he and Haseya had taken earlier. When he reached the entry cavern, he held back, moving slowly into it, and looking in every direction.

With any luck she would not know he was leaving. He built a map of the area in his mind, and plotted his course from the cavern to the heaviest woods at least twenty klicks away. He would not use the path to the second lake; rather, he'd go up into the mountains, and then down into the thick forest. If he could make it there before she discovered him gone, he'd have a chance.

Then he realized he hadn't seen her dragon form the last few times they'd had sex. He'd assumed it was a reflex brought on by her orgasms. Was she gaining better control over her dragon-self, or was it leaving her, as she said it would once she became pregnant? He hoped that wasn't the case now.. She had to be gaining control, which meant he had to be alert for animals on the ground, and the Haseya dragon above.

"Shit!" he whispered and started running.

<<>>

Two and a half hours later, he'd put ten klicks between himself and the two lakes, but was moving more slowly than he'd wanted because of the large rocks, thick brush along the mountainside. His suit was still not functioning, which stopped him from accessing the

GODDESS

survey map; instead, he relied on his memory, and his mental map, which placed him close to the area he sought. The moons were in descent, their light casting a pale, blue light over the planet.

With enough illuminated to see, he gazed down and across at the northern forest, and looked for pathway down. As he scanned the area, he took the lone protein pack, ate it slowly, and when he finished, he tried to contact the ship. The contact failed … again.

Roke no longer questioned whether she had set a com block on the planet itself. She had. Hopefully, the outgoing substrata signal Daho would send in two days, combined with several other communications bandwidth broadcasts would make it.

No, he didn't need to hope, he knew one would.

With the protein finished, and the clearest path was down-marked in his head, he half-jogged, half-scooted down the rocky tree-cluttered mountain slope. When he reached the base of the mountain, and stepped onto the flatter land, he wanted to rest. *Don't stop now, not yet*, he told himself, and pushed himself on through the trees, moving steadily north, directly away from the cavern, the lakes, and especially his ship.

As he glanced at his chrono, it flickered then faded. A ray of hope surfaced at the sight. Was this nearing the limit of the signal block? Whether he was or not, one thing was absolutely certain: Haseya was already searching for him. She was a logical to a fault, computer-like, except when it came to sex. Odds were, she would search the area surrounding his ship first to make sure he hadn't returned there.

If his calculations were correct, he was at least seven miles from the ship. Now he needed to put even more space between them if he wanted to stay free. He changed his angle from straight-northwest to a more northern slant, and pushed himself into a full jog, moving just fast enough to add distance while avoiding running into a tree. To the west, the moons had set, their light a bare line along the western horizon, while the first bands of dawn rose in east.

Slowing his pace an hour later, as daylight replaced the dawn, he stopped. As powerful a runner as he was, and at the pace he'd maintained, including the extra distances needed to avoid the trees he'd only made it another five klicks—barely three miles.

He sat with his back against a tree, his breathing forced, and desperately thirsty. He was dehydrating, his muscles were starting to cramp, and signaling his body's need for water. Although his sweat was absorbed by the suit, converting it to water, and the suit's temperature-control cooled him by a few degrees, it wasn't enough to keep him going. He wanted to take his helmet off but refused to take the risk Haseya was searching for him with her mind.

Low sounds filtered through the helmet. Night birds chattered, and the breeze rustled the leaves of the trees in passing. In the distance, came the howl of an animal.

His inner compass and his mental map—the map he'd committed to memory before landing, told him there was a lake nearby. Exactly where, he couldn't pinpoint, but it wasn't far.

'Remember what I taught you, Little Rock', his grandfather whispered. He smiled at the thought. If only it were real … But he

GODDESS

accepted the remembered advice, stood, and searched the ground, looking for groupings of animal tracks going in the same direction.

He walked for a half-mile, finding a double set of prints in the softer sections of the ground, he followed them. A quarter-mile later, he found another set of prints mingled with the first. Ten minutes after that, three more sets of prints merged into the mix; water was nearby.

He drew his grandfather's bone-handle hunting knife and went forward. A short time later, he broke free of the forest, and stepped into a grassy area. Ahead of him was a lake, larger than the two in the mountain, but small in comparison to most on the planet. He checked around the area. There were no animals near, or they'd heard him and run off. Either way it made no difference.

Reluctantly taking off his helmet, he cautioned himself to do this fast. He knelt at the water's edge, put the helmet at his left knee, and without any thought to the bacteria in the water, cupped his hands and drank until he could drink no more.

With the water dripping from his face, Roke straightened his back. He stayed on his knees while his body absorbed the water, his cells rehydrating, his cramped muscles easing. Just as he started to rise, his neck exploded with so strong a warning every muscle in his body tensed.

Two seconds later, the grass rustled behind him. A thunderous howling roar shattered the silence over the lake. A chill spread through his body. He gripped the bone-handle knife tighter.

TWENTY

Reversing the knife, Roke reacted to the threat by using the tension in his muscles like springs. He spun, and in the same motion, pulled his longer scout knife free with his left hand and braced his feet for the animal's charge.

The beast stopped when he spun. It was one of the strangest looking animals he'd seen thus far. Unlike the dog-like animal, he and Caruso had catalogued this one on their first tour, but from computer-imaging scans and not in person. The size of a Gleisien 2 Wolf, it weighed around 120 pounds, had a shaggy black fur coat, and silver-blue eyes. A double band of teeth ran the length of its long jaws and its four long, curved, viper-like fangs glistened dangerously.

It stood dead still, ears pointed directly at him; its eyes fastened like lasers on him as it started forward again. The animal's raging growls lowered into thunderous rumbles coming from deep in its throat.

The 'wolf' had six legs, which was where it differed from the Gleisien wolf. With its eyes unwavering from him, it came forward, looking more like oncoming mishappened death than anything else. He should have pulled the stunner.

The wolf stopped seven feet from Roke, who held absolutely still, and matched stares with the animal. The first chills that had raced through him at the sound of the animal were gone, replaced by a second, stronger rush of adrenaline. The thunder coming from its throat suddenly intensified. Its muscles tightened; its rear legs bent, the muscles knotting in preparation to charge.

Digging his heels into the ground, Roke twisted them back and forth, creating a cushion to brace himself. Then the wolf's growl stopped, and in a bare fragment of time, the air turned as still as space itself. Roke bent his knees as he crouched lower.

Watching the wolf's eyes, his grip tightened on the knives. The animal sprang. Roke raised both arms the instant the wolf left the ground and leapt into the air. Its long body arced toward him, jaws open, fangs gleaming deadly in the sunlight, its rear legs drawing beneath it, ready to rip through his abdomen.

When the wolf reached mid-flight, Roke uncoiled and leapt upward, using the ground cushioning at his heels, to add power to his legs.

They met in mid-air, Roke plunging his long scout blade into the softer underside of the wolf, even as the predator's rear claws ripped across his chest, the carbon-laced talons cutting through his EXO suit's metallic fabric and slicing into the flesh and muscle of his chest. He felt nothing, his concentration so singularly focused solely on his only objective, killing the beast.

Roke screamed out his pent-up rage of the past days, using it to fuel his muscles, and at the same time, forced the shorter knife up under its jaw. When the blade of the bone-handle knife reached the animal's brain, the beast stiffened and died, dropping down to crush Roke between itself and the ground.

He lay there, breathing hard and willing the pounding of his heart back to normal. An instant later, a wave of pain erupted across his chest; Instead of screaming, he turned it inward, using the intensity of the pain to maneuver his arms and hands, and get a grasp on the animal's dead weight.

Taking a deep breath, he pushed hard, and shoved the body up and off. With the weight lifted, he lay there, sucking in air and taking a mental take inventory of his body. Every breath sent streaks of fiery pain across his skin and muscles. If he were going to survive, he had to find a way to take care of himself.

Biting off the cry of pain, he took several short, quick breaths and sat up. He crossed arms over his chest, pressing them against the intense pain scorching his upper torso. Willing himself to hold strong as the worst of the pain eased, he looked down to see the suit's nanites already repairing the suit.

As the they worked, Roke hit the release button, and the suit opened so he could assess the damage. It wasn't as bad as he first thought—it wasn't good either, but the suit had helped. Six long, slicing tears ran a diagonal path from the right side his neck, across his chest, and down his ribs to the edge of his abdomen.

The flesh was split and bleeding. He lowered suit further, took off the backpack, and freed the med kit. He took out a small, thin packet from one of the compartments.

With the flick of a thumb, he opened the packet, and shook its contents over the wounds. Four seconds after the powder hit the air, it turned to liquid, separated into six rivulets, filled each of the cuts. If

GODDESS

his luck held, the med would seal them against infection. Hopefully, it would handle any dirt and bacteria the wolf carried on its feet and claws.

The pain receded in slow-but-steady waves as the healing agent went to work. With the long cuts medicated, the anesthetic in the medical agent numbed the pain. It would take the remaining two packets to heal the wounds completely.

During the next five minutes, the skin around the six cuts joined together, leaving long, angry red lines. He grunted; even with the healing agent, he had gained yet another six scars to go along with the others.

It took another seven minutes for the nanites to repair the suit. Roke forced himself onto his feet, knowing he had to move. The was a flash of pain with the movement, and then another wave of pain rippled through him as the numbness receded and the pain returned. No matter how well the healing agent worked on the open wound, its primary job was to prevent an infection, not kill pain. Infection was the most dreaded killer on a strange planet. While the medication had closed the open wound, his body would still take time to heal. The pain dancing over him was a simple message to not push himself hard.

He let out a short, barking laugh. He was running from a mind-reading alien who wanted him to give her children so her race could be recreated. "No!" he spat between clenched teeth. He had no choice but to stay free, and out of her reach until help arrived, which might be in two days, or two weeks, or never.

He pressed the switch on his arm for his map, it flickered, but did not rise. He'd hoped he'd gotten far enough for his suit to work, but not yet.

Shaking his head, he closed his eyes, and brought up his own mind map. There were a lot of areas to go, places where he could hide, but to reach them, he would have to expose himself. *No*, he thought, he needed to stay in the woods, beneath the blanket of trees. She could fly, which meant she would see him if he was in the open. He needed a roof over his head, and this thick forest was just that.

Again, a sudden tingling at the nape of his neck kicked up—and since Haseya, he was now an absolute believer. He no longer doubted his grandfather was right and had been so all those years ago. Somehow Roke knew she was near, and this sense of his, this tingling, was advance warning.

He looked up, trying to see through the cover of treetops, but he could not. All he knew with any certainty was her closeness. Surely, she was somewhere nearby and searching above the treetops for him. Knowing she was close was a strange feeling. But how had she found him so quickly?

'We are bound together,' she'd told him when they had gone out to the lakes. He thought about what she'd said, and a chill sliced through his back—a knife with a blade of ice. 'You are already bonded to me, as I am to you. This is not a simple thing. It reads your DNA and mine and blends them to make the bond. The bond will last as long as we live.'

GODDESS

The blood drained from his face as he repeated her words in his mind. He had thought of it as a manner of expression, not a statement of reality; now he had no choice but to accept whatever this dust was had effected a change to his DNA, and given her the ability to know where he was. But it was a double-sided knife, for now he knew it told him where she was. It might only be a small advantage, but an advantage nevertheless, and that was all he needed.

He took another minute to seal his EXO suit and retrieve his helmet. "What the—" he spat, looking around him. He hadn't moved more than a few yards from where he'd knelt before the wolf attacked. It wasn't there.

He wouldn't take the risk of turning on his lights, not with his neck vibrating as madly as it was. *How can I block her from finding me?* He had no idea how this DNA bonding worked. Did she sense his mind? His body? His blood ... or was it his presence?

What about her dragon nature? She'd told him it would disappear when she conceived. As soon as she was pregnant, the male and female animal, and the male DNA strands would disappear from her genetic makeup. He had seen the evidence in the way her dragon appearance was fading ... Or was she hiding it?

He pushed himself to think back to other conversations he'd had while he looked for the helmet. From the corner of his eye, he saw something sparkle in the water, twenty feet out. It was the helmet. He must have dropped it into the water when he'd fought the wolf. A moment later, as Roke went to the edge of the water, the helmet sank.

He looked around, he was in the open and his neck began to buzz again. He had to get under the trees.

Turning, and knowing the helmet was lost, he walked as fast as he could into the thicker trees. He found two trees close together, their trunks rising high into the air, the branches thick with leaves. He sat down beneath the largest of the two, faced the other, and returned to his thoughts.

While her dragon-like head no longer rose, she'd had her dragon wings, which was enough to give her the ability to fly and search him out. Today, tonight, and tomorrow was all the time he needed to stay alive and free. A lance of pain ripped through his upper torso when he arched his back to look at the canopy of leaves; somehow, he would find the way!

He sensed her approaching the lake but that she was a fair distance away. He was sure she would be using a specific search pattern. It was something he would do, fly his ship or sled in ever-narrowing circles until he found exactly what he sought. He closed his eyes. *Think*! he told himself, *Think*!

How was she tracking him? Was she using her inner senses to track him? Their DNA bond? How else? He had to move, but before he could take a single step, he needed to have a destination. He looked at his left arm. The chrono was flickering, the image getting stronger. If he could pull up a detailed map of the area, he would find a place to hide.

Common sense reared its ugly head to stop him from attempting the map. If she could track him by his DNA, what other

GODDESS

means did she have available? No, he would use nothing not a part of this world. Even if he could use the map, which drew little energy from his suit, it still used detectable energy, and it connected with the ship to function. With his eyes still closed, he built a mental picture of this quadrant— the section of Anadi he and Caruso had designated quadrant one.

Quadrant one's borders ran north from the junction of the equator and prime meridian two-thirds of the way to the pole, and a 1000 miles west. It was the largest of the northeastern quadrants. Quadrant two mirrored one until it reached Anadi's arctic pole.

A knife-tip warning stabbed him in the neck. He had a decision to make: go back and try for the ship, or run deeper into the forests? It took him five seconds to realize there was no choice. He had to remain free. He was not going back to the twin lakes. He would keep on the north-by-west angle, moving further distant from the twin lakes and the ship, making it harder for Haseya to find him. Then, when enough time had passed, and the emergency signal sent, he would return to the ship.

'The earth, the ground you walk on is always your friend', his grandfather told him more times than he cared to remember. 'The earth protects our people in many ways: it supports you; it lets you sleep upon it, and it protects you when you are within its embrace. Do not ever forget'.

He looked down at Anadi's ground. The soft upper layers of topsoil cushioned this world from the hard substrata below. In that moment, Roke understood his grandfather's words were more meaningful than he had ever believed.

The earth his grandfather spoke of was not the planet his race had originated on; rather, it was an expression fitting all worlds. The earth was the ground of any planet: the soil, the rocks, and the dirt of a world was its earth.

Finally understanding what his grandfather had worked so hard to teach him, he did not doubt the old Navajo knew exactly what his words would mean to Roke at this very moment. The earth would protect him.

Regretting his missing gloves, Roke formed his hands into claws, and dug in the soft topsoil. When he finished, he'd dug a grave-shaped opening, three feet deep. From his backpack, which he'd leaned against the bole of a tree, he took out a six-inch-long metal tube with a cap on each end. The emergency flare was intended for use when communications failed. He opened one end. A small wire with a looped end dropped from the cap to the side of the tube.

Operating the flare was simple, pull the wire after the tube is set in the ground. Roke did not set it in the ground; rather, he unscrewed the bottom cap, and looked inside at the wiring and at the chemical packet.

As if it were a bomb, which it could turn into if he made a mistake, he reached a finger in, and felt around for anything holding the chemical material to the tube. There was nothing.

He pushed the original pull-wire back into the tube, and worked the chemical packet out. The operation took almost ten

GODDESS

minutes. When the packet fell to the ground, with the wire still attached, he exhaled in relief, and pulled the wire off the chemicals. The heat at the nape of his neck grew more intense.

He sat in the open grave, and using both hands, pulled the dirt on top of him. As he continued to bury himself, he laid completely flat, when he reached his neckline, he stopped. He looked around, closed his eyes, and tried to sense her. She was closer, but he still had time.

Lowering his head, he prepared for the hardest part, burying his head beneath the topsoil. First, he put the tube in his mouth. Then pushed as much dirt as possible around his head, outlining it. He piled dirt where his arms would have to go, and then put the rest of the dirt on his chest and closed his eyes.

The EXO suit inflated, giving him a half-inch of air between himself and the dirt; the suit also adjusting to the temperature change in order to keep him comfortable.

Working by feel, he covered his face, making sure there was at least four or so inches of dirt covering him. Then he wiggled and maneuvered his arms until they were beneath the ground. Taking a breath, he sent his senses outward, seeking Haseya. He found nothing, sensed nothing.

This may work, he told himself, lying within the envelope of darkness, as his wound sent lances of pain across his chest, and the dirt pressed down on him.

He emptied himself of all thought. He didn't know if the earth of Anadi would protect him in the way he needed, but he had to try, for it was the only means left to him to make sure she did not win.

He concentrated on the darkness behind his eyes, focusing everything on it. A sudden wave of dizziness swept through his head. Then there was nothing but dark.

GODDESS

TWENTY-ONE

Something was wrong. The pain in his chest was agonizing, rousing him from the fevered sleep he'd fallen into soon after he buried himself. Weight pressed down on him. The half-inch of air separating him from the dirt was no longer protecting him, and the temperature had dropped. The suit had been in the cavern for four days without sun.

The morning following his escape, he'd spent most of the daylight hours running beneath the crowns of trees, the reach of the sun through the leaves barely been enough to keep the suit going. The batteries could not recharge properly. The skin of the suit held hundreds of battery cells. They were all dead. Now the increase in pressure from above was squeezing the breath from his chest—or was it more?

He held still, taking short gasps through the flare tube. It was as though someone were walking on him. The force on his abdomen and chest turned intense; the pain from his wounds radiated wildly with each movement from above.

Then the weight shifted, and even more weight pressed down on him, this time on his abdomen and thighs. The weight moved off him seconds later, and he took in as deep a breath as possible. But then something cold pushed through the dirt and touched his forehead. The touch was enough to galvanize every muscle into action.

Screaming with rage and frustration, Roke pushed the dirt off, and broke free of the shallow grave, only to find two large animals snuffling the ground around the hole he'd dug. They were big animals, long and round, with broad, black-tipped snouts and strangely shaded violet eyes.

He took several deep breaths of the cool air into his lungs. When he saw the moons were low in the sky, he wondered how he'd spent so many hours beneath the ground, taking short breaths because of the weight of the earth on him.

He recognized the animals. Nocturnal, they ate what was beneath the ground: worms, insects, whatever. He remembered what he'd said to Caruso when he realized how they hunted and fed. "How in the rings of Delkin, do they get so fat?"

Caruso had laughed. "Genes."

Realizing he wasn't on their diet, the pair shuffled to another spot to seek food. He watched them disappear into the woods, and then closed his eyes and concentrated on the part of him, the special sense telling him she was near.

He didn't find it.

Brushing the caked-on dirt from his EXO suit, he looked at the thin, barely perceptible line beginning to outline the eastern mountain. Dawn was close, and on Anadi daylight followed quickly. Daylight was not good for him; rather, daylight would give Haseya yet another advantage.

Suddenly woozy, he took a deep breath, exhaled slowly, and remembered the same feeling when first buried himself. He realized he had a fever—the cuts were infected. He released his backpack, took out the med kit, and opened his suit to find the claw marks now an angry, swollen red.

He took the med kit out of the backpack, and removed a second packet, which he opened and poured over the wounds. While the powder turned to into the flowing gel, he took a tab out of another compartment of the kit and swallowed it. He hoped the complex spectrum antibiotic would work on whatever has caused the infection.

When Roke flipped the backpack over his head to attach it to the back of his suit, there was a lag in the click of connection before it sealed. At least the nanites were still active, but that wouldn't last much longer. He pushed aside a quick jolt of despair, turned, and set off in an easy jog, hoping the antibiotic would hit and keep him strong enough to get away. He needed to put as much distance between him and the Forerunner installation as possible.

Moving steadily northeast, there were a few thousand klicks ahead before the forest would end, and the ground would turn cold and hostile. He had no need to go that far, just far enough to stay out of reach.

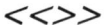

<<>>

Half an hour later, the sun broke the horizon. Five minutes after it had, he came upon a slow-running creek. Without hesitating, he stepped into the water and laid down, letting the flow of water wash the dirt off the suit. Then he stood for five minutes, waiting for the sun to give him enough of a charge to open the suit.

When the suit fell, he set it on the ground next to the creek, and laid down on the creek's bottom. The cool, almost-cold water was an unexpected gift, sending happy chills along his torso.

When the water rolled over his chest, the long, angry scratches stung as the crystal water washed the dirt from where the animal's claws had cut through the suit to open his skin.

Rising out of the water, Roke grabbed the EXO suit, hit the button to free the backpack, but could not without the suit's power recharged. Strangely, as the pain continued to increase, he wondered why there had been no backup method of getting to his supplies. Thankfully, all he needed was ten minutes of sun to get enough of a charge to energize the nanites and free the backpack.

On the west side of the creek was an old tree with branches so long they bowed to the ground. He hung the suit on a long branch in the direct path of the sun. While he waited for the suit to charge enough to operate, he pushed the pain away, and planned out his next moves.

He had to stay free, yet he needed to get close enough to the ship to be ready when Caruso and the others arrived. Alternatively, he considered getting into the ship to send Caruso a warning to stay away from the river in the valley, and the twin lakes—a warning of alien life.

But was she an alien life-form? At this point, he knew every inch of her body. How could he not after living most men's wildest and perhaps weirdest fantasies. Yes, he knew every inch of her; but the real issue was what he didn't know. The tail, the wings, the facial scales … Where did they go? And were they really gone? He thought about the different animals and insects he'd seen on a half-dozen worlds, and how they were able to manifest the changes to camouflage themselves and appear as one of their enemies.

Was that was Haseya was? Was that what the Forerunners were, beings with the ability to camouflage themselves by physically changing their bodies, not just the outer layers of their skin?

The enormity of the question staggered him. Everything about her was human, except when it wasn't. Roke closed his eyes against the veering path of his thoughts, and knew he'd placed himself into the middle of a biological quandary, one he was far from qualified to pursue.

Without trying, he could feel her arms around him, her hands pressing him closer to her, and taste the silk of her skin on his lips. Even here, alone and his body infected with an alien bacteria, the feel of the warmth and desire constantly flowing between them cried out to him, telling him she was human. The need to be with her grew unbearable, tugged at him, surrounded him with need for her.

"Stop! It's a trap!" he shouted into the air. It was the bond, he realized suddenly, the DNA-created bond.

His stomach growled, and he laughed, ending the debate he was holding with himself. He took the suit from the branch and pressed in two places. The backpack opened at last, and he took out the med kit and one of the antibiotic tabs, deciding a second dose now might be a good idea. One tab remained, along with one more packet of wound powder.

Taking the bone-handle hunting knife, he returned the suit to the branch, went back to the creek, and squatted at the edge of the running water with the knife in his right hand.

He waited, holding statue-still so his shadow didn't move on the water. When a fish long enough to eat swam near, he swung the blade down, timing his strike to the speed of the fish. He struck the silver and red fish perfectly and scooped it from the water.

He made short work of the meal, surprised by how good the raw Anadi fish tasted. He wasn't worried about parasites or bacteria from the meal, he had been inoculated against everything they'd found in the analysis of Anadi's plants and animals. He grunted. But not inoculated enough against a wolf's claws.

By the time he finished the fish, the suit was ready to wear, and fully functional. A thought he'd had yesterday dashed through his mind. She was definitely blocking outworld communications, and blocking surface com, but was it the entire planet or for a distance around the installation?

He took a chance and pressed the map switch. A half-second later the screen popped up. His breath rushed out as he looked at the map. His location was pinpointed by a blinking orange arrow.

He was thirty klicks from the twin lakes. *Not far enough*, he told himself. He shut down the image and made some mental calculations. He could run for about twenty klicks without stopping, around twelve or so miles before he needed to rest.

GODDESS

He pressed his forearm to his chest, and the pain lanced out in every direction, prompting him to change his mind. He decided to walk.

The sun floated lazily overhead, sending down slanted lines of light to break through the leaves and spotlight the way. He'd been walking for four Anadi hours, and the last two hours had been pure agony. Why? The pain should have been long gone, but it wasn't, it had gone from bad to worse. Why? He stopped, knelt, and opened his suit. As soon as the air hit his skin, the pain jumped, escalating to torment. He clamped his jaws shut to stop an unexpected scream from getting loose.

Something was wrong. He looked at his chest. The angry, red welts were swollen. The skin holding the edges together looked ready to burst. *What the hell?* He pushed a sharp exhale. The meds were the best ever created.

Suddenly, the world shifted. He took breath after breath, working to control whatever was happening. He was sick, drowsy, and dizzy at the same time. He reached out, looking for something to hold onto as the world spun around him and froze. The skin on his chest exploded; a band of colors shot from his chest and flew into the air. In the next instant, the colors separated, and circled his head, speeding and slowing in their own crazy cadence. He shut his eyes, counted to ten, and opened them.

The bands of color were now in front of him, dancing in perfect synchronization with each other, while they performed a weird undulating dance. His head spun faster. He closed his eyes again, breathed, and forced himself to concentrate. He felt drugged …

The thought pulled out a long-buried memory. The memory took life of its own and turned into a Tri-D show. He'd been thirteen and had gone to town with two friends. Somehow, one of them had gotten his hands on what they called Golden Honey. Three drops of Golden Honey would take you on a trip to a faraway place, a world where you were happy, a world you controlled, and one where nobody hurt you.

The Golden Honey's promise had failed him; all he'd found was terror.

He shut his eyes at the horror of the memory, a memory reminding him of why he'd never taken another drug. The Golden Honey took him on, what his grandfather called, 'a bad trip'. It took three days for him to come out of it. When he did, it took another two weeks to find any semblance of himself. He'd never touched another mind-altering drug again. His thoughts sent a shockwave through his mind, and the Tri-D show was suddenly replaced by the dancing colors.

Ignoring the dancing colors, he shook his head and whispered, "Impossible!" Then he traced the cuts on his chest with his fingertips, each one changing from red to black the instant his fingers touched them. He shut his eyes again but couldn't keep them closed. The second he opened his eyes the sunlight turned into a thousand shades of yellow. He snapped his lids shut, fast.

Definitely drugged, but how?

GODDESS

Keeping his eyelids tightly closed, he ignored the burning slices on his chest, which were suddenly pulsing, and concentrated on everything he'd done since waking in the dirt. Whatever was screwing with his mind let him see his memory.

"The fish! Damn," he muttered. It was the only possible explanation. If it had been something in the wolf's claws, its talons actually, it would have hit hours earlier.

They'd tested every animal, fish, and insect they'd caught. All tested safe for humans—digestible and safe. But they didn't do any testing on the drug level. Why would they, it wasn't part of the protocol. But Roke sensed … no, he knew it was the fish.

He wasn't sure what to do. The colors shifted, grew larger, longer, wider, and began to encircle his body. Should he find shelter, food, or just sit back and wait? With luck, it would end soon. He decided on the latter, and with a few quick openings and closing of his eyelids, he found a tree to sit against and wait it out.

He hoped he was far enough away from her.

DAVID WIND

TWENTY-TWO

His skin was on fire; a thousand insects dug their mandibles into his skin, tearing at his flesh. He reached for the button to open and pull the suit off when a thunderous two-word command blasted its way into his ears. "Control yourself!"

His hands froze. He opened his eyes. The colors were gone, everything was normal, except for the man sitting across from him.

"Tsé nil-ta," his grandfather said. "Stubborn Rock, when will you learn?"

"Learn what, Acheii?"

"To know yourself well enough to control yourself."

"I do."

"Then why are you talking to me?"

"You spoke first."

"How could I do so? I am dead."

He stared at him. He wasn't dead, he was talking to him. "No, you are here."

His grandfather laughed. "In your mind only, Roke. I am here because you need me."

"Why do I need you?"

"Where are you?" His grandfather's white eyebrows formed twin question marks above deep ebony eyes.

Roke pushed away the tendrils of fog doing their best to confuse him. "I ... I am on ... on ... Anadi," he finally said.

"Good; why are you here?"

GODDESS

"I am a first-in scout. I am preparing for the colonists."

"No! Why are you here?" he asked again, waving a deeply tanned, and wrinkled blue veined hand. "Why are you in this place, at this moment? What is wrong with you? What is happening to you?"

"I ..." He gazed at his grandfather, struggling for the words. He looked deep into his grandfather's eyes. "I am here, in this place, running from a ... tł'iishtsoh, a dragon, an alien. I ..." His throat closed, he tried to catch his breath.

His grandfather now floated a few inches above ground. He pointed up into the sky, where a magnificent golden eagle flew. His grandfather's eyes bored into him. "Tell me, Roke, why would an eagle give up her wings?"

He watched the eagle, knowing its breed had died out on Old Earth centuries ago. "I don't understand. There are no more eagles."

He managed three short breaths, and when he exhaled the third, he lowered his eyelids and sought the place within him, the center of his core. A place he'd discovered years ago, where he could ground himself, and shut out all distraction at the same time. It wasn't meditation; rather, it was different, a process he couldn't explain.

Now, realizing what he must do, he stayed in his mental center, and willed himself to feel nothing. It took three minutes for the first of the stinging and biting sensations to ease. Another ten minutes passed before the sensations stopped. The moment the stinging ended he opened his eyes.

His grandfather was gone, and with him, the hallucinations. Whatever poison had infiltrated his system, had caused the hallucinations; but the last one, his grandfather, was his own mind fighting for control over the whatever it was. It was the manifestation of his grandfather that led him to regain control of his mind. "Thank you, Acheii, for always being a part of me."

Looking at the chrono, he discovered he'd been down and out for almost five hours; at least the suit was fully charged. It would be night soon. He needed to keep moving. He pushed off the ground. His legs buckled. He slammed face-down into the soft earth.

He reached to his thighs, squeezed the muscles, but could only feel his fingers. There were no sensations in his legs. He made himself breathe slowly and evenly until his nerves settled. Then he pinched his left thigh. Nothing!

Had the flesh of the fish contained a drug, or was the chemical makeup something human digestion effected and changed into a poison or a hallucinogenic? Was it a paralytic as well? Those, and a dozen more thoughts bombarded his mind like a Tri-D vid epic gone mad.

Could he have poisoned himself by eating the fish? He laughed sarcastically at his predicament while his thoughts took their own journey. Or was it the water? Could the water have carried whatever caused the reaction? Was it some type of plant or seeds that had gone into the water?

The last thought was a stretch; a still pond perhaps, but not a flowing stream. Not a heartbeat later, the spot in the back of his neck began to tingle. He stiffened. It was faint, but it was there, and definitely not a drug-induced sensation. He knew this one all too well.

GODDESS

She was getting close. He tried to stand again, and failed.

Smashing the ground with a fist, he scanned every nook and cranny in the area. There weren't many. There was a cluster of smaller trees about thirty yards from him. He'd seen them before in various areas of Anadi, always within the forests; circles of dwarf trees, six feet in height, each perfectly spaced from the others. They had thick trunks in opposition to their height, and their branches were entwined with each other's to form a tightly woven canopy over the circle. He'd noted in the first survey on Anadi, there were always nine trees in a circle, and the space within their circle was clear. Although they were trees, they looked more like weeds growing within the bounds of the forest's giant trees.

He hadn't figured them out, the why they existed part, and neither had Caruso, who'd said, 'You'll find things that have no explanation on every world you explore. If it doesn't kill you, accept what you see and move on. Don't mess with these oddities, even the most innocuous plant, or animal, or insect, has a purpose to a planet. Let the scientists get frustrated.'

With Caruso's words playing in his mind, he eyes the circle of trees as, yet another thought deepened. When he wore his helmet, the connection between he and Haseya had been tenuous at best and disappeared after a short distance. When it was off, he'd been able to sense her. He figured it was the same for her, which is why she'd kept his helmet separated from his EXO suit. What if the strangely intertwined branches of the tree circle could shield him from her searches as had his helmet?

Having accepted the oddities of Anadi, he needed to put this one to the test—if his intuition was right. Instead of standing, which he couldn't do anyway, he used his hands, arms, and shoulders to lift his torso, and then pull himself forward. His hands, biceps and shoulder muscles bulged with heavy work. Halfway there, his hands were sore, cut, and bleeding, the skin torn by the small stones and pieces of branches littering the ground.

Ignoring the pain, he pulled both knives from the sheathes on his suit, and instead of using his hands, he used the blades. He stretched forward, jamming each blade as far into the ground as the metal would go, then dragged himself forward.

Halfway there, the sensation at the nape of the neck increased from the mild tingling to sharp shocks. She was getting close. He willed himself to ignore the sensations. He could not move any faster.

It took seven minutes to cross the thirty yards. When he reached the small trees, he pulled himself into their middle. The moment he did, he knew he'd been right. The roof of tightly woven branches and leaves were solid enough to muffle his mind from hers. The sensation in the nape of his neck confirmed his hunch when the tingling eased to a low annoyance. He laid back waiting for the muscles in his arms and torso to relax and return to normal.

He could almost hear her wings coming near, but knew it was his imagination. 'Why would an eagle give up her wings?' His grandfather's question came back at him; no, not his grandfather's, his. And the answer stared him in the eyes. The eagle would not.

GODDESS

"You fucking bitch!" he screamed, not caring if she heard. Then he buried what he had discovered deep in his mind.

Sunset came a half-hour later, and with dusk, the sensation of her nearness faded. Now all he had to do was figure out how to make his legs work. It never occurred to doubt his ability to recover, Guild scouts weren't built that way. And he was going to end this one way or another.

<<>>

Roke lay beneath the umbrella of branches within the circle of nine trees. All too soon his few minutes of clarity vanished as the reaction to eating the fish took over again. His body shook with exhaustion while his mind chased shadows along the pathways of his thoughts. Sometime during this torture, his mind shut down; he saw nothing, and he felt nothing as his body took charge, and forced him into unconsciousness.

When he woke, light filtered in between the thick trunks of the circle of trees. He'd slept through the night and into the day. He was hungry, but the hunger didn't bother him, for he realized his mind was his own, and whatever had caused the hallucinations was out of his system.

Hesitantly, slowly, he reached to his thighs and pressed his fingers into them. He felt the pressure from his fingers on his thighs and relief washed over him. He bent his legs: they followed his command. "Good," he whispered to the trees.

He stood, took two steps, and went down. He could feel his legs all right, but the accompanying pain shooting through his muscles was debilitating. He rolled onto his back and massaged his thighs.

There was no way he could walk yet. He went through his own mental checklist, working out what was happening, and came to the only conclusion he could. He was dehydrated. He tried to remember the last water he'd had. Yesterday, he realized, in the creek. His last food, the fish, was yesterday as well. The hunger wasn't bad; the thirst was.

He pressed the switch on his suit and the map floated over his arm. He manipulated it with his fingers until he had a view of the area around him. There was a stream about a half-mile north. Could he make it in his condition? *You will!* he told himself silently.

He took his knife out, the longer scout blade, which also had a serrated edge on one side, and stumble-stepped to one of the nine trees. He looked for a branch large enough to support him, but small enough to cut through with the knife.

Just as he decided on one, he stopped himself. These trees were anomalies, and some instinct held him back him from cutting into one. He looked around once, and then left the embrace of the tree circle.

It took no time to find a suitable branch, but he spent twelve minutes of stop-and-go work trimming the leaves and cutting off the smaller extending branches.

When he was finished, he had a walking stick strong enough to support him and help him get to the water. He took his first step and

GODDESS

froze. What if the water was the problem? What if the water contained the hallucinogen?

"No!" he snapped at the tree in front of him. "It can't be. We evaluated the water. We found nothing harmful." But then, they'd assessed the fish too.

The tree didn't say anything. He shrugged and took the first step of the half-mile haul to the stream. He walked in rough steps, the lances of pain rolling up and down his legs while his muscles twisted with cramps. His lips were dry, his tongue swollen, and time was not his friend.

Whatever had happened, whatever caused the drug-like reaction had depleted his body of more than just water ... potassium, he realized. His legs grew heavier, the pain worsened, but he trudged forward, mixing his strength with the stubbornness his grandfather had always reminded him.

His obstinacy was the only thing keeping him going, keeping him alive. And he needed to stay alive, to warn Caruso, and the others before they touched a stone. The one thing he believed above all else, was Haseya would do whatever it took to make sure they touched an iridescent rock.

First-in scouts, and Guild explorers, were not sexual creatures to begin with, not to say they didn't enjoy sex, but neither did they miss it for prolonged periods. Somehow, the Forerunners knew how to change this trait; Haseya was living proof she had done so him, turning him into her personal breeding stud.

Why else would they have created the stones, which he now considered more an egg, artificially created perhaps, but still an egg? Their entire purpose was to create ... no, he corrected, recreate their original species—the race who had seeded the universe. And they could do so, having discovered a way to manipulate another species' DNA, altering the genes of living entities to enforce procreation.

Each child of any union would be born with the full genetic memory of his race. However, the more terrifying aspect was knowing the memories not simply as part of the child's genetic history; rather, the child would be born with the complete knowledge of Forerunner history, science, and technology already in its mind.

If this was not stopped here and now, humanity, as he knew it, would not survive, not with the knowledge the offspring of human, and Forerunner would be born with. This was a fact Haseya had told him, so secure was she in her ability to keep him with her.

"Not this scout," Roke spat, the words sounding like 'noch bish scuut", through his swollen lips and tongue, and pushed himself even harder to get to the water.

It took him twenty-seven long, pain-driven minutes to reach the side of the stream. He knelt, lowering his face to the clear, flowing water, his desire to drink overwhelming, but he stopped himself, reached back, and unhooked the thin backpack. He took out the the tube of anti-bacterial water tabs.

He stared at it, looked around, and realized he had no container to hold enough water to dissolve the pill. There was no choice but to

GODDESS

drink. He put his entire face into the stream, and drank until he could not take in any more.

Sitting up, and crossing his legs, he closed his eyes, waiting for whatever might happen now that he'd taken in enough water to begin rehydrating. At the same time, he prepared himself for whatever the water might do to him, physically or mentally.

TWENTY-THREE

Standing up an hour after taking his first drink of water, Roke was fully hydrated. After his first mad bout of drinking, he'd taken his time, drinking small amounts of water every few minutes. In between, he'd applied the last packet of the healing powder to close the cuts and scrapes on his hands.

His legs no longer cramped, and his breathing was back to normal. He curved his back, raised his arms over his head, and stretched out to loosen his stiffened muscles and tendons. He took a single hesitant step. The pain was gone. He took another, and another, and as relief spread through him, his stomach growled loud and clear.

"I hear you." He opened his suit, and for the first time in over a day, he had enough liquid in his body to release some. When he finished, he sealed the suit, and walked east. It wasn't a conscious decision; it was the direction he faced.

By his third step, his mind was functioning properly, and he detected nothing of the drug in his system. He thought about what came next; he'd made it to the second day. Today, the second day of his escape was the seventh day since he'd left his ship, and by midnight, Daho's programming would send the signal to Caruso's ship.

If all went well, Caruso would receive the signal anywhere from an hour after it was sent, to a day, depending on the signal magnifiers, which were set to boost com transmissions to hyper-lane amplifiers powerful enough to generate signals into the sub-strata levels of hyperspace, and to hit exactly where it was directed. This was, of course, when they worked, which was most of the time, but not always.

Com signals could not be received in hyperspace, but not the scientific reasons they were able to move within hyperspace strata to the exact spot where a receiver orbited in normal space. None of the scientist mumbo-jumbo mattered; Caruso would be here within two days of receiving the signal.

All of which meant nothing unless he stayed free. It was the only way he could warn Caruso of the iridescent trap Haseya had waiting for anyone who landed. And, he would survive, even if it meant he'd have to live on water alone. It wouldn't be the first time, but it would definitely be better with protein.

He paused in mid-thought, realizing staying free also meant he would not know if the signal made it through Haseya's block. The only way would be to get to the ship and check it for himself.

He went back to the edge of the stream and picked up his walking stick. Then he pressed the left side of his suit, and the holster holding the projectile weapon extended. Just as he reached for it, he reminded himself the weapon wasn't silent.

The weapon would risk the possibility of Haseya's hearing it. He didn't know what defense systems she might have put in place since … was it her awakening? Her birth? Whatever it was, he couldn't take the chance.

Returning the weapon to the suit, he brought out the stunner, set it to lethal, and drew up the map. He checked the distance between himself and the ship, and then between himself and the twin lakes.

He looked at the chrono. It was midmorning. According to the map, if he started now, and followed a straight line, it would take him fifteen or so hours to reach the ship. He traced several routes to see if one was better than the other and decided on going north for a half-dozen klicks, and then west, knowing that by the time he turned west, he would be fifty klicks from the Forerunners' cavern installation and forty-five from his ship.

All he had to do now was find food. Roke went into hunt mode.

<<>>

An hour and a half into his hunt, he'd spotted three large animals, and one of the wolf-like animals, but none of the smaller ones. The Navajo in him refused to kill a large animal for one or two meals.

At six klicks, the map glowed over his left arm, reminding him of his route. He turned west. Far ahead in the cloudless day, the peaks of the northern mountains lined the horizon. The section of the forest he was moving through was thicker than where he'd been earlier.

Studying the map, he traced the line of either a wide stream or a narrow river. He moved his fingers along the map, and it refocused and magnified. It was a narrow river with a small tributary leading away from it. The tributary was a good ten klicks west, but in the direction to where he was going.

GODDESS

His stomach growled again, reminding him he needed to move. With the slim pistol-shaped stunner in his left hand, he jogged forward, moving at a pace designed to carry him over a long distance without tiring him too much.

Roke headed toward the tributary's end, knowing it was the logical place to find smaller animals. The trek took an hour through the thick woods, and the sun was directly overhead when he stopped to find a place to hide.

The tributary ended in a shallow creek seven feet wide. Nearing the water, he slowed his pace, his experienced eyes indexing the various animal tracks crisscrossing the ground. He spotted a two-toed impression of the animal he'd named a 'popper'.

Kneeling, he traced the tracks with his fingertips. The firmness of the impression was slightly more than the earth surrounding the footprint, which was caused by the pressure of the popper's foot, telling Roke the animal had been there within the last hour.

There were several sets of tracks, which indicated a trail to water for the animals. Ten minutes later, and moving not just more slowly, but in complete silence, he stopped. The creek was ahead.

There was a thick tree to Roke's right, its lowest branch a foot above his head. He holstered the weapon, grabbed the branch, and hauled himself into the tree. He climbed ten more feet, and found a thick branch notch formed by two broad branches, giving him a place to sit and a clear view of the creek, and the semi-circular pool at the creek's end.

He watched the water's movement, and knew like the river in the valley he'd nicknamed the Vale, the creek went into the ground. He was aware of Anadi's natural irrigation system of underground rivers, which fed most of the forests on the planet.

Roke had only seen rain three times in both his visits to the planet. They hadn't spent enough time to chart all the weather, but rain was infrequent. When they'd mapped the interior of the planet, they'd discovered thousands of interconnecting underground rivers and streams deep beneath the northern hemisphere, and the lack of the same in the southern.

None of which made a bit of difference right now. Food was what mattered, staying free from her was what mattered; and, at the thought of Haseya, the urge to see her, hold her, and feel her again threatened to overwhelm him. A picture of Haseya filled his mind's eye, naked, with her arms outstretched, calling to him. *What the hell?* he asked silently as the compulsion deepened.

He wanted her, he needed her. No! Was she doing this? Was she somehow creating a mental connection to him and pushing desire into his mind and body?

There was no tingling at the nape of his neck—it wasn't her.

'We are bonded,' she'd told him. 'We are one, together, our DNA is mixed. I am yours; you are mine.'

He drew in a shuddering breath as one of the poppers emerged from a clump of shrubbery and edged toward the creek. He forced the unwanted longing away and watched the animal go to the side of the creek.

GODDESS

Tightening his hand around the grip, he lifted the weapon, and took aim. He waited until the popper finished drinking and raised its head. He fired. There was a bare whisper of sound when the stun beam struck the small animal.

The popper dropped to the ground.

Roke shook off the feeling of Haseya, climbed down from the tree, and moved quickly to where the animal lay. He picked it up by its tail, but before walking away, he leaned over to look into the clear water. Rocks and stones of various sizes and shapes were on the bottom, but none with the distinctive iridescent sheen and rectangular shape of a Forerunner seedpod; nor did they follow any patten as did the rocks in the river valley.

Breathing a little easier with the urge for Haseya fading, and finding no seeds in the water, he drank deeply and went to a low outcropping of rocks. There, Roke used the bone-handle knife to skin the animal, then stretched the popper across the rocks, and finally cleaned his knife before sheathing it. He took out the stunner, which had three power settings: stun, lethal, and laser. The laser gave the scout the ability to cut or burn whenever needed.

He set it to a broad beam and held it three feet from the popper. He would have preferred cooking it over a fire, but wasn't about to risk smoke rising into the air, so he used the wide beam to roast its flesh, and when it was done, he let it cool.

He left twenty minutes later, with a stomach full of the gamey meat, and a haunch stored in his backpack. He trotted westward in a steady gate, using a V-shaped notch in the northern mountains to keep him focused on his destination. He planned on hiding in that area until he saw or heard the Guild ships. No doubt, Haseya would be in the area as well, but there was no choice.

He looked at the sun, which was on its way toward the horizon; it would be dark before he reached his destination. Dark was good. Dark meant she would return to the cavern. He hoped.

GODDESS

TWENTY-FOUR

Slowing to a walk as dusk set its grip over the forest, Roke let his eyes adjust to the oncoming night. He picked his way through the trees, his eyes tracking left to right and back again without stopping, an exercise to help speed light adjustment, process shadows, and avoid branches, roots, and holes.

A half-hour later, dusk completed the transition to darkness, as had Roke's eyes. The first band of the twin moons rising light was a distant flicker, while the stars gifted the night sky with bouquets of sparkling pinpoints. Roke glanced at the chrono: four hours until the signal would be sent. He pulled up the map, its glow eerie in the ink of night, and it showed him two hours from where he intended to make camp.

Then it hit! The explosion at the nape of his neck jammed a harsh jolt into his head; a warning so intense he knew she was close—too close. He looked around, his body and muscles vibrating with the rushing adrenaline of his fight or flee response.

Roke knelt, searching around frantically for the outline of the small tree clusters. He didn't see any. "Shit! Shit! Shit!"

<<>>

"I don't give a damn what you think! We follow protocol here, Master Scout Caruso. I told you such last time we spoke. We will not send a dozen scouts on your ... hunch!" Conrad Tyler, the Deputy Guild Administrator for the Scillion Sector of the galaxy, slammed his hand on the desk.

"It's not a hunch! Conrad, I know something is wrong on Anadi."

"We're not in the Academy, Leon, and in the twenty years since, I've learned these psi hunches don't count."

Caruso shook his head. "All I'm asking for is a seven-hour head start. I'm telling you I know for a fact the distress signal will come tonight. No scout in recent memory has gone seven full days without contact, not unless they're dead, or captured by the Scav."

"You can't and don't know this for a fact, and neither can the psi who told you ... Yes, I know it was your gypsy, Kastova, who told you. You know damned well, no matter which signal it is, it won't matter if you go now or when we get the signal. No, Leon, we wait."

Shoving down his anger at Tyler's slur, he leaned forward. "You're wrong, Conrad, and I don't give a Sarconian fuck what you have to say. Something is wrong on Anadi. Forget Sanchette Kastova's psi warning. Stenner is the best scout we've trained in a decade, and you're ready to write him off. You should be ashamed of yourself."

The skin of the Deputy Administrator's face mottled into blotches of red, blue, and purple. His eyes hardened and his hands balled into fists. "Enough, Master Scout Caruso! Friendship only counts for so much. Shut the hell up before I have to write you up. Am I clear?"

"Way too clear ... Deputy Administrator. I'll wait for the signal from Anadi. Do I have permission to leave then?"

GODDESS

Tyler stared at his former schoolmate. "In seven hours you do, and with a full contingent of scouts if the 'missing scout' signal comes in, but only if it does. Understood?"

"Yes, sir," Caruso spat, spun on his heels, and left the office. He knew Roke Stenner better than anyone in the Guild. He'd spent five years teaching, working, and fighting next to him. Stenner was the best scout he had ever trained, and he damn well knew Stenner would not let seven days go by without contact. He was either hurt, dead, or taken by whatever had found him or he had found.

Caruso's concern started three days ago while on his rounds, preparing the pilots and crews of the Explorer Guild, and of the colonists. Stenner's last signal was received four days prior, and what Tyler called his hunch, was a well-honed sense of what was right and what was wrong in any mission he was part of. But it was more than a hunch, Kastova's psi confirmation backed up his apprehension.

Spending five years with Stenner at his side, their relationship was close to symbiotic. This wasn't unusual in the Explorer Guild, where every scout's life depended on another. Caruso knew something was wrong with the mission when he realized Stenner had not followed one of the basic contract procedures.

Whatever message his intuition kept pounding him with was what drove him to see Sanchette Kastova, a level-three psychic in the Explorer Guild. Sanchette traced her ancestry to Old Earth Eastern Europe during the Middle Ages, through the stories handed down for the centuries, from family members to family members. Sanchette was of Romany blood—Gypsy blood, and space was as much the Romanies.

playground, as had been the open areas of Old Earth before space travel.

Sanchette and he were occasional lovers. She was a full-blown psionic in the Explorer Guild, as had been every member of her family since the Guild's inception.

On the fourth day without a signal, a day he'd spent overseeing the colonization prep, the same way he had since returning to Norton's Landing—he'd learned Sanchette was on Norton's Landing on Guild business.

They had a wonderful dinner, and spent the night reacquainting themselves with each other in the way long-time lovers do. But when he'd woken in the morning, he'd found her staring unseeingly at him, her green eyes glazed with swirls of white and gray.

Caruso lay there, watching her small breasts rise and fall, and knowing the last thing he should do was disturb her. Twenty or so minutes later, she blinked once, and her luminous eyes, large and now totally green, centered on him. She released a long sibilant exhalation, and then fell across Caruso's chest, flattening her breasts upon him.

He held her there, one hand gently rubbing the small of her back, and the other hand on her shoulder. A few moments later she stirred and rolled to his side. "Leee … on," She stretched his name out in a gentle call.

"I'm here."

"I know."

GODDESS

She sat up, took both his hands in hers, and squeezed them gently, her eyes locked onto his "I had a vision."

"I know."

"About a planet and your apprentice."

Caruso stiffened, no longer the relaxed lover. "Tell me."

"He is in trouble. I do not know why, not exactly. He's discovered something. A ... a ... danger for certain," she got out. Then shook her head. "No! More! He is ... trapped, or ... I ... I couldn't see clearly, which is strange because I always do. This is not good, Leon."

Shuddering, Sanchette wrapped her arms around herself, as much for warmth as for protection, but against what? She shook her head again, her face frozen and dazed, as if some inner truth had suddenly broken through. "Something bad is happening there—so bad, so ... Leon, it will affect everyone, everywhere. It must be stopped no matter the cost!"

"I will go there now."

She dropped her arms, reached to him, and cupped his face in both hands. "No, Leon, they will not let you. They will stick to their timeline."

"But—"

"Do not even think it. If you go yourself, you will ... not return. You must wait. I cannot explain my vision, it is too ... ambiguous for words. You must not to go until the right time, and you will know when. Will you trust me and do what I ask?"

He traced every line of her face, reading the concern, and more importantly, the fear in her eyes and the taut stretch of her lips. He bent and grazed her lips with his. "I always trust you ... But you know I have to try."

She leaned down and kissed him. When she drew back, she nodded. "I know. And I must leave in three hours. They will not allow anyone to go," she added. "Please do not go alone, please."

He had never in all the years since they'd met heard her speak like this, the worry in her voice, and the haunting fear in her eyes convinced him. "I will not disobey orders; I won't go alone."

"Good. Can we not waste the time talking anymore?" She bent again, pressing her mouth to his chest as her tongue slipped across his right nipple, kissed, and then nipped teasingly at its hard tip before moving slowly downward—very, very slowly.

Caruso bit off an unexpected moan.

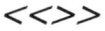

<<>>

Fifteen minutes after they'd started, the vibrations oscillating madly at his nape had not let up, and he had still not found a small tree circle. The darkness was solid, the moons' light could not penetrate the thick covering of leaves and branches, and he couldn't see further than a few feet ahead in the gloom of the forest.

"Damn it!" he snapped and turned on one shoulder light. It was the last thing he wanted to do, but he needed to find safety. Making a three-sixty, he saw nothing. He remembered from flying over the forests, the small tree circles seemed randomly placed; however, there was usually one somewhere within a klick of another.

GODDESS

Using thirty-degree angles as he walked, he went 100 yards before zigging in another direction. The constant shots of adrenaline helped power his muscles and keep him moving.

Half an hour and three klicks later, he found a circle of dwarf trees. The vibrations in his nape were now axe-strikes chopping into bone and tissue. She was close … too close.

He ran the remaining distance full-out, dove between two of the dwarf trees, hit the ground and rolled up against another of the trees. He dragged himself to the center of the trees' umbrella covering, sat with his legs crossed, and his head bent.

Breathing in deep gasps of Anadi's sweet air, he used his training to slow his heartbeat, and forced himself to stop thinking. He worked to camouflage his thoughts the way his grandfather had taught him, using the mantra of a single word and image: dot.

He repeated the word over and over, never pausing, and never thinking about anything. The universe was empty, devoid of anything, anywhere, accept the solitary white dot floating in a sea of blackness. A small dot which slowly disappeared, leaving behind darkness without substance.

So deep was his self-induced trance, Roke was unaware of the demi-dragon flying above, crisscrossing the forest in search of her mate, her human body kept aloft by iridescent wings, and steered by a tail the length of her body.

DAVID WIND

TWENTY-FIVE

Drawn from his trance by stripes of sunlight squeezing through the trunks of his umbrella of safety, Roke opened his eyes. It took a moment to realize he'd made it through the night without being discovered.

He breathed slowly, his mind steady, while the last tendrils of the unending emptiness of the trance drained away. Two breaths later, he realized he was as refreshed as if he'd slept for a dozen hours.

But his stomach wasn't, and the film covering his chapped lips told him he was not only hungry, but once again becoming dehydrated. He took care of the hunger with bites of the popper haunch he'd taken with him, his thirst somewhat held off, but not appeased with the meat.

Calling the map up from his arm, he studied the area. He was forty klicks from the twin lakes, and fifty from the vale. Somehow, he needed to warn Caruso to stay away. How? He stood, bending over to not scrape his head, and moved to the center of the circle, where he stretched out his stiff muscles. Even bent, his head grazed the branches of the trees.

The signal was scheduled for midnight plus one second. If it made it through, the earliest he could hope for a ship would be later tomorrow. In all probability, it would take another two or three days. But it was crucial to get the information out in case she found him.

GODDESS

Knowing what had to be done, and the cost to him for doing so, he made the decision to go to the ship. But first, he had to take care of himself, or he wouldn't make it.

There were several small tributaries leading off the northern mountains, creeks and streams fed by the river flowing through the center of the mountains. After picking the closest tributary, four klicks away, he crawled out of the tree cluster.

Standing and stretching again, he strode southwest toward the water. It took thirty-eight minutes to get there. The tributary was three feet deep at its center, shallower at the side, and with water bubbling over the rocks and tree roots at the sides. A few fish, most under two inches, swam randomly in little pools between the roots.

He knelt, looked at the various stones, and was relieved to find bluish algae rather than iridescent sparkles coating their surfaces. He drank his fill, letting the cool water reach his organs, and slacken the thirst. He sat for ten minutes to work out his next steps.

The only thing he could think of was getting back to the ship before she found him. There, he would find a way to reach Caruso, or the Guild. He opened the map image, and traced several routes before deciding on a straight line to the ship. The route was mostly through the woods.

Standing, Roke ignored the risk of Haseya finding him. He expected her to be looking further and further out. Of course, he could be wrong, he thought with a shrug.

His angle to get water had taken him further than the forty klicks he'd been at, and he estimated the ship was now forty-five or -

six klicks from the brook. If he maintained a strong and steady pace, he would make it just after midnight.

To get there, he would have to depend even more on his own sense of danger, and whatever connected Haseya and him together. What he had to do was trust his senses, have faith they would alert him when she was near, and leave him free to concentrate on the running.

He accepted the reality she would sense his location the closer he came. After all, they were connected now, as she'd reminded him more than once. "Shit!" he spat and started to run.

—<<>>—

The only thing keeping him going was the suit. Its cooling unit kept his body temperature at a point just below normal, allowing him to run at the steady mile-eating pace. His years of Guild training were bolstered by his formative years of training under the eyes of the Kryon planetary Council, the council responsible for the physical and mental traditions of their tribal heritages. Both trainings worked in sync to keep him moving almost effortlessly.

Roke stopped four times for water, three times for piss breaks, and once to finish the popper haunch. He was close to the ship by late afternoon and picked up his silent mantra of *dot ... dot ... dot.*

Twice, Roke sensed her nearby, and stopped to hide within the cover of bushes, while keeping the mantra rolling through his mind. When the sun finally set, he let go with a sigh of relief, and hoped she was back in the Forerunner installation.

GODDESS

His determination to reach the ship and send out a backup warning com-blast never faltered in the hours he ran. Once he accomplished the task, and if his luck held, he would release a second beacon, a notice of quarantine.

It was a risky but necessary move. Once a quarantine beacon was set off, only top-level Guild scouts of master rank are permitted to land. Roke knew the immense danger of quarantining a planet held a strong possibility he might never get off-planet. Every scout understood and accepted the risk and responsibility they carried when they stepped onto a new planet.

For now, the only way he could leave, would be when he'd proven the cause of the quarantine was overseen, and the threat eliminated. Roke accepted the responsibility for what he was going to do, as well as the knowledge that no matter what he did, it would not be easy—not by a longshot.

He looked up at the dark sky and back at his map. He had two hours left before he reached the ship. "Go," he commanded himself.

Roke took off into the night. The twin moons of Anadi rode above the mountains now, and a quarter of the way into the night sky, their pale light doing its best to aid his passage. His eyes darted left and right, identifying any object directly in his path, or near it. His legs pumped steadily, carrying him to his goal.

Two hours and ten minutes later he stopped to look around. He was at the edge of the forest, kneeling in a grassy field, 300 yards from where his ship sat, dark and silent. He waited for his breathing to settle as a cloud rolled overhead, blocking the twin moons' light. He looked at his chrono. He'd miscalculated and gotten here early.

He had only a few minutes before the ground would be illuminated by the pale blue moonlight. If Haseya or her computers were paying attention to the lenses, which he was very certain of, he needed to get there while the dark showed him as a shadowy shape.

Just as he was ready to go, a new thought froze him to the spot. If he stepped into the ship now, the missing scout signal was programmed to continue on a loop until it was stopped, or he reached the ship, which would automatically shut the message down. When that happened, he'd have to send out a direct com signal—but that created a problem!

The missing scout emergency signal operated on several bands, including sub-space and targeted FTL pulses. He was fairly certain the subspace would not be blocked. Only the regular com channels would be. On the other hand, hyper and Faster Than Light pulse signals were always a toss-up, except for the backup pulse to Guild Prime. Sometimes they worked the way they were supposed to, other times they missed a delivery point, or the pulse bypassed it completely. The pulse to Norton's Landing, and Guild Prime could take a week or longer, which was unacceptable.

Idiot! He shook his head. If he stayed here for the next two hours, there was no way she wouldn't sense him, and he needed to set the signal beacon. A low hum at the nape of his neck was vibrating. She wasn't too close … not yet.

GODDESS

There was one alternative, but it meant he might not be able to send out the quarantine signal. He could override the auto cut-off of the missing scout warning himself, send out a detailed message to stay off-planet, and hope he had time enough for the quarantine. If not—

Squashing the thought, he braced himself, and shot up and off from his squat, running bent-over and at full tilt to the ship. The 200 yards flew beneath his feet, and twenty-two seconds later, he hit the switch and gave Daho the code.

Ten seconds later, he was inside the ship. "Move," he ordered himself. The lights came on and he issued orders to Daho in a rapid-fire staccato. He went to override the computer's automatic shut-down of the lost scout signal and found it had never been sent even though he had not returned in time.

"What happened?"

```
"Your creature, Haseya, stopped it."
```

"How?"

```
"She used your codes."
```

He contained the flash of anger at himself for not expecting this. She had been in his mind; he should have known.

Working fast, he reset the codes. "Send the signal, now."

```
"Affirmative. Haseya is coming. six minutes."
```
Daho added.

"Prepare a second transmission, a warn-off. Send in two hours," he told Dago, at the same time he pushed himself to move faster. He took a step toward the console, stopped, and went to the med cabinet instead. He opened the bottom drawer and took out a packet, which he ripped open, and swallowed a single yellow capsule. Then he went to the main cockpit's console, sat in his seat, and hit a switch with his right hand. The keyboard slid out and a screen projection floated in front of him. Roke typed, ignoring Daho's comments so he could do it faster.

"Daho, finished," he called when he'd added the guts to the warn-off.

"The warn-off is prepared to be sent on all transmittal channels— Roke, she is almost here."

"Good!" Roke's fingers flew over the keys for fifty seconds before he hit the return and pressed a series of buttons on the side of the console. There was a low mechanical whine when an outside panel of the ship opened and released a signal beacon. It moved several yards from the ship, and spun in a circle, burying two feet of its four-foot length into the ground. The three low pops signaling the beacon's anchoring into in the ground was followed by Daho's voice.

"Are you sure?"

"There is no choice, Daho. It must be done. It's not a matter of escaping off planet. I am required to stay to make sure that if the messages do not get out, I can prevent the ones who land from touching a stone."

"Perhaps you should reconsider. You will be trapped here."

"There is no alternative. Regulations state this must be done," he reiterated. "Your databanks hold the information of what happened when this regulation was broken. Look them up. When the Guild

GODDESS

scouts arrive, give them all the recordings since we landed. Show them the images of the creature and the woman; show them how she changes. You do understand, yes?"

"I understand."

"Protect the ship at all costs. Protect the signals, is this clear?"

"It is clear."

"Caruso will come, I know it. He will find me. Make sure he touches no stone or rock with the alien spores on it."

"It is already in your message, but I will repeat it to him."

"Thank you, Daho." He started to stand, then stopped as a new thought struck. "And Daho, you are authorized to use low-frequency radio bands, within the 30-300 Kilohertz range, and within planetary orbit for communication. Send out a low-frequency radio signal the moment you detect a scout or an Explorer Guild ship in approach or orbit."

"You are welcome, Roke. I will communicate if your conditions are met. She is here."

A heartbeat later the hatch opened, and Haseya entered. Her aquamarine eyes locked on his. A smile broke across her lips.

"I was afraid I'd lost you forever." She knelt by him and looked into his eyes. "You can't do this, Roke. You can't hurt me like this. You and I … we are too important. We are crucial to salvaging the universe."

DAVID WIND

TWENTY-SIX

The missing scout message was sent within minutes of Roke's entry into his ship; neither Roke nor Daho knew the message did not go through—a fact of which Daho detected. At six minutes after midnight on Anadi, and mid-morning on Norton's Landing, Daho sent the second transmission.

Although the HF signals were blocked by the Forerunner technology Haseya activated; Daho's A.I. component recoded the subspace transmissions by changing its bandwidth. The problem was the message would take at least a week to reach Norton's Landing. However, buried within the subspace signal, the FTL band went undetected within the subspace transmission and reached the monitoring satellites.

Following normal protocol, when they'd first arrived, Roke and Caruso had dropped monitoring satellites within the same orbit as the moons. At midnight plus seven minutes, the Faster Than Light band buried in the subspace signal was captured by the lower moon's satellite, which routed the FTL transmission to the proper hyper point junction. The FTL message reached Norton's Landing one hour and eleven minutes later, the signal going to the Guild headquarters and Caruso's ship.

Unknown to Daho, the Forerunner communications block stopped the return signal. Because there was no return signal within its given parameters, Daho followed the protocol Roke set. At 3:00 a.m. Anadi time, Daho set off the quarantine beacon.

GODDESS

<<>>

Ninety minutes after responding to the Roke's signal, Caruso's computer informed him his message to Anadi had not been delivered. He turned to his new apprentice, Thea Laanestret, a Keplerian of direct ancestry to the original settlers of Kepler-186. "I told you there was a problem. Damn them!" he snapped, slamming his fist against the console.

He stared at the screen, and at Norton's Landing below. "Adrianne, get me Conrad Tyler. Accept no excuse, use an emergency priority." Adrianne was a Tri-D vid star he fell in love with as a twelve-year-old, and therefore the name of his ship.

It took a full minute to get through. When the commlink connected at ten-oh-five in the morning, on Norton's Landing, Administrator Tyler's angry and stiff face glared at him. "What is the emergency now? I'm in the middle of a conference."

"Did you not see the emergency transmission from Anadi two hours ago? I fucking told you what was happening. I could have been halfway there by now,"

"Slow down, Leon. Let me check." He looked at his com, then shook his head, his face pale. "Damn, that idiot shift commander didn't call me. Give me an hour," Tyler added before the screen went blank.

Still waiting an hour and a quarter later for Tyler's response, Caruso received the second signal. His normally tanned skin turned a deep burgundy as his fear and his anger grew proportionately to each other.

"That stupid—Adrianne," he snapped, "Get Tyler back."

"This is bad. Scav?" Thea asked, one long finger tracing a thin curving scar from her left ear to the corner of her lips. Caruso knew the former marine acquired it in a Scav fight, on a quarantined planet, not six weeks before her acceptance to the Guild's Scout Academy.

Caruso nodded, it was as bad as it could get, and she as an ex-marine would know just how bad that was. "If it were the Scav, he would have put it in the beacon. No, this is something else. Bad ... very bad. Stenner wouldn't have released a beacon of this magnitude for anything less than an overwhelming danger to human space—alien, bacterial, or viral."

Before she could respond, Tyler's face filled the screen. The earlier stiffness gone, worry lines creased his brows and radiated from his eyes. "The Day Watch Officer is a newbie. Sorry. Get what and who you need. Proceed to ET-87310.2."

"You saw the quarantine?"

Tyler's eyes widened. "Crispin's balls. I ... Tell me."

"Roke released a quarantine beacon. He found something, and it is dangerous. I'm on my way," he added, and cut the com link before Tyler could respond.

Knowing the admin would order him back, he turned to his apprentice. "Strap in, we're going hyper in 6-5-4 ..." he told his apprentice. "Adrianne, set course for Anadi. Jump as soon as it's set. Prep hyperspace communications. I have messages to send."

```
"Deputy Administrator Tyler is calling."
```

GODDESS

"Ignore. Jump!" He had no choice. Stenner had added one seemingly meaningless word to the quarantine warning: a phrase only he would understand: danihizází.

The jump from normal space into hyperspace was as smooth as possible, which wasn't very. Once settled, and their course finalized, he sent out four messages to four scouts before turning back to his apprentice.

Watching her, he formulated what he would say. Tall and lanky, she looked thin, but wasn't. As a bonus, she was deceptively strong, and powerfully muscled. She'd applied to the Scout Guild, but the Guild had a four-year backup, so she'd volunteered for a three-year hitch in the Marines while waiting for her acceptance into the Guild.

Her years as a marine had sharpened her, and he knew this particular apprentice would be a keeper; she would make a good scout. He understood well why she hadn't had the long, curved facial scar removed. To her, like so many scouts and marines, a scar was a badge of honor. If and when she got to retire, she could always have it removed ... if moved to. He would bet a half-year's pay she wouldn't.

One by one, as they sped through the emptiness of hyperspace, the messages came in. Rendezvous would be in twenty-six hours, give or take two hours. Caruso looked over the instruments, and turned to his apprentice, thinking about the last word in Roke's message, danihizází. "What do you know about Forerunners?"

<<>>

Roke had come to terms with what was inescapably becoming his fate. The instant Haseya entered his ship, their connection had solidified, and his need and desire for her, which he now recognized as a compulsion, had grown even stronger.

When they'd returned to the installation, and to the room they shared, she had almost attacked him in her need, pushing against him, caressing him, and bringing out every bit of desire. They had joined together in a frenzy of passion, he riding her, and then she riding him, their cries and moans bouncing off the walls. When it ended, he lay still, working to control his breathing and his emotions.

He was physically exhausted and mentally drained. His body was bruised and sore after the ordeal in the Anadi forests. Every muscle ached, the wounds from the wolf were still red and swollen, and his chapped lips hurt even more after the just-ended sexual escapade.

He had no idea how it had been possible to have an erection, or move his pain-stiffened muscles, but he had; doing so scared him more than anything else. Whatever happened when he'd touched the seedpod, had made changes that somehow gave her certain biological controls over him.

He bit down on his lower lip. Why hadn't he realized this before?

"Promise me you won't do this again, Roke."

He turned to her, to those large green-blue perfectly human eyes, and knew they were anything but. "Why would you believe me?"

GODDESS

"Because you are bonded to me. If you leave, we both suffer."

"Like an addict withdrawing from his drug?"

Her brow wrinkled. "I don't understand."

He closed his eyes in an effort to block out hers, which reflected the innocence of her response. Apparently, Forerunners did not have drugs. "Drugs are substances a person can use to enhance their mind or body; these drugs take them away from who they are, and make them feel better. They are addictive substances a user cannot stop using without having physical pain and mental … emotional suffering for a period after stopping," he explained with as simplistic terms as possible.

"No, my Roke, it is not what happens. You and I … any pair who has shared DNA will never be able to stop wanting the other. I told you we are bonded, bound together, this is not something which can be undone. You will always need me, as I do you, now, after we have children, and until we die."

My Roke … A cold chill spread slowly through the conduits of his mind, spreading to his face and shoulders, before racing to every other part of his body. He did not doubt her words. He only wondered what would happen once he was off this planet and away from her. He needed the Guild; he needed them to be here, to stop her, to end his enslavement, and to either destroy the entire planet, or put a permanent nuclear quarantine net around it. One way or another, it had to end.

A moment later, her hand slid between his thighs, and moved slowly until her warm hand cupped his testicles. He groaned. The sound contained anything but pleasure.

TWENTY-SEVEN

Leaning away from the screen, Thea swiveled toward Caruso. "This is beautiful, but strange."

"What?" Caruso asked without looking at his apprentice while he synchronized the orbit of the Adrianne to match the Daho's landing spot.

"Near his ship. There are two lakes, one high, one low, both have an unusual iridescent aura. The upper lake feeds the lower by waterfall."

He leaned toward her screen and stared at it. "That is strange. I don't remember seeing it. Send a signal to Stenner's ship."

Thea flipped a switch. Sixty seconds later, she shook her head. "Nothing. The signal isn't going through, even in atmosphere. Odd."

Caruso didn't say a word, rather, he stared at the control panel. If dynamic broadcast signals were being blocked, as well as HF channeled hyperspace coms, his former apprentice would have found another way. It wasn't in Stenner to not fight—only death would stop him.

"Scan for any signal emissions. Take your time. Run every frequency band." He didn't add there would be no way in hell Roke would activate a quarantine without a back door for Guild Scouts.

A single eyebrow rose at his command. "All frequencies?"

Caruso didn't speak. He just stared at her.

"Yes, sir." Her tone was no longer questioning.

GODDESS

He took a breath, reminded himself she'd just graduated to apprentice, and she was no longer a junior-grade marine officer. "Think back to war-com class at the Academy. It took us a half-decade to discover how the Scav communicated over interstellar distances, because they used Light Band Frequency, and pushed the LBF through hyper hops. Once we learned how they communicated, the code breakers picked apart their communications, and we stopped their advance. We also learned several ways around blocked communications by using FTL."

He looked back at his screen, which now showed the ship on the ground below the lakes. "What were you doing here?" he asked, rhetorically.

"Sending out LF frequency on the 278 MHz band. I just ran an RF spectrum and found a signal coming from the scout ship."

Without waiting, Caruso flipped a switch and matched frequency with the signal. It was Roke, and as Adrianne printed the message across his readout, each word struck struck Caruso like a solid charge projectile to the guts.

"Fuck me," he whispered, then turned to Thea, who was staring at the same message on her screen. "As we discussed after takeoff."

"This isn't possible," she said. When her words reached Caruso's ears, they sounded like something being pried from an old rusty box top. Her voice leveled when she continued. "Forerunners vanished what, at least 100,000 years ago? It was long before man even walked upright on Old Earth."

"That's the theory ... so far." He turned from her to look at his screen again. "Adrianne, communicate with the ship's computer. Find out what the hell is going on down there."

```
"On it, boss!"
```

For the next 207 seconds, Adrianne and Daho swapped spit, in human terms, or interfaced in computer lingo.

```
"Private or speakers?"
```

"Speakers," Caruso said.

```
"Converting the Daho's signal to audible.
Monitor viewscreens."
```

While the two Guild scouts, master, and apprentice, listened to the computer voice of Stenner's ship, they watched the first video, showing Haseya, in her dragon-child form, bringing the unconscious scout to the ship.

They watched on in stunned silence when the creature landed on the ground, detached what was left of Roke's helmet, and pressed the two-button sequence to open his EXO suit. The moment the suit shrank into itself, Roke's body began to shake.

Caruso and Thea followed the being as it lay next to him, wrapped its wings around him, and held him while his body shook. Whiles the creature held him, its shape transformed from the scaled dragon-like creature to a silver-haired, beautiful human girl of six or seven.

When Roke stopped shaking, the child's wings retracted into its body. She rose, went to the hatch, and pressed the small, almost invisible panel next to the hatch.

GODDESS

They saw her tap in a code with one finger, and heard Daho respond with, `You are not authorized.`

The child's next move took them by surprise. The girl turned to the emergency box on the other side of the hatch, opened it, pressed the single button, and said, "Íidoolíił."

When the hatch slid into the body, the seven-year-old returned to Roke and did the impossible. She lifted a man weighing five times her weight off the ground and brought him into the ship. She carried him to his bunk as if she had been there before, then wiped away the blood on his face. In the next half-minute, her body reformed into the iridescent dragon-like being.

When it knelt on the floor next to the bunk, and outlined his chin with a single long talon, Thea's gasp was an explosion in the cockpit. "I ... I don't believe this," she whispered after seeing the creature slowly slide its hand down the length of his side, over his hip, and along the outside of his thigh.

Then the creature stared into the vid lens across from the bunk, turned back to the scout, and leaned over him. They could not see whatever it did next, but when it finished, it stood and went to the hatch. The dragon-like creature stepped out of the hatch, and the computer switched to the outside camera. Caruso and Thea watched it stride calmly across the grass, spread its wings, and rise into the air.

"Hold," Caruso ordered. They sat in the silence, neither willing to put to voice what they'd just seen. Then, after a long pause, and carefully picking his words, Caruso looked at Thea. "Just to confirm, did you see a small dragon turn into a little girl ... and back again?"

She ran her tongue across dry lips. "It looked similar to the ancient artwork in the Guild museums—Old Earth art. But Caruso, what she did ... what it did with Stenner ... the way it touched him before it left. I swear it was ... caressing him."

"Yeah, I didn't miss that either." He sighed loudly and shook his head. "We're in this shit now. Adrianne," he called, "Get to the rest in order of importance."

"There are three more vids, the first shows her a day later, and she has grown. The second shows her seven days ago, in the lakes we are in sync orbit above. The creature is now human, according to Stenner's computer. The third vid was taken by the ship using bots to search for Stenner, following scout protocol for an out-of-communication scout. The images show the woman, although human in form, with scaled wings and tail, and flying in a search pattern. Do you want to view?"

"Is there more?"

"His last transmission is a manually encoded text."

"Did you convert it?"

"Yes, I just finished using Scout Stenner's files of Navajo code-talk."

"What the hell is that?" Thea asked.

GODDESS

"Later," Caruso said. "Skip the last vid for now. Put the message on the screen."

By the time he'd finished reading the message, he knew what had happened, and what his former apprentice wrote for him to do.

"You can't," Thea whispered.

"There isn't a lot of leeway here. He understands, otherwise he wouldn't have left the message. He knows the odds of him leaving Anadi are ... I won't even say slim; they're less. Do you want to stay up here? Protocol says yes."

She smiled, although her steel grey eyes did not. "I may be an apprentice scout, but I'm a by-God-God-Damned-Marine as well. I don't wait behind, and we don't leave anyone behind."

"Suit up. Gloves and helmet. Projectile and stunner. We touch no stones or rocks. The helmet and gloves stay on unless we are in a ship and—" He paused as another thought rose. He nodded to himself. "Sealing spray and an S-three-six-zero. Understood?"

Her eyes widened slowly, comprehension dawning. "Precautionary ... Understood!"

"Good. Move your ass." Caruso glanced at the screen when she left the cockpit. "Adrianne, tell Daho we are on our way. He is to allow us entry—use Guild Authorization code seven-nine-zero-A and prep the sled. Remain in stable orbit above the Daho."

`"Be careful,"` Adrianne responded.

TWENTY-EIGHT

Haseya sat up and turned to him. She was naked, as was her habit when they were together. "There is a ship in orbit."

He sat up quickly, moving to cover the wave of relief washed through him, and fortifying the wall around his mind: dot—dot—dot. "What craft type?"

"Small. Similar to yours."

His eyes widened in feigned surprise. "A scout ship?"

She nodded. "How are they here? Communication is blocked."

"The ship would have signaled me missing. But if coms are blocked, I have no answer." He shrugged. "Perhaps something has happened, something we are unaware of?"

She studied him for a full quarter minute before turning and standing. "I will see about this." She put on the robe-like garment she always wore now, and striding forward, slipped it on.

Moving fast, he rolled out of bed, grabbed his pants from the floor and followed her. He paused only long enough to get his pants on. He caught up with her at the computer section and went to the large screen with her.

He stood next to her and saw the Adrianne centered on the screen. "How did you know it was here?"

She pointed to her left ear, where a barely visible tiny bud perhaps a few centimeters in diameter lay in the canal, and was surprised he hadn't noticed it before. She pointed at the screen. "Look," she said, as the sled separated from the ship, and began its

GODDESS

descent. "I know the one with the green helmet, he was with you the first time. Who is the other?"

Of course she did; she knew everything in his mind ... almost. "Most likely his new apprentice. I do not know who."

"Does this mean the colonists will follow?"

Seizing on her question, he nodded. "I can't be sure, but it's possible."

She glanced at him, her mouth curving into a cupid's bow of a smile. "This is good. They must find their seedpods."

"They will have to go to the river."

Haseya shook her head. "No, here." She shifted to face the computer next to her, put her palm on its surface, and closed her eyes. A moment later she opened her eyes. "It is done."

Alarmed, he stepped closer to her. "What is done?"

"I've added the rest of the seedpods into the lakes. I have not released them into the underground channel. The two who have arrived will awaken two more seeds. This is as it should be. Soon there will be many children." She accented her words by rubbing one hand in circles over her abdomen.

Roke prayed to whatever gods were listening that she wasn't already pregnant. Dealing with her was hard enough, having a baby dragon to deal with was nothing to look forward to. And if she wasn't pregnant, he promised she would never become so. If she was, he would have to ...

He cut the thought off before it became too solid, and concentrated on the screen, watching the scout sled touch down by his ship. He instinctively moved closer to her before she could turn to look at the screen, pulled her to him, and pressed against her.

Knowing how volatile her reactions were to sex, she couldn't help herself. The instant his hands touched her breasts, a low hum sounded from deep in her throat. When he caressed her, his fingers slipping over her stiff nipples, the hum turned to a low rumbling groan, and she pressed against him. The heat radiating from her was so intense he started to draw back. He stopped. Why so hot? Was she ovulating?

"Roke, not now," she whispered. Instead of releasing her, he covered her mouth with his, and drew her even tighter, playing on her weakness, using her own genetic programming to interfere with her mission logic.

Shuddering, she turned, a moan drifting from deep in her throat as she gave into his urging. She gripped the muscles of his back, her tail extended, and wrapped around both of them.

For Roke, the relief of her tail holding them together was a weight lifted. If she was ovulating, she wouldn't get pregnant now, the yellow pill he'd taken shipboard would see to that. He drew his lips from hers, lowered his mouth to her neck, and kissed the pulsing artery in her neck while he snuck a glance at the monitor, and watched the two scouts enter his ship.

"Let's go back," he whispered in her ear, training his tongue down until his slipped her nipple between his teeth.

"No." Her voice was husky with need, her hands pulling at his pants. "Here, now!"

GODDESS

<<>>

Before Caruso's fingers reached the outer switch, the neo-titanium veneer of the hatch slid hissing into its pocket, letting Caruso and Thea in. The second hiss signaling the hatch closing happened the instant Thea's foot cleared the entry.

"What's happening, Daho?"

"Welcome, Master Scout Caruso and Apprentice. Roke Stenner is captive to a female alien who says she is fully human being. Scout Stenner believes she is from a race known as the Forerunners."

Caruso's brows rose. "Forerunner? Really … Where is he?"

"Somewhere inside a massive cavern constructed in the mountain, which they entered through the channeled water of the upper lake. He is a prisoner. He is being used to impregnate the alien."

An unbidden jerky laugh got away before Thea could hold it back. "This has to be some mad Tri-D vid Stenner thought up. This can't be real," she said to Caruso. "It's insane. Computer, this planet was uninhabited by intelligent life. Where did this alien come from? How do you know it is a Forerunner?"

It took a moment for the computer to respond. "My name is Daho. Please have the courtesy to address me properly and introduce yourself to gain informational clearance."

Her eyebrows snapped up like the two sides of a drawbridge. She turned to Caruso. "Are you fucking kidding me?"

Caruso shrugged his shoulders. "Roke has aah … his own way with things. If you make it through the next five years, Thea, you will have your own as well. Humor him … and Daho."

She snorted, shook her head, and said, "Thea Laanestret, serial number G-A-S-387942."

"Welcome, Apprentice Laanestret. No one is fucking kidding you. Roke Stenner fell from the side of a foothill into the river at zero degrees prime meridian. He used the talons on his glove to secure himself to a rock in the river. The glove held, but the force of the current put enough pressure on him to separate his hand from the glove. The glove remained on the rock while the current dragged Scout Stenner under.

"When he sought to return to the surface, his hand brushed across a stone, which he'd used in his effort to steady himself. The stone was coated with an iridescent substance; the stone was a seedpod, as he now references them. The alien who captured him came from the seedpod. To better understand, call the seedpod an egg.

"This seedpod changed soon after it was touched. Within a day, it had grown into the size of a rock, but with the same shape. The next day it was gone, and the alien was here."

"And I suppose you don't have visuals?"

GODDESS

"I always follow first-in protocol. The drones send back all findings and images and I record and file and—."

"Stop!" Caruso half-shouted the order. "Daho, play everything you have other than what we have already seen ... please."

The main screen went bright as the first recording began. An hour and a half later, Caruso looked at his apprentice. "This is not good."

Thea, her features showing exactly how stunned she was, said, "Not good? Leon, finding this planet was a catastrophe if this is true."

Caruso's eyebrows rose. "Only if the alien gets out."

"Master scout?"

"Yes, Daho?"

"It will not become catastrophic if the alien does not procreate, does not leave the planet, and no one else makes landfall."

He shook his head once. "No, it will; the Guilds are greedy. They'll want whatever Forerunner tech they can find. Something will happen and—"

"—They will get out, Murphy's law. *Anything that can go wrong, will go wrong,*" Thea quoted verbatim. "Chaos Theory fits as well."

"Nothing fits this situation, because this has never happened before, or not in the last few hundred-thousand or so years."

"I have calculated the probabilities."

"Which probabilities?"

"That you and the apprentice will touch either a seedpod; or the Guild will come, and many of those who come with it will touch seedpods. Haseya will spread the stones everywhere there is water; and the resulting children will spread the seedpods everywhere in the universe, everywhere there is humanity."

"What are the probabilities?"

"The present probability of Roke Stenner having a child with the alien is zero. The probability for yourself, Master Scout, if you do not leave now, is one hundred percent; and the probability for Apprentice Laanestret is one hundred percent. For those who may follow, the probability is also one hundred percent."

GODDESS

TWENTY-NINE

Caruso was stunned. Thea stared at the blank console screen, her jaw dropping with Daho's words. "How can you know this?"

"There are several formulas leading to my conclusion." In emphasis to Daho's next words, the screen lit up with a graphic to aid by visualizing its explanation. "To begin with, when a human touches the seedpod, there is a DNA exchange. This decides the sex of the being who will emerge from the seed. At the same time, the DNA, the iridescent particles coating the stones are absorbed into the human's skin, altering the human's DNA, while simultaneously bonding the human to the emerging being. The DNA creates both a bond and a compulsion in both, this bond and compulsion will last for life."

Caruso stared at the images of the DNA strands. "What sort of compulsion?"

"Its most driving force is sexual desire, created by a genetically predominant need to reproduce; and, over time, generates an overwhelming need to be with the other, regardless of anyone or anything."

Caruso stared at the screen, his mind working to find a solution. "This is all controlled by this new DNA?"

"Yes."

"What happens when the pair is separated?"

"When Scout Stenner escaped, and spent two days free, Haseya, the Forerunner, spent every daylight hour searching for him, returning to the cavern to sleep for a few hours before searching again. They are bonded. They do not know exactly where each other is when separated, but they know the general vicinity the other is in. Once close enough, they will know each other's exact location. From my observations, if Roke leaves the planet, she will do whatever she can to continue her search for him. Scout Stenner's compulsion will never completely end."

"Unbelievable!" Thea spat. "How will she get off-planet if it is quarantined?"

"Scout Stenner noted she, Haseya is her name, has all the memories, not just racial, but the actual memories of her ancestors. What she doesn't know, she can find in the computer banks in the Forerunner installation. She will build a ship. She will leave Anadi. She will find him."

"What if we kill her?"

"Apprentice Laanestret, such an act would be counter to common sense. How would the scientists be able to understand this being if Haseya is dead? It would do Scout Stenner no good because her death cannot revert his changed DNA. As noted previously, his compulsion for her will never end. It makes no difference if she is dead or alive."

GODDESS

"But—"

"—Enough!" Caruso cut her off. "We accomplish nothing by talking in circles. We don't know what will happen; all we know is Roke Stenner is a scout. He is strong physically and mentally. As a part of the Kryon-Three nation, he was trained to ignore pain and mental suffering since early childhood. He is the one who made the decision to set the planetary quarantine in spite of whatever DNA changes have occurred. If he goes off-planet, it will be because he knows he can survive whatever happened to him here."

"If what the computer concluded is correct, he will be impaired."

Caruso turned to her, his eyes flashing angrily, and with his words spat out in staccato rifts. "You have been an apprentice for almost two months. You may have been a marine, but you have no understanding yet of what a fully trained Guild scout is capable of doing. Tell me what you can't do in five years ... if you survive!"

Thea closed her eyes against the chilling blast before slowly nodding. "Yes, sir."

"Daho," he snapped. "Tell me how to get to Roke."

<<>>

"They are in your ship," Haseya informed Roke. "What will they do?"

Roke, sitting cross-legged in the center of the room, and as naked as she, shrugged. "It is hard to know. Caruso is a master scout who has survived twenty-plus years as a first-in scout. Whatever he does, it will be careful and thorough."

"You will protect me?"

"Why would I do that? You have made me a prisoner."

"Only to protect you. You are too important to take any chances. You will protect me. This, I know."

He was about to say something, when he went deeper into his own mind and thought about his conversation with Daho. "Yes," he finally said, smiling at her while he continued to consider his options.

Knowing his compulsions were triggered by certain aspects of his DNA, he had to find a way around those. When he'd had asked Daho to analyze the DNA changes before Haseya had taken him, Daho, had spent hours going through his DNA changes and delivered the results. Because Daho was a computer, the emotional aspects of its words to Roke were non-existent.

The computer explained how his altered DNA now identically matched several strands of her DNA. He ventured protecting her was as important an aspect of the alteration, as was the urge to procreate, and would be triggered when her life was endangered. To Roke, it was an untested theory.

"We must have him touch a seed."

"He will not; neither will his apprentice."

"He will," Haseya stated, matter-of-factly.

Standing, Roke drew on his pants. He walked to her and turned her to face him. "He is important to me. I do not want him harmed. Allow him to leave. Others will be here."

"How can you be so certain?"

GODDESS

"Because he will send his report, and the scientists will come to find us, to analyze you primarily, and then me. They will examine everything from the way trees grow on Anadi, to how the iridescence clings to the stones and rocks. They will find the stones, and because they will do this, they will release more Forerunners. That is your goal, yes?"

She raised her right hand, stroked his cheek, and with a smile said, "Yes."

"Then allow me to speak with him, to tell him to leave."

Nodding, she dropped her hand. "But the female must stay."

His frustration built, igniting a low flame of anger. "They both go."

She stepped back, her expression startled. "We need her."

"There will be others."

Her face changed, her aquamarine eyes darkened, and her mouth formed a straight and narrow line; her lips paled. "Either she stays, or they both stay. They are necessary."

She stiffened. Suddenly, her eyes widening, and turned to point at the screen. "It doesn't matter, now. They are here."

Shit! Too soon, was his first thought "What are you going to do?" he asked, studying the images on the screen, and saw his last spare helmet hanging on Caruso's suit.

"They will be fine."

She bent her head and closed her eyes. He watched the screen, waiting for whatever Haseya was planning. Within the time it took Caruso and the apprentice to cross the first chamber, the watery entrance flooded with the dog-like animals charging directly at the pair.

"No!" Roke said and took a step toward her.

Two seconds later, the dogs stopped charging, only to circle the pair. Caruso held his projectile pistol in his right hand and his scout knife in his left. The apprentice had both projectile and stunner out.

"They will kill the animals. Do not do this."

"I am doing nothing. The … what did you call them, dogs? The dogs are there to contain. Wait here. I will bring them."

His anger surged, forming a hot, fiery ball he barely contained within him. He wanted to grab her, stop her, but something him held him back. "Yes," he said, forcing himself to speak softly, "I'll wait."

The instant she left the chamber, he pulled on his shirt, and chased after her, the inner force trying but unable to stop him. He wasn't following her; rather, he went back to the living section, having seen exactly where she stored his EXO suit.

The helmet Caruso carried was the only way out. From hiding beneath the umbrella trees, he knew it would block her mental ability to locate his exact position. That was his only chance. She would know approximately where he was, but that was all.

He went into the storage room, and pulled out the suit, only to discover his weapons were gone. *It doesn't matter*, he told himself. But before he left the room, he looked for his weapons.

Out of the corner of his eye, he spotted the tip of his bone-handle knife. He grabbed it from the shelf, but the other weapons weren't there. He spent another quarter-minute looking as he pulled on the EXO suit and sealed it.

He did not find the larger scout knife nor the other two weapons, but could wait no longer. He had to get to them. He ran out of the Forerunner sector, through the connecting caverns, and upward along the wide coiling steps leading up to the main cavern.

Stopping just before the opening to the final cavern, he hugged the wall, and readied himself for what had to come next.

<<>>

Following Daho's instructions, and after watching the vid of Roke walking through the water, Caruso and Thea left for the lakes. They skirted the lake until they were next to the entrance. Caruso was the first to step through the watery opening and into the large first cavern. Before they were halfway though, there was a rush of sound.

Caruso watched the cavern flood with the dog-like creatures he'd seen on Daho's screen. The moment he'd turned, Thea backstepped until her back pressed to his. Both held their weapons at the ready.

Thea raised her pistol toward a menacing animal. "Don't shoot. Not yet," Caruso ordered, seeing the dogs were not coming closer.

"What in all the hells do they want?"

"I'm sure we'll know soon enough," Caruso said dryly.

His words proved prophetic when, thirty long, animal-staring seconds later, Haseya stepped into the cavern. "Back," she commanded in English.

The animals backed up a half-dozen paces while she walked toward the two. Caruso turned to Haseya, and was startled by her nakedness. "Stop. I don't want to hurt you."

"You will not." She halted ten feet before them.

Caruso raised his knife, the blade in his right hand angled down and out in preparation for an attack. The barrel of Thea's weapon tracked toward Haseya.

Before either of them could react, Haseya's tail emerged and struck whip-like, hitting their hands, and knocking the weapons free before either could dodge.

"Do not move," she ordered. The dogs circled tighter around them, their mouths open, slow, menacing growls emerging from their throats.

"Remove your other weapons and place them on the ground ... now!"

When Thea looked at him, Caruso nodded. They took out their weapons and placed them on the ground. "Now your helmets and clothing."

"No," Caruso replied, his eyes holding hers.

Haseya's lids closed for a bare two seconds. When she opened them, four dogs slinked forward, their growls growing louder. "Do not make them harm you. Remove your clothing."

"How do you speak our language so well?" Caruso stalled as he reached for the release buttons.

"From Roke's mind. Your mate will learn from yours."

"My what?" he asked as if he were unaware.

GODDESS

"You will understand soon."

Thea moved then, stepping forward, she spun and launched a kick at Haseya. Her well-muscled leg struck the back of Haseya's knee. Instead of her knee folding, and her body hitting the ground, the only effect from the kick was for Haseya to turn and strike out with the back of her hand. The power behind her muscles knocked the apprentice a half-dozen feet back.

Thea hit the floor and skidded another foot. The moment she stopped, two of the dogs stood over her, their triple rows of teeth close to her neck.

"Take off your helmet and clothing," she repeated, her voice was soft, yet the scouts were more than aware of the steel within her voice.

Holding her eyes, Caruso silently removed his helmet and reached for the release of the EXO suit. Before he could open it, there was a flash of steel behind Haseya as Roke stepped through the watery entrance..

THIRTY

Turning, Haseya saw Roke, with a knife in his hand. Her eyes widened. He took a single step and stopped dead in his tracks, his knife still at the ready, but unable to attack her.

It wasn't that he didn't want to attack her; rather, it was whatever had been changed within him. His legs refused to let him finish his charge, or use his ancestor's knife to end her.

Nor could she strike him.

The moment she turned to Roke, Caruso launched himself at Haseya's back, his body arcing off the floor and toward her, his hands reaching for her neck. Somehow she sensed him, and before he could complete his attack, her wings burst from her back.

Instead of his fingers going around her neck, he struck the iridescent scales. His hands were deflected, and his airborne body slammed against the iridescent scales of her wings. He struck, bounced off, and fell to the floor.

Thea flipped herself to her feet and, running towards them, scooped up the projectile weapons. With her next step, she raised the pistol-shaped weapon and squeezed the trigger. At the same instant, Roke, who had been watching everything through a slow-motion lens, reacted.

He bent and jumped forward, his shoulder plowed into Haseya's abdomen, knocking her out of the path of the projectile. The long, thin, needle-tipped round hit Roke's shoulder, carving a groove

GODDESS

through the EXO suit, skin, and muscle, before striking the wall behind him.

Roke didn't feel the hit, yet. He turned to face the apprentice, his stance wide-legged, his bone-handle blade ready to strike. The dog animals surrounding them growling angrily, eyes locked solidly on Thea.

At the same time, Caruso scrambled to his feet and grabbed Thea, compressing her arms to her sides before she could do anything else. "Stop!" he ordered.

Thea sagged in his arms. He put his lips close to her ear. "We bide our time," he whispered just as Haseya rose and went to Roke.

Roke held out his arm, his palm toward Haseya. She stopped, looked from him to where Caruso held Thea. Before anyone could move, Haseya's tail whipped out again and caught the weapon still in Thea's hand. She yanked it roughly from her fingers.

She took the weapon, gripped it properly, and pointed it at the two. She closed her eyes for a flash of a moment. When she opened them, two dogs went to their other weapons and stood over them. "My Roke cannot harm me. You can. Go over there." She pointed to the opening Roke had come in through.

"Lead them down," she told Roke.

Roke looked at Caruso, giving him a barely perceptible nod, turned, and started back. The master scout and his new apprentice followed. Once on the steps, Roke spoke in a low voice, "You listened to Daho?"

"Yes."

"Good. She will not harm you. She needs you here to bring out two more Forerunners."

"We won't."

"If you touch a stone you'll have no choice. But to do this, she has to bring you to the lakes outside. We will work this out. Say nothing about the quarantine to her."

At the bottom of the curving steps, Roke led them into another cavern. Once through it, he stopped at the entry to the Forerunner installation.

"Come," Haseya said, catching up to them, and taking the lead. She brought them to the living section, down the pale grey hallway, and past where Roke and she slept, to another set of rooms. She opened the door and turned to Caruso. "You sleep here."

"You." She then pointed to Thea. "Sleep there." She pointed to a door across from them. "Go inside and take off your clothing. Wear what you find there, or wear nothing. Do this now and bring me your suits."

Thea looked at Caruso. Caruso looked at Roke, who nodded once. The two Guild scouts went into their rooms. They came out a few minutes later, dressed in the simple coveralls they'd found, and handed Haseya their EXO suits. "Go back to your rooms."

Once they were inside, Haseya locked each door with a button set flush to the doorframe. Alone in the hallway, Haseya looked at Roke's shoulder. Although the suit's nanobots had repaired the suit, the wound beneath bled.

GODDESS

"Let me fix you. I can feel the pain." Her voice was tight and low. "Here," she finished, her hand pressing her own shoulder at the exact same spot as Roke's wound. "Come."

She led him into another room and pressed a wall switch. The wall split in two, revealing a wide cabinet within. Roke took off the EXO suit, exposing his blood-drenched shoulder and left side of his chest. The projectile had sliced across the skin on the meaty curve of his shoulder, and cut through two small veins when it opened a quarter-inch channel through his skin and muscle.

Haseya poured an amber liquid into the parted skin. Whatever it was frothed in a swirl of orange bubbles before evaporating. When the foaming disappeared, the wound was clean, and the bleeding stopped, she applied a white gel, which dissolved the pain instantly, and the area around the wound went numb.

He looked at his shoulder and saw the skin was already closing. "What is this?"

"Medicine."

"It's still good after all this time?"

Haseya smiled briefly as she stared at his rapidly healing wound. "Time did not exist in here. Everything below the upper cavern was sealed in stasis." She paused to wave her arms in an all-encompassing gesture. "When I came here after you gave me life, I …" She paused, her eyes went blank for a moment, the green-blue irises tracked up and left, as if searching for an elusive word or thought. "I … rebooted the facility. Everything is the same as the day it was put into stasis."

"How could you know about it? You were not born yet."

She stroked his cheek, her fingers trailing delicately along his jawline. "Did you forget? All stones are imprinted with instructions and our memories."

He closed his eyes and took several slow deep breaths. He knew it quite well; he just didn't want to accept the truth of the matter. And that truth was in a question: *How*, he asked himself, *can we possibly fight a race who had not only discovered a way to recreate themselves, but a race who left genetic instructions on what to do, and how to do it?* His question was not only rhetoric, but pointless; no matter the answer, it was done.

"Are they a family?" she asked.

He understood what she was asking, and shook his head. "No, why?"

"When we spoke ... a few days ago, you told me families would come, and they do not believe in procreation—in sex outside their family. Yes?"

"Yes," he said, wondering where this sudden sidetrack was leading. "And you spoke about a god, yes? This god told them to do this?"

"Yes, they believe their god told them so."

"Tell me more."

He studied her for a moment, trying to understand why she'd brought it up. "Many religious people—you understand religious?"

"I do. But only in your way of thinking of it."

GODDESS

"They believe there is a single god, and this god created rules by which to live. One of the rules is it is wrong to have sex outside the marriage … the bonding."

"This makes no sense. Do you know what this god looks like? Is it like a …" She paused, closed her eyes a moment, then nodded to herself. When she opened her eyes, she asked, "Does it look like a Scav?"

The word made him stiffen. He forced himself top ease off. "No, what is believed, is their deity made them in his image, and afterward, created the rules for them to live by."

Her features remained puzzled. "So their god looks like you?"

"Yes and no. No one knows what God looks like. But they believe he must look human if he created humans in his image."

She stared at him for a long quarter minute. A puzzled expression crossed her features. "No, this is wrong. We created the human life found on all habitable planets."

Roke raised his hands, palms up, and shrugged. "They believe humans—people—were created in God's image. Perhaps your species, whom we call Forerunners, are the gods seen through racial memories, because when you seed a habitable planet, the resulting life is what you created. So perhaps they are right."

Haseya laughed, then wagged two fingers in front of him. An instant later, she brought out her wings and tail. "Do I look like you now?"

Roke exhaled slowly. "No."

"Do you still not understand? We did not create you in our image. Your earliest ancestors created us through procreation, and we grew into your image, not the other way around. Before you point out the obvious, the answer is yes, humans as you aware now were millennia from evolving into intelligent, rational beings before my ancestors died out. Their ... our technology, our computers, and our scientists discovered the potential intelligence of your race might rise to be among the highest we ... they had ever found, closer to ours than any other race."

She paused to look deeper into his eyes. "They set out seedpods and left a small colony, as they did on every planet, to guide the process along."

"Guided to make certain Cro-Magnon discovered the seedpods, yes?"

"For that I have no memory, nor is there anything in the record banks. But I will assume it was so. Once we conceive, and the extra strands of DNA are gone from our bodies, or, when a male rises from a seedpod and makes a female pregnant, the remaining DNA becomes the race of the planet, and we leave the future to evolution."

"Why?" he asked, his mind repeating *dot ... dot ... dot*.

Again, the look of puzzlement crossed her face. "It always has been and is our infinite duty to see humanity survive in this universe."

"You mean to create human life?"

She laughed again, and took his hand into both of hers. "No. Roke. Not create, to continue to ensure humanity survives."

GODDESS

This was getting into areas where he could not afford to go, not with his recent revelation. And his special sense of warning that had been keeping him alive, was telling him to be careful. Something wasn't right, and he needed to find out, but not now.

Yet, he could not help but to stare at her for far too many seconds before he could speak. "We've lost track of our conversation. Haseya, what will you do with them?"

"Let them be alone for now. Tomorrow, during the day, I will have them swim in the lake. Then they will pick up stones, so the DNA transfers are done. Afterward, they will do what we do," she smiled with her last words. "Make children."

He saw her eyes change, saw the heat, and desire appear, and stepped back. "I need to talk to them and explain what is going to happen before more time passes."

"Will they accept this, or will I have to force them?"

"If you force them, they will fight you to the death. If they are away more than seven days, or if they die, signals will be sent throughout the galaxy. No one will be allowed to come here until a full Guild investigation is done."

She tilted her head and said, "I do not see the problem. The more humans who arrive, the more stones will be activated by their touch."

"No, they will not land. They will send bots and drones and robot search mechs. The bots and robots will be armed. Nothing human will touch the ground until they know exactly what happened here." He paused, took a deep breath, and willed his face to hold steady as he spun out the next lie. "I will talk with them, and make them understand how important what you are offering them is for our future."

"Offering?"

He smiled. "If it is an offer rather than an order, they will consider it in a different light."

Her eyes widened with comprehension. "Yes, I understand this logic. Go, do this."

He was a little surprised to find her sudden desire for sex had abated with his words, which gave him pause. He wondered if this were so she could listen in, and see exactly what they were saying and doing, or there was yet another reason.

He would find out eventually, but for now, he had a plan … he hoped.

GODDESS

THIRTY-ONE

Roke spent the next hour with Thea and Caruso. He showed them how to operate the different buttons and switches in their rooms, and after, he brought them to what he called the food dispensary.

"Dispensary?" Thea asked, looking at the eight shiny metal cabinets along the wall.

"This … facility is self-contained. The synth food is produced by computerized machinery and perfectly suited for the human diet. There are proteins, carbs, and fats in the precise proportions needed to keep us healthy and alive. I believe there's a sexual stimulant compounded into the food. My body has been reacting differently since being here."

He pointed to one of the tables. "Sit."

When they did, he pressed the table directly in front of him, and three panes opened, allowing the food to rise. "All the food here looks and tastes the same." He pointed to bowls. Caruso shrugged, picked up the single utensil, and scooped out a slice. Thea watched him until he swallowed.

"It's fine," Caruso told her.

Roke remained silent while they ate. He used a spoon with his right hand, and rested his left on the table, his fingers moving casually on the table. The movements of his fingers, while seemingly random, were anything but; in reality, he was tapping out words in Guild code. The single, double, and triple taps, similar yet vastly different from the ancient Morse code of centuries before, was succinct and direct in warnings and instructions.

When he finished, he put down his spoon, and leaned back. "Get as much sleep as you can. Tomorrow, Haseya will take us all to the lakes for you to swim. Don't try to run because she will be watching closely."

"There, you will swim, find one of the iridescent rectangular stones, pick it up, and bring it to the edge of the lake. That's it. Once this is done, we return to the installation below, and wait."

"We wait … for?" Caruso asked, already knowing the answer.

Roke stared at him. "Your mate."

"And if I choose not to ah … mate?"

Roke's lips twisted in a lopsided smile. "You won't be able to."

"I will," Thea challenged, staring at Roke.

"No, apprentice, you won't. No matter how you try, you will not, but you can try."

"We'll see," she said, her eyes locked on his.

"Time to get some sleep, shall we?" They stood, and Roke guided them back to their rooms, and went to his.

Entering his room, he found Haseya already there. "They are ready for tomorrow."

"Yes, I know." She confirmed his own thoughts that she would be listening in, somehow.

"They did not sound as though they will do what is asked of them. Will they?"

GODDESS

"We'll know tomorrow, won't we? I'm tired," he said, not wanting to prolong the conversation.

"Then we should sleep."

Nodding, he got undressed and sat on the side of the bed. Moments later, Haseya sat next to him. Her hand went to his back and gently rubbed his skin. "Does your shoulder bother you?"

"No," he said with a shake of his head.

"Good," she whispered and leaned her head on his unwounded shoulder, her hand no longer rubbing gently, rather, she caressed his back and kissed his shoulder, her other hand now stroking his chest, her fingers grazing his muscles before moving slowly downward.

"Haseya …"

"Yes," she whispered, pushing him backward on the bed, she covered his mouth with hers, and shifted smoothly to straddle him.

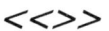

<<>>

"What the hell," Thea snapped once inside Caruso's room.

"Hush," he said, his voice low. He grabbed her right wrist, and began to tap her skin. "You weren't paying attention," he whispered. As he tapped the skin on the inside of her wrist, he said aloud, "We have no choice. If we don't do what Roke said, we're at even greater risk."

While he spoke, the message he was actually imparting was simple. *We have taken our precautions. Even so, regardless of what happens, we cannot allow any birth. She is not human, no matter what she says, no matter how convincing she is, there is more at play here than we know. Roke has a plan. Be patient.*

"I won't mate with one of them." Her low spoken words were aimed more to herself than to him.

Just be ready, he added in the silent Guild code before he replied to her terse statement with, "We have no idea what or how this works, not yet. Roke said our bodies will react differently if we interact with the seedpod. Didn't he tell us we would not be able to control our sexual urges?"

She looked thoughtful, but still shook her head.

Caruso smiled, inwardly. She had a lot to learn about the life of a scout. In his message, Roke told him he would distract Haseya when they were in the lake. When he did, they were to swim to the waterfall, go over, and into the lower lake. It was a long drop, but the lower lake was deep. From there, they had to get their sled, and fly to the ship. They were not to touch any stones.

Doing his best to ignore his self-loathing and anger, Caruso exhaled harshly, knowing he would have to leave Roke behind as his former apprentice already told him. The problem was, he knew it was the only way—until he could figure out something better.

<<>>

Waking suddenly, Roke grabbed the back of his neck. Since the day he first orbited Anadi, his sense of danger had grown more sensitive. Now, it was screaming at him with a warning oscillating from the base of his neck, throughout his entire body, and he needed to know why.

But no matter how hard he tried, he couldn't concentrate. *This psi shit sucks!* he decided. He looked over his shoulder at the other side of the bed. It was empty; with a sigh of relief, he got out of bed, pulled on his pants, and left in search of Haseya, and the reason his neck was hammering out warnings. If she was up to something, if she was the reason his ever-growing psionic sense was blasting his nerves with lightning bolts, he needed to find out why.

She was in the vat room, standing before the middle vats, studying the readout on the front of one of the huge metal tanks. While he walked toward her, he looked over the seedpod assembly line. Just before he reached her, she made an adjustment, hit a button, and then a second. There was a metallic groan from the first tank. Before it stopped, the noise rose from the tank next to it. The sound of rushing water filled the room.

"What are you doing?"

She turned; a smile tweaking the corners of her mouth. "Adding stones. The colonists and builders will be here soon."

"We don't know that."

"Why would the two have come if this was not correct?"

She had no idea, and he wasn't going to enlighten her yet. He went with the flow, smiling inwardly at her mistake. "Yes, you're right. But there are more than enough stones already. And so many more have grown larger." He looked from her to the high rock ceiling above, pushing only a single thought through his mind before saying it aloud, "You'll have to unblock communications so they can send out the all-clear signal."

"Yes, it is the reason I am releasing the stones. I reprogrammed them to achieve a higher data survival rate."

The vibrations in his neck spiked madly, pounding into his head until he deciphered what his senses were telling him. He took in a long deep and calming breath before saying, "Data survival rate? I don't understand. What have you done to the stones?"

She smiled. "I've brought their knowledge up to date." But would say no more. "It's time to go to the lake. The sun is up, and the water is warm."

<<>>

The four emerged from the mountain forty minutes later. Haseya led them to the side of the lake and pointed down to the growing cluster of stones at the bottom of the upper lake. "When you enter the lake, dive beneath the water, it is not deep, and rub your hand across a stone. Once you touch it, there is no need to pick it up."

Both scouts leaned over the water to look down at the sparkling rocks. Somehow, the sun's reach extended beyond the lake's mirror-like surface to caress the stones beneath, setting them aglow.

Caruso glanced at Thea, then at Roke. He gave an imperceptible nod, and dove into the water.

"Damnit!" Thea mumbled and followed the master scout.

The moment Thea dove, Roke walked behind Haseya and pressed himself to her. "I missed you this morning." He wound his arms around her, settling his hands at the spot just beneath her breasts, his thumbs rising to rub against the underside curve of her breast. He sensed her reaction, which he knew would happen, as it did to him when she played the aggressor.

GODDESS

She covered his hands and drew them up onto her breasts and pressed tightly. Her nipples were already stiff and pointing. She pushed her buttocks against him, moving her hips slowly and seductively, her heat flowing through the thin material of their clothing.

"Roke," she whispered, arching her neck back when his lips traced the skin of her neck. "Roke, you have to stop," she whispered, her buttocks grinding against him when he hardened.

"Wait," she whispered, her voice clogged with desire. She stepped forward and looked down to watch the master scout and his apprentice dive to the bottom and each graze their hands across the stones.

When they rose to the surface, Caruso looked at Haseya. "We have done what you asked. Can we stay out here for a while?"

She knelt at the side of the lake to stare at him. "Why?"

"To breath fresh air. To feel the sun."

While she studied Caruso silently, a hot poker slammed into the back of Roke's neck. This time, the sensation was acute and painful. Why was this happening? he asked himself, doing his best to acclimate the ever-changing nature of his growing psionic senses. This time, the sensation was harsher, more violent. Did it mean the danger was escalating? If so, what was it warning him about now?

She spoke softly to the master scout, but the tone of her voice was as hard as titanium. "Do not try to get to your ship. You will fail."

Caruso met the challenge in her eyes. "Understood."

While he listened to Haseya and Caruso, he dug hard trying to find what the warning could mean. When Caruso swam back toward his apprentice, the warning sharpened, painfully. He could not mistake what he felt. Both of them were in danger.

Oddly in the midst of this, a new realization formed in his mind about the psionic bursts in his neck, and now his head as well. It hadn't been reaching Anadi that amplified what had been a minor annoyance, no, the changes, and the increase to his inner senses had begun after falling into the river, after his hand scraped across the seedpod, and he'd unwittingly initiated the DNA transfer.

That was it! The increase of his psychic senses coincided with the alteration to his DNA. A chill spread through his stomach. What else had changed? And how deep had her psychic probing of his mind gone? Could she actually read his mind? Yes—of that he had no doubt, but he was certain there was something else. An empath? If she was an empath, she could also read the emotions and extrapolate…

Stop, he ordered himself as his last thought triggered yet another spike in his head. What was behind her warning to Caruso?

"Come," Haseya whispered, turning to face Roke after Caruso swam away.

The look of hunger was in her eyes again, reminding him of what he'd started three minutes before. "Why did you say that?"

She frowned. "Say what?"

"Warn Caruso not to try to escape."

She cocked her head to the side and studied him. "Because he will not survive if he does."

GODDESS

Roke looked from her to where Caruso and Thea swam. "Why?"

"Why does it matter?"

"He is important to me."

She raised her hand, stroked his cheek, her eyes searched his face slowly. "Am I important to you?"

"Very important."

"Then tell them not to do anything foolish."

"You think they will try to run?"

She stared at him. "You did."

He drew his eyes from her face to look at Caruso and Thea swimming. The vibrations turned painful. He winced, nodded, and went to the edge of the lake. "Leon."

When the scout turned, he motioned him back, nodding slightly to reinforce his hand signal. Caruso tapped Thea's shoulder, and signaled her to the shore. They came out of the water together and walked to Roke. "What?" he asked, looking from Roke to Haseya.

"You two should come inside."

Caruso raised a single eyebrow. "Now?"

"Now."

THIRTY-TWO

"Do you feel anything?" he asked in a voice so low it barely reached the others while he searched their faces. He had been in this area many times, and knew there were no lenses, which is why there were here. Certainly not for the food.

Caruso and Thea were seated across from him in the food section, each had a cup of a warm broth-type substance. They looked at each other and then at Roke. "Nothing."

He took Caruso's hand and tuned it palm-up. There were no remnants of iridescence on his palm. He did the same with Thea. "We have some time. She's working on the vats. You used the sealant?"

"Contraceptive too. Why did you stop us?"

He met Caruso's eyes. "She was prepared. The dogs would have stopped you—possibly maimed you so you can't leave. She has strong psi abilities." He shook his head. "When she realizes the stones aren't turning, she'll know you did something."

"She'll retaliate?"

"Probably, but she won't harm you. She needs you and Thea." He looked around, his voice going lower. "She's planning to use every person connected with the colonization. If they land and touch a stone, she'll succeed."

"Does she really think she can breed her race back into existence?"

Roke studied the apprentice. She had a pleasant enough face; the battle scar didn't change that. It was her marine cockiness at issue.

GODDESS

"It's much more than what you think. Do you believe in God, or gods, apprentice?"

She blinked. "That has nothing to do with anything."

Roke smiled. Religion, ever since the rebellion of 2214, was a taboo subject. Every person, and every race, kept their beliefs private when off-world. "It has everything to do with our situation."

Thea arched her neck, her eyes going wide. "How?"

"Do you understand who and what the Forerunners were … are?"

"The accepted theory is the Forerunners were a race of humanoids who travelled freely in space, and the race who came before us."

"No, Thea. They are the race who seeded the galaxies. They are the race who Haseya says created us … or our version of humanity. When a child is born to a Forerunner mother or sired by a Forerunner father, the child is a hybrid human who carries all the genetic memory of the Forerunner race. They also carry the memories of their science and their mistakes. When they realized they, as a race, were dying out, Forerunners created a way to reprogram their seedpods to embed instructions into the minds of the child who … hatched, I guess is the best word, from the seedpod. These instructions detailed what must be done to recreate their race.

"I was told most of this by Haseya. It was easy to work out the rest. Haseya made improvements … upgrades to the memory component of the seed to correct two massive errors."

He pause for a breath, and to read the two scouts faces. Both stared at him as if he were insane, yet, behind the initial doubt, he saw a light of belief in belief Caruso's eyes.

Then Thea spoke, "I don't understand. What has this to do with religion?"

"Patience." Roke looked at Caruso, then back at her. "Of all the galaxies and planets in our universe, only on Earth did our particular line of humanity evolve the way we did. On all the other planets, humanity as we know it, either did not evolve, or did not survive.

"On Old Earth, seedpods were placed by the Forerunners, and our cave-dwelling ancestors found them. I'm not sure why, but something in our ancestors' genes did not fully accept the DNA transfer, and they did not become versions of Forerunners; rather, it took thousands of years of evolution for us to gain the level of intellect we have.

"In the centuries since, we've reached the stars, we've discovered enough evidence of Forerunner remains, on too many planets in the various galaxies, to doubt their existence. We've found remains of lifeforms on many planets, not just the planets supporting biologically human life, but others, right?"

When the two nodded, he went on. "We've explored hundreds of planets in three galaxies, and found, of the species on all the planets that supported human life, only two reached deep space capability; another discovered and created basic intra-system travel; and yet another was a species which had devolved from a technical society into a primitive one.

"Several others are or were at the stage Old Earth was during the second millennium." He looked from Thea to Caruso. "Every one of these life forms, these humanoid species, were created from Forerunner seedpods. I'm sure there will be more discoveries."

He stopped for another breath, and shook his head. "I know when we reach other galaxies, we will find more humanoid type life. But the most important thing you need to know is the Scav were created by the Forerunners—"

"—Woah," Caruso spat. "Wh—"

Roke held up a palm. "Wait. Haseya told me they made a grave mistake when they mated with the Scav. They believed them human, but evolved differently than they had expected. I think this happened on many worlds including ours. But we also should consider how, as humanity evolved, somehow our own genetics continued to evolve side-by-side with the Forerunner genetics, and during our evolution, we did not become fully assimilated into their race. But our racial and genetic memories did blend with theirs, and in the minds of our earliest intelligent ancestors, they saw the Forerunners as gods who created us in 'their image', and saw as well, angels with wings."

"But that is ... crazy."

"No, the crazy part is how the Forerunners made more than a few massive mistakes. Their single biggest miscalculation was in how they literally bred themselves out of existence, by sending all their embryos to other worlds, and depleted themselves of their offspring.

They compounded this error by continuing to do so until it was too late to reverse."

He paused to read their faces. Caruso was still with him, and Thea was beginning to accept his ideas as well. "Mounting a last-ditch effort to save themselves, they seeded this planet, because it was and is the absolutely perfect Petrie dish to create human life, and to recreate their race."

"But they aren't gods," Thea whispered.

He searched her face. "What is a god? A creator, yes? What is a Goddess? A creator as well. Their egos—as they spread their own race through the universe and discovered races whom they considered to be budding humanity—spoke more to who or what they believed themselves to be, which were the saviors of what they consider humanity."

He shook his head once in emphasis. "If Haseya is successful, they will become the gods of the universe again; because, as I said, she upgraded the seedpods … modified a component of their DNA coding to better integrate with our DNA—to control us. She did this because we're an evolved intelligence based on the original seeding of Old Earth; I don't think she understands our … Old Earth's human evolution. There are no Forerunner records newer than 100,000 years, so how could any Forerunner know what our branch of humanity has become?"

Caruso's stoic face grew a smile. "An ego can bring even a goddess down."

"Yes, Leon, it can, and our will to survive is our weapon."

GODDESS

"But that still doesn't give us a way out." Thea's eyes flicked from Roke to the master scout.

"It does," Roke stated.

"Stenner—"

"No choice, Leon," he said with a lopsided smile, his eyes tracking to the apprentice. "Ego," he reiterated, "And sex, will get you out. Haseya's ego, and the Forerunner's dominant procreation gene. Have you been on Xenor?" he asked Thea.

She nodded, her eyes questioning. "During the last incursion."

"Did you see the herds of solax?" With her second nod, he went on. "Then you understand why they keep the male and female separate?"

"I was told it was because if they didn't the animals will overpopulate and destroy the environment."

"Yes, but why?"

She shrugged. "A need to copulate?"

"Indirectly, but it is a deeper dive: the need to procreate, and that particular need is the chink, the weak point in the Forerunner's armor. Above all, they are driven with an unending demand from their subconscious to procreate, to bring forth a new civilization, and one with them sitting on the top, guiding their offspring to retake and control the universe."

The apprentice's expression sped from bewilderment, through a series of endless possibilities, until finally she understood. "You are going to—"

"Yeah," he said dryly. "It's her only weakness: it's the only way." Ten minutes after explaining his plans, going over the escape route step-by-step, and getting their agreement to follow his instructions to the letter, he returned to his room. Just before he left them, he settled his hand on Caruso's shoulder, as he made clear how timing was the most essential aspect of the plan. One misstep and it would be over.

What he hadn't told them, because he wasn't absolutely positive, was of his doubt the human species, which evolved on Earth, had ever been fully integrated by the Forerunners' gene manipulation. His sense of danger, which was growing into much more since the DNA exchange, told him he was right. He was as close to certain as possible, that Haseya's explanation of the Forerunners being responsible for changing Earth's evolution was not a lie, but the twisting of fact. Finding out why, his now-throbbing head and neck told him, was important ... no, more than simply important, it was critical.

<<>>

Dinner time found Caruso, Thea, Roke, and Haseya with plates of synthetic protein before them. Thea was the first to take a bite of the food. When she swallowed, she put her fork down and turned to Haseya.

"What will happen now that we've touched the stones?"

Haseya stared at her for several drawn out seconds, a frown breaking the smoothness of her forehead with a crease. "They are assimilating your DNA. Sometime within the next few hours, the pods

GODDESS

will grow, and at the same time, your body will accept and adapt to the seed DNA."

"Will I feel anything?" the apprentice asked, her face showing a tinge of fear.

Haseya reached across and covered Thea's hand. "No. If you have any psionic ability, it may or may not become enhanced, nothing else."

"What happens when the seed grows?"

"Your seed will become a male, and he will make you pregnant. It will be extremely pleasant, I promise." A smile spread on her face; she turned to Roke. "Is it not?"

Roke looked directly into her eyes. "Very."

"How long does the process take?" Caruso asked.

"Four days, perhaps a little longer."

Thea snorted. "And then we become what … breeders? Do you keep us in pens too? Bring us out when its time?"

"Thea," Roke snapped. "That's uncalled for."

"Is it? Do you like being a … a …"

Roke shook his head. "You'll understand in a few days."

"I won't understand shit!" she spat and stood. "I'm going back to my … quarters."

When she strode from the room, Caruso stood and turned to Haseya.

Roke grasped his arm. "Will she be okay?" he asked, while his fingers tapped Caruso's forearm.

He nodded to Roke and looked at Haseya. "Apologies, she is young. I will calm her."

When he went after Thea, Haseya turned to Roke. "They will get used to everything," she said confidently. "As soon as their mates can join them. Do you have a need to talk with them?"

Roke shook his head. "Maybe later." He reached out and stroked her face. "They need time. Remember how it was for me."

She covered his hand, pressing it tightly to her cheek. She leaned forward and kissed him, slowly, tenderly at first. Just as the kiss deepened, she drew back to look at him.

He was prepared for her, with his block up and set. Ever since discovering the increasing of his psionic ability, he worked on maintaining the block against her, and found it easier to maintain his mantra without having to concentrate on it.

With his embrace of his ability, a wave of realization filled his mind. The DNA changes had not been only for the Forerunners' benefit; rather, the unexpected adaptation had enabled his psi abilities to expand. The mind protection he'd so hesitantly built had grown stronger, and without his recognizing it, the walls protecting his mind were already in place—Moreso, he told himself, with the intuitive knowledge his mind block was now a firm and constant part of him. Then he wondered if anything else had changed.

The heat from her skin increased on his hand. "Let's go to our room," he whispered.

GODDESS

THIRTY-THREE

When the door closed behind them, Thea turned to Caruso, about to speak; he shook his head and motioned to the bathroom. Before she could turn, he grabbed her shoulder, and his finger tapped out Guild code.

Nodding, she marched to the small room where she hoped there were no lenses or listening devices. She looked everywhere, but found nothing to indicate there were. Perhaps the Forerunners liked privacy when at their bodily functions. With the thought a low chuckle escaped her lips.

Caruso followed her in, and when the door closed, let out a whoosh of held breath. Thea spoke first, her voice a bare whisper. "Are we really going to get out and leave him?"

Caruso's eyes locked on hers. "Do we have a choice?"

"We do. We can stop her. There are three of us, one of her."

"Except in the cavern, when he got here, we've have no knowledge of her physical or mental capabilities—but we know she is stronger than any of us. We can't take the risk of a fight. Our objective—our only objective—is to warn the Guild. The quarantine signal will not stop them from searching for the source of the quarantine if there is no one to tell them to stay off. They'll come military-style with bots first, followed by a full master scout team.

"Thea, if we don't get off Anadi, the threat to every colonized planet grows exponentially."

She shook her head, but did not take her eyes from his. "It's wrong."

"It's necessary."

"Fuck that," Thea spat, her voice raised. She held up her hand. "Sorry," she whispered. "Did Stenner tell you where our suits and weapons are?"

"He did ... Thea, understand, one misstep and it's over. You need to think of Roke. You heard what he said. This woman has created ... no, she has chained him to her. If he leaves the planet, what happens to him?"

"That's his choice for him to make, not ours. But if we escape, and he stays, she'll retaliate. She'll hurt him, possibly kill him."

Caruso shook his head. "She can't, no more than he can hurt her. You saw what happened when he tried to attack her. He stopped dead in his tracks. It will be the same for her. The Forerunner-encoded DNA will prevent either from hurting the other ... but not us—we did not absorb any DNA off the stones. We are dispensable. She can kill us, or imprison us here, because she knows more will come unless the warning is strong enough to keep them away."

Thea sighed. "After three years in the Marines, I learned one thing; dangle food in front of a hungry animal and it will do whatever it can to get to it. When the Guilds learn what's on Anadi, nothing will keep them away. They will land ... no, they will swarm the planet like a plague of Centurion ants, and they will touch the stones and the rocks in their effort to get Forerunner tech. And they will—"

GODDESS

He gripped her shoulders. "Now you're beginning to think like a scout, not a marine. One more thing: Roke told me he doubts what Haseya told him about Earth evolution. He said Haseya may be trying to create a new race of Forerunner, one that will control everyone and everything. He thinks the Scav are a part of the plan."

He paused and squeezed her shoulders gently "So, Thea, what do we need to do?"

"Get off-planet," she whispered.

Caruso smiled. "Good. Let's get ready for his signal. Then, Apprentice Laanestret, you will have the opportunity to know exactly what scouts do in situations like this."

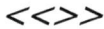

<<>>

Without being able to tell time, Roke relied on the only thing he could, his own intuitive sense of time, which was usually reliable. *It had better be now*, he told himself as he and Haseya walked toward their room. He walked on the left, Haseya on the right, and just as they reached the room, Roke tripped, then stumbled-stepped to his left, where he slammed his shoulder hard against the opposite wall.

"Damn," he whispered when Haseya grabbed his arm to steady him.

"Are you—"

"—I'm good," he said quickly, looking back at the floor as if he'd tripped over something. "Just a misstep." But she didn't take her hand from his arm for the rest of the way.

At the door, he pushed the switch, and the door whooshed upon. When it closed behind them, he set his internal clock and turned to her, his eyes traveling from her feet to her head. A slow smile spread across his lips. "It's been a long day. Come, let's clean off together."

Her green-blue eyes tracked across his face as a matching smile spread across her face. "Yes, let us." She dropped her clothing to the floor and stepped back to wait for him. He took his off, purposefully moving slower than usual and, from the corner of his eyes, he watched as she followed his every movement.

Was this what the rest of his life was going to look like? *No*, he promised himself, *this won't happen.*

When he was as naked as she, she took his hand, and led them into what he called the shower room. Not more than eight feet square, and ten feet high, the center of the ceiling had a swirling pattern of hundreds of waterjets in a circle five feet in diameter, and motion activated.

When Haseya went to the center the water rained down, Roth joined her beneath the warm water. But when she reached for him, he stepped back. "Wait," he whispered. He pressed his hand to the wall, and a shelf rolled out, a teardrop-shaped bottle filled with a cloudy liquid was the sole occupant. He poured some of the liquid into his hands, knelt, and began to wash her.

Moving smoothly, he started at her left foot, slowly messaging it beneath the rising foam. Then he went upward, his hands and fingers pressing gently along her calf. He stayed there, kneading the flesh and muscle for a moment before edging closer to her knee. When his

GODDESS

fingers roamed across the skin at the back of her knee, they skimmed sensually across the skin.

Carefully, slowly, and maddeningly, he rose higher, his fingers never still, never rushing, and always moving in small smooth circles. He trailed over her knee to her thigh. Her muscles spasmed with the touch of his fingertip. A low moan resonated deep in her throat while her leg trembled in his grip. He kept his pace maddeningly slow, stroking, kneading, and moving upward along the pliant skin of her thigh.

Forcing his mind to concentrate on her skin and nothing else, he reached the top of her thigh, stopped, and leaned forward to press his lips on the taught skin of her lower belly before reversing the direction of his mouth and hands to go teasingly back down the same leg.

He drew his fingers along her inner thigh, the tips gliding ever-so-lightly continued downward until he reached her ankle. The moment his fingers touched her ankles he drew them away. An instant later, he moved to her other leg.

Once again, and moving slowly upward, he pressed harder and then softer as he crisscrossed her skin with swirls of caresses. When he reached her upper thigh, she cried out. Her knees almost buckled, but she grasped his shoulders to steady herself. A second later another low moan bubbled from between her lips to dance in the raining shower.

She lifted her hands from his shoulders to cup his cheeks before moving to each side of his head. He traced his fingers across her moist vagina drawing out another low moan, the quivering sound matching her trembling body. Then her fingers wound through his hair, and she tried to pull him up.

"Not yet," he said, his voice low and firm. He stared up at her, his hands slipping to the back of her thighs, before rising to cup, and then to grasp the cheeks of her buttocks. He pulled her tighter to him, his lips pressed once again on the tender skin of her lower abdomen while he kneaded her pliant skin and muscles. She tried to pull him up once again; he stopped her.

"Wait," he whispered, looking up into the wild-eyed desperation of unfeigned sexual need blistering through her eyes—eyes that did not see him but only what she needed from him. Her breasts heaved with her forced breathing, her mouth opening and closing soundlessly.

He had never seen her this sexually driven before. It was as though her entire being was focused on him and what had to happen this moment. And as her sexual craving blazed through her eyes, a chill sliced into him, tunneling deep into his mind, and showing him what the future would bring.

Staring up at her, his hands still cupping her rear, he caught an almost imperceptible change to her pupils. A flash of iridescent sparkle shimmered around her head for a nanosecond before it vanished, making him doubt he saw anything other than light reflected from falling droplets of water.

He shook away the thought of what he knew it was. *Don't think! Keep her busy.*

GODDESS

She released his hair, but did not take her hands from his head, her fingers silently urging him to stand. He did so, as he rose ever-so-slowly, his mouth never leaving her skin as he trailed higher, his lips encroaching the landscape of her skin like a commando as he moved upward from the patch of silvery down and over her belly, his tongue flicking along her skin while his hands massaged her back in ever-increasing circles. Beneath his fingers her body vibrated madly, her hips moving and bucking against him, while moans pushed their way into the waterfall of the shower, until he was suddenly pulled to his feet, her tail locking them together.

In that instant, he knew she was beyond self-control. The problem was, so was he. Then, as his lips reached her breasts, she grabbed his hair and pulled his head back.

She stared down at him, the black pupils within blue-green irises were no longer round, but the oval of her animal DNA. Her chest rose and fell in powerful heaving gasps. "I … I can't stand!"

<<>>

Moving silently through the hallway, two full minutes after hearing the thump on the wall, and confident Roke was keeping her away from any security, Caruso led his apprentice around three turns and to the storage area Roke had described, right down to the glyph embossed on the door.

He pressed the indentation on the wall. The door slid back revealing a room of shelves lined walls. To his left were their EXO suits, but no weapons other than their long-bladed scout knives.

"Damn, Roke was afraid of this. Look around, see if you can find any weapons. Be quick."

While Caruso pulled off the Forerunner clothing, and dressed in his EXO suit, not taking the time to put on the under suit, Thea ransacked the shelves, uncaring of the noise or mess she made on the floor.

"Here," the master scout called, and when she looked at him, he tossed her suit to her. She let it fall to the floor when she spotted a box on a shelf across from her. She pulled it down and opened it. Inside lay four weapons, not hers, and not Caruso's. "Stenner's weapons."

Putting the box on the floor, and picking up her EXO suit, she dressed as fast as she could while Caruso took out the weapons to check them. He tossed her the projectile gun, and kept the stunner for himself. He put the two knives into a pouch on his side.

"Helmets?" he asked, looking everywhere.

She shook her head. "Not here."

"Let's move. Any of the ... dogs, take them out."

"What about her?"

"She is not to be harmed, no matter what."

Thea's eyebrows rose. "Okay, boss, I'm ready, let's get the fuck out of here." Then she paused. "What if she comes after us?"

Caruso closed his eyes for a moment. "Yeah, about that ..."

She looked at him, and waited until he spoke. When he finished, she said nothing; rather, she gave him a quick and curt nod. Then she smiled.

GODDESS

<<>>

"I ... I can't stand," she cried and, dislodging his hands, she pushed him backwards, her face flickering between an iridescent shimmer and pale skin.

Roke was caught within a fog of near uncontrollable desire. He tried to tell himself it was the changes in his body, but knew it wasn't, it was her and her mind taking control, separating his mind from his ability to think. He did his best to focus but failed. Then he realized she was using her own abilities to increase his desire—she had been ever since she'd pulled him from the water.

His body was overloaded with the physical need for her, and there was no chance of prolonging this; he only hoped the others were on their way out. She loosened her tail from around them and pushed him to the floor, and all while the iridescent scales flashed on and off her face as the maddening compulsion deepened. When she knelt next to him, her mouth seeking his, and her tongue pushing its way into his mouth, he accepted everything.

She pulled back suddenly. "Off!" she shouted. The water stopped instantly. She pressed down on his shoulders, pushing him flat onto his back, and rose above him. She held still for a moment, her entire body trembling, her face shifting back and forth between skin and scales.

Before she could lower herself and take him inside, the sound of footsteps clicked behind her. She tried to turn, but was too late. Something grabbed her long, silvery hair, and with a single swift jerk, yanked her back and off Roke.

THIRTY-FOUR

Haseya's body flew across the small space and slammed into the wall. She struck face-first, and slid to the floor, a scream of rage tearing from her throat. She staggered to her feet and spun to face the intruders.

When she turned, her entire body shimmered. Before Thea could react, Haseya's long, powerful, and iridescent wings burst from her back, her face and head no longer flashing back and forth; rather, it glittered with the iridescent blue-green scales that had replaced the skin on her face. Her hands were sharp, taloned claws.

Roke took a step toward her. Caruso reacted instantly by grabbing Roke's upper arm, pushing the barrel of the stun gun into his belly, and firing. Roke crumpled to the floor; Caruso turned to face the demi-dragon, moving at his apprentice.

Haseya's tail whipped out and lashed across Thea's body, sending her spinning backwards, and forcing Caruso to sidestep so he wasn't hit by the backlash.

Catching and rebalancing himself, he spun toward Haseya, as the Forerunner launched herself at him. Before she reached him, he fired the stunner and stepped aside. Her body froze, her muscles unable to stop from hitting the far wall.

Paralyzed by the stunner, she ricocheted from the wall to the floor, where she lay staring up at the ceiling. The only thing moving on her body were were her eyes. "You are done," Caruso told her. "No one else will ever land here."

GODDESS

When he saw a taloned finger move, he increased the stunner's charge, and shot her again.

Turning on his heels, he squatted next to Roke, and motioned Thea to him. "No one is leaving you behind." He handed Thea the stunner, pulled Roke up and across his shoulders, and stood. "Go!" he commanded his apprentice while resetting Roke on his shoulders.

<<>>

They made it out of the cavern, and to the bottom lake thirty minutes later, where the dog-like animals greeted them. This time they were more a horde than a pack. Hundreds of sharp-toothed, long-fanged animals surrounded them, their growls reverberating like unending layers of rolling thunder.

They backed up against the rocky, mountain slope, where Thea helped Caruso set Roke on the ground before turning to point both stunner, and projectile weapon at the dogs. The dogs held still. "How the hell could she have sent them?" Thea asked.

Caruso stared at her. "Roke said she had psi abilities. The stunner can't stop her thoughts. Watch them," he ordered before kneeling next to his former apprentice, whose color was returning to his face. He slapped Roke twice. "Wake-up time."

Roke's eyes rolled, he shook his head as feeling flooded his body, bringing burning tingling explosions as his nerves came back to life.

He'd been conscious through every minute and every step, cursing Caruso for doing this when he could have held her back without being stunned. "Whhuuie?" He he pushed the word out with his tongue as he tried to moisten the stunner-induced dryness around his mouth. He shook his head and tried again. "Why?"

"We both know you wouldn't have been able to stop her. Can you move? Can you think? It was a light charge."

Roke nodded. "Having trouble focusing."

"Thea, suit."

Thea reached behind her and pulled his EXO suit from her pack. She held it out for him while Caruso helped the scout to his feet.

"I'm good," Roke said, taking the suit from her and stepping into it. Thirty seconds later, he pressed the collar button to seal the suit.

Caruso pulled out Roke's knives and handed them to him. "We've got another fifteen minutes if we're lucky before the stun wears off her, but I don't know her body ... So, let's move, yeah?" Caruso asked, staring directly into Roke's eye "You can do this, right?"

Nodding, Roke held a knife in each hand. "Where are the helmets?"

"We couldn't find them," Thea said.

"Shit! That's what blocks her from finding us—I think. My ship is a klick from here. We need to get within a few hundred yards for its defenses to pick us up. Daho will respond with the ship's weapons."

One of the dogs crept closer. Thea shot it in the head. The other dogs closed the semi-circle surrounding the three, their growls loudening with the death of one, but they did not move toward the three.

Roke looked at his chrono. "You're right, Leon, the stun won't last much longer. Her body is different, stronger than ours, and her physiology different and powerful in other ways. We need to get the hell out of here, now!"

Caruso looked from him to Thea and nodded. "On my count we move. Kill anything in our path. Understood?"

Thea nodded, but when Caruso met Roke's eyes, the first-in scout shook his head. "Kill anything except her. If you go after her, I … I won't be able to let you."

"Why do you think we stunned you?," Caruso said, sharing a quick look with his apprentice. "Let's hope we make it to the ship first, yeah?"

"Yeah," Roke agreed. "Thea, how many rounds in the gun?"

She did a quick check. "Thirty-one. It should be enough."

Roke glanced at her. "Don't waste any. "

She looked at him, her head cocked to the side, and her eyelids half down. "I don't miss."

Roke smiled. He liked her response. "Good."

"Enough chit-chat, children. Form up! Triple backs."

Caruso took the lead. Roke and Thea went back-to-back and perpendicular to Caruso's back, giving them a three-sixty-degree field. "Now," Caruso whispered, his voice so low only the two behind him heard it.

Moving forward, Caruso took half-steps while the two sidestepped behind him, all looking to fall into a smooth rhythm. The dogs charged. Caruso fired the stunner, sweeping it across a group of charging animals. A dozen hit the ground to lay motionless. They made it another fifteen steps before the dogs reformed. One group shifted behind them, not to fill in the circle, but to move forward against them.

"Hold," Roke called. "Thea, watch the ones on your side. Caruso, watch front and sides." Three dogs charged forward; Roke went into a half-squat. When the first of the dogs leapt at him, its mouth open, and the rows of razor-sharp teeth seeking his jugular, Roke raised his left forearm, hit the dog on its shoulder, and struck with the bone handle knife.

The blade sliced across the dog's belly; its intestines exploded outward. As it fell, the second dog was already in the air, going after Roke's now-exposed left side.

Reversing his left hand, Roke pushed all eleven inches of his scout knife into the dog's open mouth and pierced its brain. When the dog dropped, it yanked the blade from his hand.

The third dog stopped, giving Roke enough time to bend and pull blade from the dead dog's mouth. The instant he straightened up, he shouted, "Run, now!"

The three abandoned their maneuver and raced forward. Thea and Caruso fired their weapons. Within seconds Roke spotted his ship in the distance just as a molten spike was hammered into the back of his neck. She was close.

GODDESS

He stopped, turned, and saw the dogs were no longer chasing them. "She's here. Run. Get to the ship ... I've got this."

He heard Thea's low "Fuck," and Caruso's sharply indrawn breath, and knew they were about to come to him. "Don't!" he shouted, freezing them both. "Go! Now!"

Caruso looked at her. "We go! Now! Get the warning out."

The two turned and ran the last 300 yards while Roke stayed behind. A half-dozen dogs chased them, gaining quickly as the two scouts closed in on the small scout ship.

They were 100 feet from the ship when two of the dogs reached attack distance. Before the animals could get to the scouts, Daho's front laser port opened, and an intense beam of purple swept across the dogs, killing all six with pinpoint accuracy.

When Caruso was fifteen feet from the hatch, it hissed open. Thea and Caruso literally blew in. The hatch closed, and the engines went on. "Daho, get to Roke, hover above him. Give me a full view."

The ship lifted instantly and flew to where they'd left Roke. They watched the scene beneath them, and saw Roke facing Haseya. There was twenty feet between them, the dogs circling both of them.

"Daho, can you get audio?"

"Of course. Master Scout Caruso, shall I use the laser on the Haseya creature?"

"Negative, Daho. It will harm Roke."

"Not physically."

"Yes, Daho, physically," Thea countered.

"I do not understand. I will not touch Roke when I fire at Haseya."

"Computer, this is Master Scout Leon Caruso, GMS29876TTR initiating emergency directive 921, taking control. Acknowledge."

"Acknowledged and granted, Master Scout Caruso."

"The command is do not fire. Understood?"

"Understood, Master Scout."

"Audio, now!"

GODDESS

THIRTY-FIVE

Following the dogs' eyes, Roke looked up at the shimmering wings arrowing toward him along the same angle as the mountainside, while the air behind him danced with the sizzling pops of defense lasers striking flesh.

He held still, staring directly at the growing glimmer speeding toward him. Just as she neared, his scout ship lifted off. The moment the ship went skyward, Haseya's wings spread wide, stopping her forward flight. He watched her come to ground ten feet from him.

She moved toward him, her scales disappearing, and her human shape reforming into the the beautiful woman he knew as Haseya. "Why?" she asked.

She was a magnificent feast for his eyes, one he could not resist; and even though he knew what she was, he couldn't deny the truth of the need she evoked within him. She stopped halfway to him, her eyes searching his face.

Haseya's skin gleamed in the sun as he held her stare while his need for her pulsated through him. It took a few seconds for what was happening to filter into his mind, and to realize what he felt was not sexual; no, it was far more than sexual. The emotions slithering through him, turned into a single need, winding itself around his mind, and loading it with emotions that drilled deep into his primal instincts, sending messages to his brain, instilling within him the need to protect her against anything ... and anyone.

His neck was on fire, sending bolts of pain to explode in his head, until somehow he managed to raise his mental barriers and block her. The instant he created the mind-wall, the sense of need fled. He gripped both knives so tightly his biceps shook, and the anger flooded his every sense.

"You lied to me. Everything you said was a deception. You're not human. You are not a woman, but you are a female with a solitary goal: to reproduce. You put the compulsion in my head, the day you pulled me from the river. I saw you do it on the vid. You're not human. You never have been."

"You made me a human woman. You and you alone."

He raised his right arm, the tip of his ancestor's buffalo knife pointing direct at her. "Your form ... the form you are ... wearing now is because you read this in my DNA. But this isn't you. The dragon ... the creature is you!"

"No, Roke, I am human, and I am not a ... a creature. I need you; I will never harm you, and together we will recreate our people and our race."

Pinpricks of warning danced along the nape of his neck, warning him of something, but he had no clue as to what. He drew up a mental picture of the area, remembering were he'd rested or hidden during his first escape.

He had to get away from her. He had to. There was a group of small umbrella trees about three klicks east, but how to get there ... he exhaled and shook his head, doing his best to clear his mind.

GODDESS

"You've been manipulating me, forcing me to do things I would never do. But I did stop you from conceiving."

She smiled. "That is impossible. I have been ovulating for four days."

He smiled for the first time in days. "Not impossible," he said in a voice so low he didn't think she heard him. But when her eyes widened, and her body stiffened, he knew she had. He looked up at the scout ship, hovering eighty feet above them, and knew Daho was watching and listening, along with Caruso and Thea.

"You have been in my mind. You learned all about my branch of the 'human race' from my brain, from my memories, from my studies. So you know what a contraceptive is, and now you know I took one."

"You could not have done so."

"Look at my eyes, and tell me I am lying."

She stared at him for a moment before her mouth turned into a straight line, and her eyes hardened. Before she could say anything, he went on. "I should tell them to kill you." He pointed to his ship.

"But you cannot. You cannot harm me. You cannot leave me. You have my DNA in you—That is the truth, and it will not allow you to harm me, or leave me. You do not have your helmet to communicate."

He ignored her words. "Or I could ask them to cover me when I run from you. I could ask them to wound you, or shoot your wings off so I can escape from you."

"You cannot leave me without both of us suffering every minute we are parted. That too, is the truth."

"I can't ask them to protect me from you by killing you, but know this; I don't believe I will suffer when I am away from you."

"You are wrong."

"Am I?"

"You do not want to try, Roke, I do not want to hurt you." Haseya smiled and took a step toward him. "We will return to the cavern."

"You don't want to hurt me?" he asked, staring at her as his every sense turned to ice. "You don't want to hurt me," he repeated, louder. He looked up at the ship. "Now!"

<<>>

Thea turned from the console. "What is he trying to tell us?"

"To protect him, and not kill her, to help him escape so we can pick him up."

She frowned. "He said he can't let her … *it* be harmed."

"Killed. But he's telling us how to protect his escape. He's telling us he can manage whatever she throws at him."

"Do you believe he can?"

Caruso took Thea off guard by smiling. "I told you Roke Stenner was raised Old-Earth style on Kryon-Three, so yeah, he can. You know Kryon?"

She nodded once. "Who doesn't? Every child raised in the GU is taught Old Earth history.

GODDESS

"Then you know he was raised old-style and to fend for himself from eight to twelve. When he was thirteen, he was brought into the male lodge to build body and mind under the supervision of the Diné Elders. Roke has a backbone of steel and a mind to match. If he says he can do it, then he will. He's playing the odds. If he gets away, he'll deal with whatever repercussions there are, if he doesn't get away, then he's ... fucked."

"Literally," Thea said before she could stop herself.

`"Master Scout. I have detected a signal."`

"One of our ships?"

`"Negative. Outward bound."`

"From?"

`Unknown language and code. I have identified the beamed emanations originating from the Forerunner installation in the mountain.`

"Break it!" Caruso snapped, "And fast!"

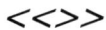

<<>>

The first shot came two seconds after he stopped talking. He didn't think—he reacted.

Spinning as dirt billowed into the air between them, Roke ran straight into the woods. Behind him, Haseya started after him. Three shots hit the ground in front of her, followed by streams of laser fire crisscrossing the ground in a circle around her.

Stopping and spinning from the fire, she ran, her wings expanding to lift her from the ground. She rose low and banked to come around. When she did, a streak of red laser sliced into her right wing. She screamed, the rage in her voice following her to the ground, where she tucked her head into her chest, hit hard, somersaulted onto her feet, and raced into the woods for protection.

<<>>

The instant the laser tore through her wing, Haseya's scream ripped through Roke's body. His right side erupted with pain. The muscles in his right leg seized. He lost his balance, fell, and spun on the ground until a large tree stopped him. He lay there for a breath before forcing himself to his feet, Haseya's scream of pain and rage still ringing in his ears.

Pushing aside the pain, knowing he was uninjured, Roke ran, his mental map guiding him as he wove between the trees. He was a powerful runner, balanced and smooth, and moved fast within the forest.

He went deeper into the woods, heading due east. Ten minutes after he'd started running from her, his warning level lowered to a barely perceptible sensation.

Only then did he change direction and jog north toward the umbrella trees, and what he hoped was safety.

<<>>

When Roke disappeared beneath the crowns of the tall trees, and the wounded Forerunner entered the tree line, Caruso flipped a switch on the console. The screen shifted into the infrared frequency, and he watched Haseya's heat signature turn south toward the mountain installation, and not follow Roke. "Daho, follow Roke."

GODDESS

"Master Scout?"

"Yes, Daho?"

"There are three ships thirty-thousand klicks out and heading for orbit."

"Yes, the rest of the scouts."

"Negative, Master Scout, they are not GU. They have no identity markings; the hulls match known Scav transport designs."

A chill sped through him. Unmarked ships were always bad. This deep into this sector could mean Scav. "Can you communicate with our ships?

"Using sub-space range is possible; but if they are not listening—"

"Do it anyway. And fast!"

DAVID WIND

THIRTY-SIX

"Daho, open communications with the Adrianne."

"Is that wise, Master Scout? The Haseya creature may be listening."

"It doesn't matter. Contact the Adrianne."

In seconds, Caruso was giving Adrianne orders, and even as he spoke, his ship moved toward the Daho. They were side-by-side in under two minutes and continued to track Roke who was moving beneath them.

"What are we doing?" Thea asked, looking at the screen showing the Adrianne next to them.

"Waiting for Roke to stop so we can pick him up."

"In the forest?"

A low chortle rolled out. "No, so you can take the Daho's sled down and bring him back."

"Of course," she whispered.

<<>>

Spotting the circle of small umbrella trees, Roke veered toward it. Stopping just before entering its sanctuary, he moved to where there was a wide enough space between two tree crowns, and looked up, wondering if the Daho was there. At the same time he hoped Caruso had listened to him, and fled the planet to the open reaches of space, where he could get a solid communication link to Guild Prime.

GODDESS

He didn't expect a ship and wasn't disappointed. He knew what he'd said, and what had to be done. His understood his life was no more important than those living on the other worlds of the Galactic Union; just as he knew if he and Caruso did not contain Haseya to this planet, those lives would be forfeit and humanity lost forever.

He knelt where two of the umbrella trees had grown with a wide enough separation for him to enter, while doing his best to ignore the growing and gene-modified need to find Haseya fought with the intuitive knowledge he could not give in to its call—not until he knew the planet was sealed.

Slowly, an almost imperceptible tingle crisscrossed the nape of his neck. As it grew, it did not turn painful; rather, its warmth held a strange, comforting feel.

Now what? He shook his head. It didn't matter, all that did, was to keep Haseya occupied with hunting him until Caruso and his apprentice were off the planet and on their way to Guild Prime.

From above and behind, he heard the familiar sound of a sled landing. He turned just as Thea glided between the leafy crowns of two huge trees to land the sled twenty feet from him.

Standing, he went to her, but stopped when he saw her lift the stunner. "Are you coming with us? Can you break the hold on you or are you staying?"

He looked into the steel gray of her eyes, and slowly raised is right hand. A single finger pointed skyward.

<<>>

With three people crowding the small cabin of the Daho, Roke took his first real breath of freedom. The pull from Haseya was strong, but nowhere as heavy as on the planet's surface.

"You good?"

"Yes," he said quickly, then, "How badly is she injured?"

"She can't fly, that's all. Hit her wing."

"The Forerunner med tech will take care of her faster than you can imagine. What's the plan?"

"First is to get the fuck outa here. second is to find out who in the seven hells is coming toward us."

"Who—"

"We have company. Any luck, Daho?"

"I don't understand, Master Scout. What do you mean?"

Caruso shook his head. "Have you broken the code? Who are the incoming ships?"

"No. The code is in symbols. I have no basis to apply to it."

"The ships?"

"They are now 5,000 klicks out and on orbiting trajectory. They will be here in four-point-two minutes. Hold." Daho paused. Three seconds later it said, "Two Guild scout ships are 10,000 klicks behind the three."

Caruso turned to Roke. "Can you handle this ship?"

Roke nodded. "Yeah, get to the Adrianne."

GODDESS

"We need to move fast."

"Go," Roke ordered even as he went to the console and sat. "Daho, prepare for evasive actions, all weapon systems online. Get Caruso off-ship."

"Opening lower hatch." Four seconds later, Daho said, "Hatch closed. Scouts Caruso and Laanestret debarked. Roke, it is good to hear your voice again."

"Same here, *ak'is*." Even as he said it, calling the computer and ship his 'friend', he realized he meant it.

"Two GU scout ships are closing. The three ships heading here are slowing to match orbit."

"They are either graverobbers or Scav. Either way, they can't be allowed to land." He hoped they were grave-robbers, the outlaws who went to Sol-type planets to steal Forerunner tech before the guild could guard it.

"The transmission being sent is going to those ships."

"What signal?"

"I reported the transmission to Master Scout Caruso. It emanates from the installation in the mountain."

"You are certain?"

"One hundred percent."

"Warn Caruso, now!"

Four seconds later, Caruso's voice broke through the silence. "Three ships are closing on us. Get here now!"

Without waiting for Daho, Roke hit a row of switches. The ship shot upward with enough power to break gravity's hold and still allow him control. "Pinpoint Caruso and the others," he ordered Daho. Five dots glowed on his screen, two incoming, and three orbital. Then Caruso's ship entered the field, moving fast and directly for the two guild scout ships.

According to his screen, he was twenty-seven seconds behind the Adrianne, enough time for the three bogies to strike. "Daho, give me sixty percent boost."

`"Dangerous."`

"Do it!"

Before the word was completely out of his mouth, he was slammed back and the combined force of the boost and the ship's powering through Anadi's gravity added another ten Gs to the load on his chest. He gritted his teeth and stared at the screen, watching the dots grow larger, while his breathing turned shallow, and his vision blurred.

It took another eleven seconds of torture to reach the point he judged right before he shouted, "Cut!"

Daho cut the boost as the ship broke through the last band of atmosphere and into space above the scout ships. He shifted the screen to view, and saw the three unknown ships heading toward them. The instant his eyes caught the first one, his neck exploded with lances of angry fire.

"Scav!" he shouted after flipping the comm switch. "Caruso, cut left!"

GODDESS

The Adrianne cut left, Roke went right, and the two orbiting scout ships shot forward, firing solid-charge weapons at the incoming ships to break down their shields for the lasers to cut through the hulls.

When Roke was parallel to the bogies, he hit the thrusters and went up ninety degrees, did a reverse roll, and when the bogies centered on his screen, fired three shots at the ship closest to him. Without waiting, he released two timed laser strikes at the exact spot the solids had just struck.

Caruso had taught him the trick in their first firefight with the Scav. The three rapid solid projectile explosions left the shields wavering for two to three nanoseconds, just enough time for a laser to get through before it solidified.

Now, the nose of the Scav ship had a seven-foot slice through it, and atmosphere was exploding outward. They would have to switch power from all shields to concentrate on the front and seal the leak. The instant they did, their ship became vulnerable.

This one didn't; it headed toward one of the scout ships, and was on a direct collision course. "Shit!" Roke's hands flew over the controls, turning the ship 100 degrees on an intercept with the Scav.

"Daho, set a two-laser concentration at the point of strike, fire one nano second before the projectiles hit the rear shields. Stream fire, do not pulse," he ordered as he made a half dozen adjustments with the firing mechanisms.

`"In range. release when ready."`

Roke used his thumbs. The ship bucked as it fired the projectiles at the Scav ship. Although he couldn't see them, Daho was already locked onto them. The instant the third projectile hit the same spot as the first two, Daho fired the laser.

Before he could take a second breath, the Scav ship exploded. The two remaining Scav ships split, each doing a ninety-degree turn, and moving up and away from the planet.

"We can't let them go!" He flipped the controls and took off after them. Caruso's Adrianne followed suit, and the two scout ships below them were soon on their tails.

"Caruso, Stenner, someone want to fill me and Prince in?" came Chan Wu's high-pitched voice. Wu was a first-in scout with ten years behind her.

Roke replied. "Simple. The Scav cannot get away. No matter the cost, they can't get away."

"An explanation better be there when they're gone," she snapped, her screen blip turning into a streak.

Roke punched his acceleration to match Wu's and the others. Soon all four scout ships were gaining on the two Scav, who had joined each other again. As soon as the scouts were in striking distance, the Scav ships split again. "I'm on the right," Roke called.

"With you," came Wu's voice cracking sharply when it through the speaker.

```
"Perhaps voice box alteration should be
suggested to the scout."
```

Roke laughed. Wu's soprano voice even irritated a computer. "Don't think she would appreciate it, Daho, but a good suggestion. Only actionable talk now." He fixed his eyes on the Scav ship ahead.

GODDESS

Wu dropped low to fly under him a few seconds before they reached strike distance. "Wu, we do a double, back me up." He caught a glimpse of Caruso's ship diving toward the second Scav ship.

Before anyone could react, the second ship did a backflip and was face-to-face with Prince's ship. Roke held back as he aimed for the Scav and fired. The instant the projectiles hit the ship, Daho fired the lasers and pulled up, while Wu fired her projectiles, timing them to hit two nanoseconds after Roke's lasers struck.

The shields wavered, shimmered madly, but held beneath Roke's attack. Before they could solidify, Wu's projectiles hit the shields, and cracked them open enough for her lasers to penetrate. The beams reached the hull at the same time the Scav shields shimmered and fell.

Seeing the shields go down, Roke hit the firing stud again, sending a wave of hot, slicing beams through the hull, and followed up with a single hard shot. The ship exploded and split in half, the Scav inside dying before they knew what had happened.

"Prince is hit," Caruso's voice boomed through the speakers. "The Scav is descending, following Prince down. I'm going in."

Once again, Roke's neck screamed with blistering heat. He knew better. "No! He's going to the installation. He needs to be stopped."

"Not by you. Wu, go after Prince. Stenner, stay in orbit. You can't get too close."

Roke had no choice but to disregard Caruso's orders. He had to go after Haseya. He'd bet his life she'd sent the signal to the Scav, which was exactly what he was about to do. Those ships had answered her call too fast for them not to have been there, hiding behind the twin moons, and waiting for her signal.

Roke stared at the screen; his mind torn. Haseya's pull grew stronger as he neared the edge of Anadi's atmosphere. "Leon," he said to Caruso, his voice calm and low. "This is my planet; this is my job. I clean it up."

"Roke, you—"

Roke shut down the com. "Daho, bring me to the upper lake."

"It is dangerous."

"I know."

"You might not be able to leave."

"I know."

"You might die."

"I know, but Daho, we all die at some point."

"Yes, humans do that."

Roke half snorted a laugh. "Yes, we do. Now, get me down there."

"As you command, Roke."

Reentry was gentler than when he left, a fact he didn't notice because he was concentrating on his mind and body's reaction to getting closer to her. In space, there'd been just the shallowest of pulls, but the moment the ship cracked the atmosphere, the draw grew stronger.

No matter what he did, he was fucked. He shook his head, closed his eyes, and let Daho take control. He thought back to Kryon-

GODDESS

Three and the day his grandfather had come for him on his thirteenth birthday. His fear of not being out there, not being free any longer, had been a hard hurdle.

The old man had knelt before him, spoke several words in Navajo he had never heard before and did not understand, and then smiled. When his grandfather smiled, a myriad of lines radiated from his eyes and the corners of his mouth, and something inside Roke told him everything would be all right.

But today wasn't his thirteenth birthday. His grandfather was long dead, and he was about to go face-to-face with an alien who wanted him as her breeder-stud. One thing was suddenly crystal clear, more so than it had been since he landed here the very first time. Haseya had been using half-truths to play on his need for Anadi to be the perfect planet for the Galactic Union to colonize, except he knew exactly who and what she was.

"Shit!" He punched the console.

THIRTY-SEVEN

"He's not listening to you," Thea said, turning her seat to face Caruso.

"Appreciate, the reminder ... apprentice. Let's take out the bad guy first, yes?"

She looked at the screen, at the spot where Prince went down. "He's only a few klicks from the lakes. Let me take the sled to back up Roke."

"You aren't trained yet."

"For fuck's sake, Caruso, I know what to do."

Caruso looked at her, a single eyebrow raised, and cocked his head to the side. "Don't touch any rocks when you're down there."

Thea's body relaxed; a smile played at the corners of her mouth. The thin scar on her left cheek formed a second grin. "Yes, Master Scout."

"Wu, I'm air-dropping the greenie, stick with me."

A heartbeat later, Caruso opened the lower hatch and dropped his apprentice into the air. Then he banked the ship and arrowed down to where Prince's ship hit the ground, and dug a thousand-foot trench along Anadi's surface. Luckily, he missed most of the trees ... except for the last two.

"Shitfire," Wu shouted. "How the hell did Prince do that?"

Before Caruso could think of an answer, the Scav ship laid down a barrage of fire at the downed scout ship. Caruso flipped his ship and came headlong at the Scav. When there was barely 500 feet between them, he released two explosive rounds, and went vertical.

Both missed the Scav.

From above, Wu's scout ship dove toward the alien ship, her weapons firing without stopping, rocking the Scav ship with an incessant torrent of projectiles and laser strikes, disrupting the pilot's ability to fly as the shields went from clear to opaque, over-stressed with the continuous barrage of strikes.

Caruso, seeing Wu's tactic, joined with her, firing projectiles, but at the same time, using the shell-laser technique to get through. He wasn't sure who had gotten through first, but the Scav shields went down, and the ship fell, smoke billowing out its sides.

He followed it down, until it struck. The pilot survived the crash well, and the ship hit with less than the results the Master Scout expected. "Cover me," he called to Wu before he went nose down.

As he dove, one of the crew half flew, half jumped out of the craft, rolled on the ground, and tried to jump into the air, but one of its wings hung down. The Scav looked up at the incoming ship, turned, and started for the trees.

He made it a half-dozen steps before one of Wu's lasers split him in half. Caruso brought the ship down next the Scav ship. "Adrianne, life signs?"

```
"One dead, one living not moving."
```

"Open the hatch," he ordered, pulling on his helmet. Roke's warning about blocking Haseya's psi abilities rose in the corner of his mind.

"Keep me on your scan, and don't miss me too much," he told the computer.

"I miss you already, Leon."

With that, he was out and moving toward the alien ship. "Leon, I've got Garon."

"Prince is alive?"

"Alive; broken arm, not bad."

"The ship?"

"Gone," Garon Prince said, before groaning, then, "Easy, Chan, I'm not one of your antique porcelain dolls."

"You wish you were, don't you?"

Ignoring their stress banter, he said, "What about the ship?"

"Backbone is gone. She won't fly without full skeletal reshape. Ain't happening here."

"Damn ... Your ship has to be destroyed. No other way." With that, he walked into the Scav ship.

He took one look around, and saw the Scav lift its blaster. Caruso fired until his handheld was empty, and nothing was left of the Scav. He went to the rear of the ship, looked at the engine compartment, and opened the panel next to it.

There were several lines of Scav writing, which looked vaguely similar to the Forerunner glyphs he'd studied in Haseya's lair. Thankfully, he didn't have to read whatever it said. Every Scout knew the layout of the various Scav ships. The two green buttons, four inches from his hand, were the ship's self-destruct triggers. He looked at the Scav writing once more, shrugged, and hit the two buttons simultaneously.

It didn't take a single breath of the foul-smelling, heated air before the ship's bells and whistles clamored. He turned and walked out. The explosion came fifteen seconds after he was airborne and headed for the mountain and the stacked lakes.

<<>>

The moment Roke stepped on the ground, he sensed her on every inch of his body, which now vibrated with the need he knew wasn't real, and was not a component of who Roke Stenner was, even if it was now a marker on his DNA.

No matter what he thought, he could not deny the mental and physical need it created within him. He held no weapons because he couldn't hurt her; but he knew what had to be done—destroy the computers in the installation, and the vats of seedpods from the face of Anadi.

He'd put on Caruso's backup helmet and secured it tightly to the fastener on his EXO suit. He was positive it would dull her abilities to get into his mind. He would add his increased psi ability as well. Only the DNA factors couldn't be stopped.

This time there were no dogs to herd him. He walked through the water, went straight through the cavern, down the circular passageway, and into the installation below. Once there, he turned toward where he sensed her to be—with the computers and the vats.

When he entered the gray-walled room, she was already walking toward him with smile on her face, her features and body fully human. There were no wings, no tail, no scales. His heart kicked up another twenty beats per minute and his breathing deepened. He held his mind-block tight to add to the helmet's protection, and took a long slow breath, exhaling just as slowly. He did it once more before she reached him. With his hormonal rush calmer, he concentrated on her.

"Take off your helmet so I can kiss you."

"No."

A flash of anger tweaked her features before she could contain herself. "Roke, please, I need to feel your lips on mine. My wing still aches, even though it has been healed."

"You need to back away from me."

She took another step forward. Her breasts touched his chest, but the EXO suit stopped any sensations. She raised her hand, reaching toward the helmet securing buttons on the neck band of the EXO suite.

He grabbed her wrists and stopped her. "No."

"Roke, I have sacrificed my entire life, my future for you. I have given you me. Now you need to give me you."

"You already took me. You gave me no choice. But there will be others, Haseya, others who will be happy to make little dragons with you."

She shook her head. "You know I cannot mate with anyone but you."

When he looked into her eyes, he saw fear for the first time, and he knew she was telling the truth. It cut through him, but he ignored it. "You are a fraud, Haseya. You tricked me. You don't want

GODDESS

a universe of humans, you want what you and the Forerunners who came before you have always wanted, to bring your race back to rule the universe. And you want to be the goddess who rules all."

"Roke—"

"No, Haseya, I know now who you are."

"You don't know, Roke, you don't."

"You … the Forerunners were the precursors to the Scav. We humans didn't exist when your race was dying, did we? The stories you told me about Cro-Magnon man, and Neanderthals were drawn from my mind, not your genetic memories. You seeded our planet, I'm sure, but it didn't go as planned. Our intelligence evolved in a different way."

She shook her head, about to say something, when Roke continued, "Your ancestors didn't make a mistake when they mated with the Scav. No, the Scavs were supposed to be the rebirth of your race; but instead of evolving, they devolved from what was left of your race."

"Roke, you are making a mistake."

"You made the mistake. When I awakened you … no, even before, there was something, some sort of a connection, wasn't there? Is there a field around the planet sensing life in the atmosphere; something that creates a signal of approaching lifeforms to activate the pods' dust? Whatever it was, it didn't become clear until I touched your seedpod, did it? Until it was too late. You expected a Scav, not a human being."

She shook her head, started to speak, but he ignored her.

"This planet was a set-up." He waved his hand around, "This installation was built for the day your descendants arrived here through the hints your ancestors left for them as they re-evolved into a more intelligent species. That was the plan, wasn't it?" He shrugged. "I mean, your original memories came from pre-human time—from 100,000 years ago. Once the Scav were here, and awakened the seedpods, a new race would evolve—no ... no, by mating with the Scav, your race would arise and retake everything they'd lost. Every galaxy, every solar system, until every planet with a breathable atmosphere would be occupied by your race."

"No, Roke, you must believe me," she pleaded, her beautiful aquamarine eyes widening as they filmed with tears. "You are wrong ... I..." She shook her head, reached for him, but he backed away. Her eyes flickered, and for half a heartbeat, the vertical pupils flashed and disappeared.

Glaring at her, he could not hold back his anger. "You will never leave this planet. Your race will not return. They are dead, gone, and I will never allow them to rise again."

A half-smile edged across her face. "You can't leave, Roke, the pain you will have to live with will destroy you."

"Bullshit! You picked the wrong race to mess with, lady dragon, and the wrong scouts." Thea's voice was loud and harsh, as she stepped into the cavernous room, firing her words at Haseya like shots. "We don't give up," she finished, and stopped just out of Haseya's tail-striking distance.

GODDESS

From somewhere inside, Roke found a smile. He nodded to Thea. "Shoot her in the legs if she tries to stop me."

"You cannot hurt me," she begged Roke.

"It won't be me." He jerked a thumb at the apprentice. With that, he went to the computers, set two of the charges between the four huge, monolithic cases, and then placed a charge at each vat.

When he returned to where Thea held her weapon on the Forerunner, he looked at Haseya. "If you want to live, come to the surface; if you want to die, stay here. Thea, we're outta here."

The two scouts, first-in and apprentice, started out. They made it to the doorway before Haseya's scream of rage tore through the air.

DAVID WIND

Author's Notes

Dear Reader,

If you enjoyed this novel and would like to lend me your support and help spread the word about *Born to Magic,*, please tell a friend and share it by writing a review on the site your purchased your book. Nothing fancy, just tell the world what you think—even just a sentence or two is welcome.

Reading your reviews, and receiving emails from you, means a tremendous amount to me. I would like to thank you in advance for your help in spreading the word about Areenna and Mikaal and the people of Nevaeh.

Thank you for taking the time to read *Goddess.*

David

◇◇◇

NEWSLETTER

For Information about Special Give-A-Ways, Free Books (from myself and other authors), New Releases and other news, please visit my website to sign up for my newsletter. This newsletter goes out approximately 8 times a year.

BONUS MATERIAL

Bonus Material:

The *GODDESS* Bonus material is available to newsletter subscribers. To begin with, the first of the *GODDESS* bonus material is a short story about Leon Caruso, Master First-In Scout. Sign up to the newsletter and as a thank you, Download the GODDESS bonus story after signing up/.

You can always eMail me at colsawpub.davidwind@gmail.com

GODDESS

THIRTY-EIGHT

Spinning on their heels, Roke and Thea stared at the apparition Haseya had morphed into a humanoid reptilian with iridescent scales for skin, a face halfway between human and Scav, and a talon-clawed and winged creature charging straight for them.

She was almost on them when Roke stepped in front of Thea to block Haseya's attack. But the Forerunner couldn't stop her raging momentum and slammed into Roke's chest, striking him so hard he flew up and over the apprentice. He hit hard and slid a dozen feet on his back. The instant he stopped, he flipped himself onto his feet and charged forward.

When she'd collided with him, Haseya let loose another scream, this one a deafening shriek of pain. She turned to Thea; her hands curled into claws with two-inch talons.

Dropping to her knees, Thea pointed the barrel of her Z33 Marine Assault Defense Weapon and ripped off two shots. Both struck Haseya in her left leg.

Haseya's third scream turned into a roar of pain and anger as she rolled on the cold-stone floor and struck the wall. Blood pumped from her left leg, and Roke, still shaken from the pain of Haseya hitting him, and the exploding and echoing shock of the Z33's slugs to her leg, limped toward her.

The Forerunner lay writhing on the ground, her body still in its dragon stage, her lips drawn back, exposing sharp, pointed, predatory teeth.

Before Roke could reach her, Thea was there. The former marine swung the butt of her Z33 into Haseya's head. "No!" he cried out as the sound of the strike echoed like a hammer against rock. Her shrieking stopped instantly.

Roke stumbled and fell, his head exploding within the DNA ricochet of Haseya's pain. He dropped the detonator and tried to grab his temples, but the helmet blocked him. He started to open it, but stopped, knowing there was nothing he could do but wait it out.

Thea knelt beside him, put an arm around him, and pulled him to her. "Lean on me. Hang in, Roke." Her voice was low. "It had to be done."

She was right, but it hurt like five hells. He gulped in some air, tried to nod but the pain pulled him up short. "Pa—patch her up," he managed to say. "Make a tourniquet—give me a minute."

"Leave the bitch in here."

"I can't, and I can't let you do it either. I don't know what her death will do to me if she dies, and if I survive. The connection is …" He took another breath; the pain was easing. "Stop her bleeding."

Thea moved quickly, using her knife to cut a strip of Haseya's coverall to use as a tourniquet, and tied it three inches above the wounds. "Now what?" She stood at the same time as Roke.

Roke sucked in a breath, shook off the pain, and squatted. He lifted her, and like a weightlifter, rose in one smooth movement, her weight almost buckling him until he braced his legs. Somehow, he had never noticed just how heavy she was. Or was it because she was in her natural form? He had no idea, but he got her across his shoulders and carried her down to where the medical equipment was.

When he lowered her, a section of floor rose to form a pallet, which he placed her on. He pressed a button on the wall. A grouping of lights flashed, two metal arms unfolded from the wall, and dropped to six inches above her leg wounds. A soft violet light scanned the damage.

When the light went off, a third arm extended, and a bright white light was directed over the area. One of the arms dipped down. A long tweezer-like instrument opened and dipped into the first wound. Ten seconds later, it came out with the metal round. It repeated the maneuver on the second wound, removing the other round. Then one of the arms sprayed each wound.

In the space of forty seconds, the skin closed, and the scales began to glitter.

"Damn, we could use this."

Roke eyed Thea. The pain was all but gone, so he knew Haseya was okay. "Let's get her up and out before we blow the computers and vats."

Thea searched his face, roaming over every inch of it. "Are you okay?"

"Physically, yeah. I just need to work on the other parts."

She smiled. "Let's get dragon-lady out."

They worked together, Thea lifting her with him, then adjusting her across his shoulders, her head hanging on his right, her legs hanging on his left. Her tail hung and dragged.

It took them almost an hour to get to the top, and through the large cavern with its calendar windows. When they were at its entrance, Roke knelt, and with Thea's help, lowered her to the ground. When he stood, he turned to Thea. "Contact Caruso, find out what's going on."

She tried, then shook her head. "This is a dead zone. I have to go outside."

"Go. I'll detonate in three minutes."

Thea nodded toward Haseya. "What about her?"

"We leave her here. She'll survive as long as she can."

"And you?"

He shrugged. "We'll have to see what happens."

She gazed at him for a long second, nodded, and turned. When she was outside, he started to turn back, when something wrapped around his ankles and yanked him off his feet. He hit head first, shattering the crystal faceplate.

His nape erupted with fire. Before he could do more than react, Haseya was on him, holding him down, her fingers swiping across the helmet's buttons. She knocked the helmet free, and snaked her tail around his neck, cutting off his air. At the same time, her own throat replicated Roke's choking, and she loosened her grip enough for both of them to breath.

"You will not leave. We need you, and I will not let this happen." Her body shifted into a part-human form. She put her hands to the sides of his head, and tried to penetrate his mind the way she had done before, but his psi powers had grown stronger on Anadi, and his block was up and was holding her off.

Knowing it would hurt him as much as her, he balled a fist, and prepared himself for the pain. Then, lying on his back, with her legs on each side of his chest, he tensed his muscles, took a long, deep breath, and bucked his chest. She reacted exactly how he expected: by pressing down harder and bending closer over him as her tail tightened slightly around his neck in warning.

The moment she bent, he swung up with everything he had, and struck her in the throat. Both of them choked, her tail slipped from his throat, but Roke was prepared for what would follow his throat chop.

While she fought for breath, he exhaled the breath he'd taken in, giving him enough space to slip his left hand between them, with enough leverage to push up, roll onto his side, and dislodge her. As she fell, he rolled over again, jumped to his feet, and grabbed her silvery hair, slamming her back onto the ground.

Before he could do more, Thea's Z33 was pressed against Haseya's forehead. "Move and it will be your last."

Haseya didn't move, but her body transformed back to reptilian.

Thea eyed Roke. "My finger is getting really itchy. Can we get this over with, please?"

He held out a palm to Thea, his eyes fixed on Haseya. "Was I wrong? The Scav are what you have been waiting for. Is that why they had the star map?"

"What difference does it make?"

Roke favored her with a wide smile. "None, just my curiosity."

"Yes."

"And then what? A Scav touching a stone would make you—" He bit off his words as understanding came from her mind, not his.

When she did not answer he knew he was right. "You were waiting for the Scav to follow your star maps, not humans. You didn't know there were humans in the universe until I touched your seedpod. Human intelligence is a higher level than Scav. You understood the threat, the danger we humans are to your race, which was the reason you changed the way the dust would affect human DNA—it was to suppress us."

Roke paused to shake his head. "None of this matters, not any more. I've already told you: no one will ever land here again."

Strangely, she smiled. "You do not know this."

"I do. When we leave here, we will make certain of it. We will seal the planet by placing a nuclear net around Anadi. Nothing will pass through without setting it off and destroying the entire planet."

"And you will die alone."

He shrugged. "Maybe, maybe not. Your race has never mated with a human before—there were none 100,000 years ago, at least none with the degree of intelligence needed to be attracted to a seedpod. In truth, neither of us know for sure what will happen, do we? It's a risk I'm more than willing to take."

She glared at him. "Our genes will always dominate. You cannot stop us."

GODDESS

It wasn't her words that caught him off guard, it was the confidence in the way she'd said them. Before he could puzzle out the direction his thoughts were heading, the engines of a scout ship hovering outside pulsed through the cavern. He looked at Thea and tossed his head in the exit's direction. "Go. Now."

"No, I don't trust her. I go with you." She kept the Z33 on Haseya.

He sighed, stared at Haseya, and pressed the detonator. He motioned Thea to leave, said, "Goodbye, Haseya," and walked out with Thea. Haseya's screams echoing from behind them were cut off by the blast.

<<>>

Two hours later, Wu, Prince, Caruso, Thea, and Roke sat in a circle, their three ships behind them in a level field on the opposite side of Anadi, going over plans to quarantine the planet. First Roke filled in Prince and Wu on what happened, detail by detail.

Caruso followed Roke, telling his former apprentice that the crashed Scav ship was destroyed, and the self-destruct activated on Prince's ship as well, after salvaging everything they could. With the two ships gone, no one saw a way off-planet for Haseya.

Then they began brainstorming. It took them less than a quarter-hour to come up with a viable solution, one good enough to hold the planet secure until the military arrived and set up the planetary net.

Each scout ship carried two warning satellites, which add to the quarantine beacon and notify any ship approaching the planet to stay away. Each satellite was armed with laser weapons, a self-destruct nuclear device, and an activated shield surrounding it.

Any ship approaching would be warned. If the ship did not respond with the proper authorization code, the satellite would shoot the ship down. If the ship escaped the laser fire, the satellite would self-destruct, and the nuke would destroy the ship. The only flaw in the system was the trespassing ship had to be within 200 miles of the satellite.

What had to be done, while they returned to Guild Prime, and until the planetary net was in place, was for each ship to set their satellites on overlapping orbits, making it a redundant system.

"Then we should get on with it. Who's taking Prince back?" Roke asked.

"I can't," Caruso said, nodding to Thea.

Wu looked at Prince and winked. "I will."

"Okay, let's get the satellites dropped and get hyper."

Roke's neck began to vibrate. His first thought was Haseya, but the sensation was a dull light pull. He closed his eyes and delved inward. What where his senses trying to tell him? Surely, it was a warning, but not of immediate danger, it was something else. He pushed, replaying his last word with Haseya. And then …

"Damn it all to hell!"

Everyone stared at him. "What?" Caruso finally asked.

"That star map … the one we got from the Scav—you remember it, right?"

GODDESS

"Of course. It's why we're here," Caruso said while Prince and Wu nodded.

"This was one of three planets on it. Was it just luck I got Anadi?" He swept his gaze across each face, but not seeing comprehension in their eyes. "I'll bet everything I have that the other two have Forerunner installations exactly like Anadi's."

The four of them, three scouts and the apprentice thought on his words. A moment later, Caruso closed his eyes before saying, "Gomez is on the third. Guild teams are on the first, the one where we got ambushed."

"We need to drop the satellites, get away from the com blocks as we planned, but we have to notify Guild Prime about Gomez before we hit hyperspace. They have to know."

No one argued; rather, Wu and Prince went to Wu's ship. Caruso stepped close to Roke and placed both hands on his shoulders. "You did good, Injun. Real good."

Then Caruso turned to Thea. "You too, greenie."

Roke smiled at that, went to Thea. "Thank you for having my back. I wouldn't have made it without you."

She smiled and winked. "I know."

Roke couldn't stop his bark of a laugh.

THE END

---------<#>---------

**A special preview of *Born to Magic,*
Tales of Nevaeh follows.**

DAVID WIND

About the author

David Wind is an International award winning hybrid author, and has published 46 novels of Science Fiction & Fantasy, Mystery Suspense Thrillers, and Contemporary Fiction. A double B.R.A.G Medallion honoree, he is a member of the SFWA, and member of the Author's Guild, the past President of the Florida Chapter of the Mystery Writers of America. He lives and writes in Boynton Beach.

Born to Magic, Volume 1 of David's EIGHT-volume Sci-Fi Fantasy series *Tales of Nevaeh*, is an international genre Best Seller, and received the Silver Medallion Award from the Drunken Druid International Literary Awards, Born to Magic was a Kindle Awards finalist for best fantasy of the year. To date over 150,000 copies of *Tales of Nevaeh*, have reached readers' hands.

Among his thrillers are *The Hyte Maneuver,* (a Literary Guild alternate); *The Sokova Convention, The Morrisy Manifest, Desperately Killing Suzanne, The Whistleblower's Daughter, and Out of the Shadows. Angels In Mourning*, is a contemporary take on the noir private detective thrillers of the 50's. *Angels in Mourning* won the Amazon.com Book of the Month Reader's Choice Award.

David's novel, *A Better Place to Be,* is based on the Harry Chapin Song, and was named a B.R.A.G. Medallion Honoree, signifying a book of the highest literary quality, and written by an Indi writer. *A Better Place to Be* was also awarded the Bronze Medal from Ireland's Drunken Druid International Literary Awards.

A hybrid author (Traditionally Published and Independently published) David's novels have been translated into eleven languages and published in fifteen countries.
To learn more about upcoming books, please sign up for his Newsletter.

GODDESS

David's Links

David's website: http://www.davidwind.com

David'sNewsletter:

https://tinyurl.com/DavidWindNewsletter

Follow David on Facebook at

https://www.facebook.com/davidwindauthor

Follow David on Twitter at https://twitter.com/David_Wind

Visit David's Website at http://www.davidwind.com

Visit David's Goodreads page at

https://tinyurl.com/davids-Goodreads-Page

Visit David's BookBub page at

https://www.bookbub.com/authors/david-wind

DAVID WIND

Currently Available Novels by David Wind

Sci-Fi & Fantasy
Born to Magic, Tales of Nevaeh, Volume I
The Dark Masters, Tales of Nevaeh, Volume II
TRINITY, Tales Of Nevaeh, Volume III
Dream Weavers of Nevaeh, Volume IV
The Legend of Ailish, Tales of Nevaeh, Volume V
WARLORD: Arrival, Tales of Nevaeh, Volume VI, Journal 1
WARLORD: The Rise, Tales of Nevaeh, Volume VII, Journal II
A Dance of Light and Dark: Queen Inaria, Volume VIII
Tales of Nevaeh, THE BOXED SET
Queen Of Knights – 35th Anniversary Edition
Infinity's Doorway
GODDESS: A Forerunner Story

Thrillers & Suspense
Out of the Shadows
Desperately Killing Suzanne
Angels In Mourning
The Sokova Convention
The Morrisy Manifest
The Hyte Maneuver
The Whistleblower's Daughter
Cops Spies & PI's

Boxed Sets:
Cops Spies & PI'S
Tales of Nevaeh
  (The 8 Volume Complete Box Set)

Contemporary Fiction:
A Better Place to Be: Based on the Harry Chapin Song
A B.R.A.G. Medallion Honoree for literary excellence

Non-Fiction:
The Guardian at The Edge Of The World – Published in André Norton's **Witch World 2** anthology, TOR Books

GODDESS

A SPECIAL PREVIEW OF

Born To Magic

The Tales of Nevaeh

Volume I

>◇◇◇◇◇◇<

The Post-Apocalyptic Epic

Sci-Fi Fantasy of Earth's Future

>◇◇◇◇◇◇<

By

David Wind

DAVID WIND

This is a work of fiction.

Copyright © by David Wind. All rights reserved, including the right to reproduce, distribute, or transmit in any form or by any means. For information regarding subsidiary rights, please contact David Wind.

3rd. Edition 2/2021
ISBN-10: 0990003531
ISBN: 978-0-9900035-3-3
Cover by Steven Novak
Map by Jamie Noble
Edited by Terese Ramin

© by David Wind

◇◇◇

Other novels written by David Wind are listed at the end of this book.

.

GODDESS

**This book is dedicated to.
Sawyer Micah
A special person who holds the future in his hands
&
In memory of two very special women of power who had faith in me:
Andre Norton (1912-2005)
Katherine (Kate) Duffy (1953-2009)**

◇◇◇

'It is not in the stars to hold our destiny but in ourselves'.
—William Shakespeare
*'Change is the law of life. And those who look only to the past or present
are certain to miss the future.'*
—John F. Kennedy

◇◇◇

ACKNOWLEDGEMENTS

I would like to thank everyone who has helped me on this journey into the future. To Bonnie Wind for all her support and love, to my fabulous Beta readers who gave me the feedback necessary to make this story special—Terry Vanlandingham, Sandra Kitt, C.B. Pratt, Lia Verge Higgins, Vivienne Mathews, Christian Bunyan, Makiela Vasquez, Amanda Rabinowitz Tibbets, Brenda Hiatt, Kyra Betheil, Joe Manber, and a special thank you to Effrosyni Moschoudi for her invaluable insights. To Lou Aronica for his advice, to Terese Ramin, my editor.

DAVID WIND

>◇◇◇◇◇◇<

Born To Magic

The Tales of Nevaeh

Volume I

>◇◇◇◇◇◇<

GODDESS

CHAPTER 1

Nevaeh: The Fifth Millennium
5267

DESPITE THE HEAT of the summer sun, the deep forest was cool. From a distance, the crackle of a branch stepped upon by a large animal drifted to her. The breeze rustling through the tree leaves cooled the sweat beading young Areenna's brows. She was on the last day of the traditional cleansing period before her fourteenth birthday. She had spent the time wandering the forests, adjusting to the changes within her body and her mind—changes that had begun weeks before with her first flow of blood, and had increased a hundredfold in the past days.

Her mother had explained—not for the first time—how the final five days leading to her return home would be among the most important days of her life. During these days, she would find her aoutem, her object of guidance. For some it was a bird, for others an animal. Her mother's aoutem was a gorlon, a four-legged huntress of incredible strength. "Remember," Her mother had said in parting, "be vigilant, always, for you do not choose an aoutem, it chooses you."

There would also be changes in her body, her mother had warned. In their maternal line, it would most likely be a darkening of her skin from its almond shade to a deeper pale brown hue. Conversely, her mother had added, there could also be a lightening of her dark blonde hair.

In the branches high above her, she sensed something watching. Looking up, she spotted an unusually large treygone guarding its nest. The silver feathered male bird, lethal to any animal unfortunate enough to weigh less than its own twenty pounds, stood guard over two hatchlings.

Areenna sensed the treygone knew she posed no threat, yet it watched her closely.

Areenna smiled at it and started forward. The lands she was upon belonged to her family. Few people came to this area, which bordered the outlands of the Blue Desert, a place where hideaways and outcasts lived. The people who inhabited the desert were not those one wanted to meet—thieves, murderers, runaways, and other criminals were the mainstay of the Blue Desert's population—yet her father had made a truce with them years before. It was a strange truce, but one which still held.

Before Areenna could take her second step, a shock tore through her head. She stumbled and fell to her knees. She clutched at her head, fighting off the lance of pain that burned into her. A scream built in her throat, but died, unable to pass her lips while she stared helplessly at the giant treygone falling from its high perch to the forest floor.

A bolt had pierced its body and driven into one of the two hatchlings. *How is this possible?* Hunting was not permitted on this portion of the lands. *Not a hunter...a poacher.*

From above and behind came a scream unlike any she had ever heard. She looked up at the sapphire sky from where the sound had come. Between two tall trees, a magnificent cinnamon and black female treygone appeared, its triangular head pointed at a spot twenty paces from where Areenna knelt. It was the mate of the treygone just killed, the mother of the hatchlings, and the hunter of the family, and its rage tore through her mind like a brand.

Turning in the direction the bird arrowed, she spotted the poacher sitting in the joint of two large branches, his crossbow already set with a new bolt. He was looking up at the charging treygone, its wingspan nearly blocking the sun. In that instant, Areenna acted without thought.

Raising her hands toward the hunter, she allowed her pain at the male's death to create a storm within her. An explosion of heat spread through her and her hand glowed white. As she was about free the weapon her mother had trained her to use, a command within her mind stopped her.

The sensation lasted but an instant, yet it was time enough for the hunter to release his bolt, and for the bird to strike the hunter. A second blast of pain tore through Areenna's heart and head when the two met. The hunter shrieked as the bird hit him and buried its talons into the unarmored flesh of his face. Locked together, they fell the thirty feet to the ground.

They lay still at the base of the tree. Areenna saw from the angle of the poacher's neck that it had been broken in the fall. The treygone's breast had been pierced by the bolt. Its gasps for breath were forced.

Areenna fought to rid her mind of the pain she knew was coming from the huge bird. She staggered over to them and scooped the treygone to her. Despite its weight, she held it gently, looking to see if there was a way to remove the bolt and save its life.

While she struggled to find a way to save it, the treygone looked at her. Its eyes, black circles buried within cinnamon feathers, stared up at her. Again, something tugged inside her mind, and she knew it was the treygone.

She was not surprised by this, even though it had never happened to her before. For years, she had listened to the stories of people who had become paired with treygones. Then she remembered her mother's parting words to be watchful when she had started this *becoming* walk.

Sadness for the treygone weighed heavily on her. The bird had prevented her from using her powers to stop the hunter from shooting it, but she knew why. Treygones mated for life. When one mate died, the other found a means to follow its mate. Today was no different.

But the hatchling…what about the baby?

The answer came as a gentle tug in her mind, not the forceful scream of moments before. She shook her head, trying to understand how this was happening when the bird's chest gave a final rise and fall, its large head falling backward.

Areenna walked to a small clearing where she scooped out a grave and placed the mother within. She returned for the male and the hatchling, brought them to the open grave, and laid them next to the female. She filled the grave with loose earth and used a star shaped

GODDESS

stone she'd uncovered in her digging to mark the grave. When she finished, she climbed the tree to the nest.

Carefully scooping up the remaining hatchling, she cradled it to her chest and returned to the ground. She held the cinnamon, black and silver hatchling against her for warmth and started homeward, leaving the poacher to his reward…dinner for the scavengers.

Why was this happening on the day before her fourteenth birthday? Areenna wondered while she hummed a soothing melody to the hatchling.

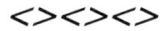

<><><>

5271

"There is no choice." Cupping the sides of his head, the High King of Nevaeh held himself as if trying to ease a headache of astonishing proportions.

"There is always a choice." The High Queens's voice was as soothing as was the hand stroking his back. While smaller than most men of Nevaeh, the King was broad across the chest and shoulders, narrow at the hips with powerful legs and arms. Yet none would have pictured him a king for his size combined with the delivery of his words served to make him appear slow-witted. He, however, was far from slow-witted. He considered every word he spoke carefully before allowing it to pass his lips.

His special combination of strength and intelligence had allowed him to defeat the sorceresses controlled and led by the Masters of the Circle of Afzal—the leaders of the shadowy empire across the sea. These witches had held Nevaeh in virtual slavery, using the fighting between the ten dominions to keep their Dark Masters' strength high—for the fed not upon earthly food, but by keeping the rulers of Nevaeh at each other's throats, living, and growing in the power created by the dark energies born from the fighting.

By defeating the Afzaleem, he became the first person to unite the dominions of Nevaeh under a single rule while at the same time denying the Circle their Nevaen puppets.

The king lifted his head to look into the gray eyes of his mate. "There is no choice," he repeated. "We must keep the trust and willingness of all rulers to allow themselves and their families to be led rather than forced."

"There are still those who resist what we do to help them," she said.

"No, it is because those few have no faith in me," he whispered. While his words were simple, they were true.

"Perhaps…Yet I know there will be one who comes to your aid, when the time is right," she whispered. "I have foreseen it in my dreams, My Lord. You have changed much since you became high king, and you ask the people to do the same. And remember, what follows this change is what you seek to guide, not the change itself. The rest will take more time than you and I have, which is why you must wait for the right person."

"How long is the wait? We both know the situation grows dire. The lords of the ten will start feuding again as the remnants of the Circle try to rise. The Afzaleem are all but dead. But we know the Circle will find new vassals to fill with darkness…if they have not

GODDESS

done so already. Soon there will begin fighting. The people will be easily swayed should the dark power find a way to regain a foothold…and such can only happen when dominion fights dominion. They almost won, and they will try again—they will never stop. How long must the wait be?" he repeated, not seeking an answer but putting forth the question to the very air itself. "Days? Weeks? Years?"

In from the window floated the voice of their sixteen-year-old son, Mikaal, as he trained for combat in the courtyard below. "This person will come. It will not be…overly long, my husband, my…Lord. It will happen—perhaps not in the way you think it should, but it will come about the way it must."

CHAPTER 2

5273

"AREENNA."

When her father entered the chamber, Areenna smiled while at the same time noticing how tired he appeared. So much had happened in so short a time it had aged him prematurely. Though only in his forty-fifth year, his hair, which had been jet black, was now pure silver and contrasted sharply with his dark skin. His eyes and face had barely changed in the eighteen years since her birth, except perhaps for the increased paths of lines radiating from his eyes, yet the pain trapped behind those forest green eyes was so powerful she could feel it.

"Father?"

"A messenger from Tolemac has arrived." He went to the large window to look out at the lands spread before him. He turned back. "The High King has called for a council."

Areenna was puzzled by her father's concern. "This is not unusual. Why are you troubled?"

His features were thoughtful. "There have been rumors of fighting between the dominions."

"This can't be." Her eyes darted over his face, trying to read what had not been spoken.

"Hence the King's call for council."

"How long will you be gone?" Since her mother's death, two years before, Areenna had acted as queen in her father's absence.

"No, Areenna, it is time. You come as well."

GODDESS

"Father..."

He stopped her with a single look. "You are eighteen. Old enough to counsel me in state matters, as your mother would do had she lived."

She shook her head. "I'm not ready."

"What your mother taught you in the two years since you returned from the school would take anyone else a decade to learn. We leave in the morning. Going to Tolemac will give us an opportunity to put the rumors to rest and to learn for ourselves what is happening."

His eyes softened. He placed his hands on her shoulders. "See to the packing and make certain everything is arranged for our departure tomorrow. Oh, the messenger will be joining us for the evening meal."

<><><>

The formal eating hall was filled with sound. Four musicians played string instruments at the far end of the dining hall. Today, the oval table was set for three, although it could accommodate many more. Areenna's father, King Nosaj II sat at the head of the table, his chair slightly elevated. Areenna sat on her father's right, signifying she was the right hand of the King—the King's highest advisor.

To the King's left sat Duke Yermon of Llawnroc, messenger of the high king. The duke was the twin brother of Olrac, King of Llawnroc—Yermon was the younger twin, born two minutes behind Olrac. Areenna had met him and his daughter when her father had delivered her to the School of the Lords, upon her eleventh birthday.

The King of Llawnroc was childless and so the King's niece, Nylle, daughter of Duke Yermon, would be the successor to Llawnroc's throne.

"You have grown into an enchanting woman, Princess," the duke said.

"Thank you, Duke Yermon. And your daughter, Nylle, how does she fare?"

Glowing with pride he said, "She is well, Princess Areenna. She is betrothed to the King's second son, Theron of Lokinhold."

"That will be a good match, Duke Yermon. They were good friends at the school. From what I remember, Theron will make a good Father Guardian for Llawnroc and a good mate for Nylle."

"It is our greatest hope," he said. Although he smiled, his eyes reflected something else.

"You are troubled," Areenna's father said. He motioned to Areenna and himself. "Can I...can we be of help?"

"You are as kind and as perceptive as ever, Highness," the duke said, careful to use the proper title. The title of My Lord was used only toward two kings, the High King, and the King of a person's 'dom'. The other kings were either Highness, or Sire. "But fear not, all is well."

"Is there a reason for the high king's call to council? There have been rumors of raids upon the northern kingdoms," King Nosaj asked.

"I have heard the same. I have no answer for the high king's convening of the council."

GODDESS

"Unusual," Nosaj said thoughtfully.

"These are unusual times," the duke admitted.

<><><>

A few hours later Areenna stood on the parapet of the north tower, three stories above her bedroom. Stars filled the sky, and the air was quiet. Her eyes were closed, yet she was able to see everything—the trees below, the animals foraging within them, and those few people who were still awake. She saw two lovers fall into each other's arms beneath a sprawling old gazebow tree outside the castle's south wall and wondered if such would ever happen to her.

She also thought about the duke's daughter and wondered if she, too, would be so lucky as to find a noble son of the ten-dominions to become her husband and, when she became the Queen, Father-Guardian to the future heir of Freemorn. Or even if she'd find any man to be her mate? Sadly, yet without rancor, and barely past her eighteenth birthday, Areenna knew well that the sons of the kings and brother-regents of the other domains wanted women they could mold to reign as Queen over their own lands. None of them would serve beneath a Queen who already ruled her own lands, even though it was only to a small degree. And Freemorn's men of title could not court her because she was their princess, the future mother of their next king, and as such was inviolate by law and untouchable to them.

No, it would be her lot to be a maiden queen without a king. The line of succession would fall to one of her cousins.

Her thoughts and the sights of the night were cut short as a giant treygone landed on the balustrade surrounding the parapet. Its long talons grasped the masonry while the giant bird arched its neck, rotating its triangular head left and right before thrusting its curved beak toward Areenna. The folds of its six-foot wingspread appeared more like fabric than feathers; her long body and elongated, tightly feathered tail were what artists of millennia past had envisioned as dragons.

The treygone's job was done for the day. She had flown high and wide in order for Areenna to see the land through her eyes and know all was well.

Reaching out, Areenna stroked the female's head, cooing softly. "Gaalrie," she said to her aoutem, "how will you fare in Tolemac?"

In response, Gaalrie arched further and spread her wings to their full six-foot width before she leapt from the edge of the wall and soared upward into the night to hunt and play. The giant bird sent a parting thought—a feeling to Areenna—it was one of calmness and strength.

<><><>

Morning came swiftly for Areenna, who had woken long before dawn to finalize the preparations for their departure to Tolemac. A half hour after sun-up she was seated with her father and the duke at breakfast. The servants moved quickly about them, following her orders to waste no time.

"Will you be going to Tolemac with us?" Areenna asked the duke.

GODDESS

Duke Yermon glanced at her father and then at her. "If I could... My brother sent me a message asking me to sit his throne while he attends the council." He paused to sip the heated spice water, and then smiled off-handedly. "In another year my daughter and her husband will handle such chores."

Areenna studied him silently. In the space of a breath, a familiar feeling swelled within her. Unable to stop, she reached out to touch the top of the duke's hand with three fingertips. There was a sudden rush of colors across her eyes from palest yellow to the inky darkness of a black mud bog that sucked her mind toward it. She flinched, snatched her hand away, and said, "I...you must allow Nylle to sit the throne in Llawnroc." A dark blood-red flash replaced the inky bog and she returned her fingers to the back of his hand so the pieces of the vision would finish playing out.

When it finally came, her gasp was loud and uncontrolled. It took her another minute before she could speak. Her voice was tight, almost choking. "You have to be at court. Your daughter must stand in your place. If you are not there...I fear...I am afraid of what might happen."

She pulled her fingers from his skin as if they'd been burned. "My apologies, Sir, I—"

"No, Areenna, no apologies," the duke said quickly. "What might happen to whom? What saw you?"

She looked first at her father, who nodded. To the duke she said, "I cannot be sure, but there is something dark, something foreboding at Court. Your brother is in grave danger, which is all I know. I...the seeing, it is not yet strong within me," she explained.

"But stronger than any other woman your age." Her father looked at Areenna with great concern, and then turned to the duke. "I would suggest you listen to my daughter, Sir."

Duke Yermon glanced from the King to Areenna. "I fully intend to, Highness, I felt something at her touch as well. I will return to Llawnroc first and meet you at Tolemac as swiftly as possible."

"Do not fail in this," Areenna said, her voice carried the disturbance of her vision.

◇◇◇

Duke Yermon left shortly after breakfast. Llawnroc was a full day's ride Southwest from Freemorn and another day and a half to Tolemac.

Nosaj, Areenna, and ten of the King's most trustworthy guards left the castle two hours after the duke. Normally, the journey to Tolemac would be done in a day and two-thirds, with one night of encampment. This time they left at midmorning. There would be no encampment on this journey, in order for them to arrive the following morning. Sleep would come only to those who had learned to sleep astride their mounts.

Her father was a few paces ahead of her, sitting straight and emanating strength from every pore. His deep brown kraal stood almost seventeen hands, its flanks powerfully muscled, its legs thick and strong. Larger and longer than its un-mutated equine ancestor, the kraal's body was broad, its coat short and dense. The kraal's flaring triangular shaped head was high and proud, and its powerful gait smoothly consumed the distance.

Her gray and black spotted kraal, a hand smaller than her father's, moved swiftly. His wide silvery gray mane spiked upward as he sped gracefully along. Above her and the muscular kraal she had named Hero flew Gaalrie. With Gaalrie's sharp sight, Areenna saw the road ahead with full clarity. Gaalrie would give timely warning of any danger along their route.

She urged Hero to her father's side. They rode silently for several minutes until he asked, "Are you ready to tell me what you saw on Duke Yermon?"

"Yes Father. It took me a while to fully understand."

Her father waited silently. "When it happened, a sheet of red…of blood washed across my sight. I felt danger to the duke's brother. I have been working the vision, as mother taught me, and was finally able to open the blood curtain."

She took a breath. "What I saw was a knife flying toward Llawnroc's king. He had been unprotected. The killer was someone seated at the council. I feel certain of it, but I did not see a face, nor could I sense who it was. I am sorry, Father."

"Never!" her father growled. "Never apologize for something like that. What you saw was a gift given to you. You get only what is given freely by those who watch. You must never apologize for them or for yourself."

While Areenna had at first stiffened at her father's tone, the words themselves served to ease her tense muscles. "Yes, Father, I shall remember."

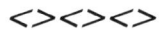

<><><>

"My Lord," Enaid called.

Turning to his wife, the High King of Nevaeh raised his eyebrows.

"All but two have arrived. They are quartered and being fed. Freemorn and Lokinhold will be here in the morning."

"Thank you," he said.

She took his hand and gently squeezed it. "You must go and greet them."

"In a moment," he whispered.

"What troubles you?"

"The past," he said, seeing not the woman standing before him, but the world he had come from, and knowing every aspect of his previous life was gone…except for memories.

<>

To read more, or purchase, Go to

https://www.books2read.com/BornToMagicVol1

Made in the USA
Columbia, SC
28 March 2023

9a532ada-9d75-4d14-a372-1a5b455fe9d2R01